THE VESSEL

Peggy Christie

Cover Illustration by Sean Seal

Cover Design by Rich Bloom

Edited by David C. Hayes

ISBN-13: 978-1-945940-16-3

www.sourcepointpress.com

SOURCE POINT PRESS

DEDICATION

For my best friend, Jo. From our crash-course first meeting, through chicken pox and mud fights, thank you for sharing your awesomeness with me over the past 46 years.

PROLOGUE

CHINA: 1238CE, South Song Dynasty, City of Guang

The flame of the oil lamp flickered against the black wood of the surrounding walls. Rice paper scrolls decorated the north wall, five in all. The dark brush strokes stood out in stark contrast to the paper, the characters representing the five elements: Earth, Wood, Water, Fire, Metal. Qíng Shēng knelt on a red silk pillow, facing the altar positioned below the scrolls. Curls of smoke rose from the pots of burning incense placed in a circle surrounding him. He inhaled their cleansing energy.

Red paper lanterns adorned with drawings of golden dragons hung about the room. Hundreds of dragon figurines sat on shelves and tables. Each was carved from a different material: jade, alabaster, amethyst, wood, resin, stone, and more. His master, Héng Lóng Wĕi, had collected them from every corner of the world. Some may have thought it impossible for one man to have found so many trinkets in one lifetime but considering Master Héng was already five hundred and seventy years old, it hadn't been difficult.

Qíng Shēng could sense the master behind him. Héng was preparing the ritual implements in a slow and deliberate manner. One does not rush any aspect of a high ceremony, particularly this one. The Master planned to bring Qíng Shēng into the fold of the línghún chī, better known as Soul Feeders. The more popular name was xī-xuèguǐ, or vampire, a name that struck fear and despair into the hearts of most men.

Qíng Shēng, however, was not most men. And his duties, once turned, would be to protect mankind, not feed off it. True, he would have to feed in order to survive but he was bound to obey the order's strict moral code and laws, the primary being permission to feed only off a willing sacrifice and the secondary forbidding him to turn anyone unless deemed necessary by the council elders.

As in every society, there were the lawmakers, the law keepers, and the law breakers. It was no different with the línghún. The elders created all of their laws, starting when the línghún first existed in large enough numbers. As societies and the world changed with time, fresh rules would be added. Qíng Shēng would become part of the law keepers as he had no interest in creating laws but every fiber of his being screamed out for action at every injustice he witnessed. What better way to protect the people of this world than to become a quán pì rén?

The unfortunate downside of his transformation would be the loss of his soul. Because their souls had to be sacrificed to the gods for this higher purpose, all their emotions would disappear along with it. Qíng Shēng had never been jubilant or overly expressive in his life, even as a child. Would his lust for justice wane once his transformation was complete? The Master reassured him that even in his turning, Qíng Shēng's quest for justice was a logical and rational need and would never disappear.

The línghún weren't blood feeders and herein lay the need for the law keepers. When the time came for a línghún to feed, he would ingest part of a mortal's life energy and absorb whatever emotions the person had at the time, good or bad. It would last several hours, or possibly days, depending on the strength of the emotion and the life energy of the individual. Many línghún became addicted to the high that sometimes resulted after a feeding. Being an immortal creature with no feelings was not an impossible burden to carry but for some, once the rush of joy or hate or lust entered their bodies after a long absence, it was a feeling that was hard to let slip away again. So, the wú lài, or rogue vampires, traveled from town to town, feeding off as many people as they could find, usually killing them in the process.

Fortunately, the línghún could only be created by a ritual of blood. The feeding off emotions was enough to sustain them but in order to perpetuate the species, a Master must feed off his apprentice, physically and emotionally, and then transfer his own blood back to the apprentice. Being chosen for such a ceremony was a high honor among the people of Qíng Shēng's village.

Qíng Shēng took a moment and looked to his left. His family – mother, father, and four younger siblings – stood against the west wall. Each held a fat stick of incense as they continuously bowed and straightened, mumbling prayers to the gods for success in the ceremony. His youngest sibling, Ài, looked up from her bowing for a moment and locked eyes with him.

Long streaks of tears cleared tracks in the dirt on her face. In a village consisting of families of farmers, even the youngest of children needed to perform various tasks and work, some rather difficult, to help the village survive. Ài was no exception, not even at the tender age of eight. But despite all their hardships in life, Ài was always a bubbly and happy child, one who looked up to her older brother as a role model, a hero, and a friend.

Qíng Shēng felt a momentary pang of guilt. No longer would they share a bowl of rice or pick berries in summer. The bedtime stories he told her of adventures with dragons and wizards would fade like the inked page left in the sun too long. Their snow fortress, built as a refuge against their siblings in their winter snowball fights, would melt into memory. Ài would be left alone forever without her favorite older sibling once he became línghún. Before he could let the emotion drown him in its complexities, Ài smiled at him then returned to her bowing. He felt the corner of his mouth tug upwards in a half smile, grateful for her strength and love, and turned back to face the north wall.

Master Héng stood over him and Qíng Shēng flinched. He'd never heard the Master move from the south wall to the north. Héng held a small golden bowl filled with oil. The tiny script decorating its sides was difficult for Qíng Shēng to read in the dim light. The bowl itself looked impossibly small and delicate, something that would crumple in the ancient hands of the Master but he held it with a soft ease and grace in his long delicate fingers. He looked down at Qíng Shēng and began the ritual.

"Gang Qíng Shēng, you have been chosen by the community of línghún chī to be brought into the fold of our great tradition. Do you accept this honor?"

Qíng Shēng nodded. "Yes."

The Master dipped his thumb into the oil and placed it against Qíng Shēng's forehead, drawing the hanzi for quán, or 'immortal', onto his skin. He spoke again.

"Gang Qíng Shēng, do you accept the laws of our community and promise to uphold them in order to protect mortal-kind, even if it may be necessary to kill a fellow línghún?"

Again, Qíng Shēng nodded. "Yes."

The Master knelt down in front of Qíng Shēng, taking a moment to lock eyes with him. He felt a tremor of anticipation quiver in his stomach as Master Héng reached forward and pulled open Qíng Shēng's shirt, exposing his bare skin. After dipping his thumb into the oil once more, Héng drew the hanzi for 'protector' onto Qíng's chest. All the hairs on his body stood at once and he shivered.

The Master stood and faced Qíng Shēng's family. They stopped bowing and silenced their prayers.

"Do you accept Qíng Shēng's sacrifice, knowing that even as he embarks on this great and honorable quest, you may never see him again, forever cut off from his existence, and he from yours?"

The six of them bowed as one but Qíng Shēng's father spoke. "We do."

Master Héng bowed in return. He walked over to each family member, dipping his thumb into the oil and anointing each forehead with the hanzi for the five elements. When he reached Ài, he knelt before her. As she looked up into his eyes, fear and awe lit up her face. The Master dipped his pinky into the oil and spoke to her.

"Ài, you are a light among the dark powers of this world. I foresee many great things for you in the life ahead. You are filled with strength, courage, integrity, and," he placed his finger against her forehead and drew the last symbol, "Love."

She smiled and clutched the incense close to her chest. Master Héng patted her head in an uncharacteristic but tender manner. It was meant to comfort Ài, and seemed to do the job, despite his awkward attempt at affection. The Master turned to Qíng Shēng's father and spoke in hushed tones so that Qíng Shēng couldn't overhear. Within moments, his father bowed and ushered the family from the room. Ài looked back at Qíng Shēng one last time and waved her tiny hand. He smiled and nodded to her.

Qíng Shēng then studied his master's profile as he moved. Master Héng returned to the altar where he placed the gold bowl and wiped his hands on a dark brown cloth. Qíng Shēng watched him as he raised his arms over his head and brought them together in front of his chest. He mumbled a string of words in a language Qíng Shēng didn't recognize.

When he finished speaking, Master Héng raised his face toward the ceiling. As he held his arms out to his sides, Qíng Shēng could see the Master's body begin to tremble. His fingers stiffened and he threw back his head, as if he were pulling energy from every corner of the room, or even the village, to continue with the ceremony.

After a few minutes, Master Héng became still then snapped his head forward. Four of his teeth had extended, his eye teeth further than the others, and gleamed in the faint light of the lamp. His eyes remained closed for a breath and when they opened,

Qíng Shēng could see they had changed from black to gold. He sucked in a breath of surprise and Master Héng turned to look at him.

He moved so quickly it seemed as if he had disappeared in one moment and reappeared at Qíng Shēng's side in the next. The Master grabbed Qíng Shēng's head with both hands and pulled him close. Their noses almost touched and the Master stared down at Qíng Shēng's mouth as he spoke. For the first time since meeting him, the Master was feverish with need and desire.

"Now begins the first part of the ritual. I must feed from your soul and transfer it to the gods. Are you prepared?"

Qíng nodded and the Master pressed their foreheads together. The warmth of Qíng's life energy drew up from his feet, his legs, his stomach, and down from his head and his arms to gather in his chest. Just as it felt like it was burning a hole through his flesh, it moved up and out past his lips. A white light flew into the Master's mouth and his eyes shone brighter as Qíng Shēng's energy flowed into him. After several long minutes, Master Héng pulled away and closed his eyes. Qíng Shēng's body sagged as weariness washed over him.

Master Héng sat quietly for a few moments, only a brief shudder or quiet murmur alluded to his processing of Qíng Shēng's energy. Soon Héng lifted his face toward the ceiling and released the soul energy to the gods. He opened his eyes and their amber radiance added to the animation of his face. Qíng Shēng had never seen so much emotion coloring Master Héng's features before. Earlier he might have felt awe or amazement at this transformation but now he stared and noted the changes as they took place.

Master Héng moved forward again and whispered.

"Qíng Shēng, now we must complete the ceremony with blood. Are you prepared?"

Qíng Shēng answered his master by tilting his head to the side, making access to his veins easier. He heard Master Héng lick his lips before he plunged his teeth into the exposed flesh. The pain shocked Qíng and he arched his back in a self-preservation move to escape.

As he struggled, Master Héng wrapped him in a vise grip and would not let go. The Master had multiple centuries working in his favor and was also in the middle of a blood feast. Qíng Shēng would never be able to break free. He doubted Master Héng would either, even if he wanted to.

Qíng Shēng felt his body weaken. Master Héng eased him to the floor even as he continued to feed. When the Master finished drinking, Qíng Shēng closed his eyes and waited for death to come. As he lay on the floor, he could hear rustling off to his right. With great effort, Qíng turned his head to see the Master as he gathered more implements to complete the ritual. Qíng Shēng knew he must now drink of the Master's blood but passing through the veil of death to see his ancestors would be just as accommodating right now.

He didn't know when but Qíng must have fallen unconscious. A gentle pressure on his chest roused him and he opened his eyes. Master Héng knelt beside him, his hand warm against Qíng's cold flesh. He held another small gold bowl in one hand as he slid his free hand under Qíng Shēng's shoulder to help him sit up. Qíng could smell the blood as the Master lifted the bowl.

"Qíng Shēng, you must drink to complete the transformation. Are you prepared?"

The master's eyes shone, not with gold this time but dark red, the color of fresh blood. Qíng Shēng nodded in response and Master Héng held the bowl to his lips. He tipped it into Qíng Shēng's mouth and at first he gagged on its acrid taste. But within moments, it turned sweet on his tongue and soon he gulped down every drop.

Fiery pain exploded in Qíng's chest. His body arced backwards and he knocked the bowl from Master Héng's hand. He contorted, twisting with a forward motion, and his knee connected with the bridge of his own nose. Strangely it only tickled compared to the pain flaring in his stomach now.

As the pain subsided in one part of his body it flared up in another. Soon his arms and legs felt as if fire flowed through his veins. The agony burst into his head and Qíng could picture his skull as it exploded into dozens of bloody shards. Just as it became almost unbearable, the pain eased away into a throbbing discomfort and then it was gone.

Slowly, he sat up. His body felt normal. In fact, better than normal. His muscles felt fuller, stronger, his eyesight clearer and more focused. He could hear the wind rustling through the trees outside as well as the villagers milling about their daily lives. He turned at a loud scraping noise only to see a small moth fluttering around the flame of one of the lamps.

He stared down at his hands and turned them over. His skin had taken on a pale golden hue and he could make out the faint traces of blue veins under the skin. Qíng Shēng stood and felt the solidness of his body. Master Héng smiled and nodded at him.

"Now, you are one of us. You are no longer your old self and so I give you a new name. From this day forward you will be known as Héng Fā Xīn, my protégé, my apprentice, my son, my blood."

Qíng Shēng felt nothing.

CHAPTER ONE

"Hello, Nora? Anybody in there?"

Nora continued to stare out the break-room window. Only when she felt a tap on her shoulder did she turn away from the city view to see her friend standing before her.

"Huh? What?"

"Wow, you're really out of it today. What's going on?"

Nora shrugged. "Nothing. Didn't get much sleep last night. What's up?"

Janet eyed her friend dubiously, but to her credit, didn't push the matter further.

"I wanted to know if you had a chance to proof that presentation."

"Oh, yeah. I did. It's on my desk."

"Cool, thanks. Sorry to disturb. Go back to your daydream."

Janet winked before she turned on her heel and left. Nora looked back out the window. She wished she had been daydreaming but the pictures flying through her brain today were not of her or anyone she knew. And they certainly weren't dreamy. Envisioning a small house on fire, an entire community engulfed, was not her idea of a good time.

She stared out across Hart Plaza toward the Detroit River. The sun, high in the afternoon sky, dazzled in diamond sparkles across the flowing water. From here the surface of the river looked calm, belying the rushing current underneath. Several fishermen stood on the nearby walkway, manning several lines.

She couldn't fathom why anyone would want to eat anything caught from that river. *Ha, fathom.* She made a nautical joke without even trying.

Nora sighed. Janet was right. She just couldn't get her head focused today. She had drifted through her morning routine, barely registered the presentation Janet asked her to proof, and had only managed to check off two of fifteen tasks from her 'to do' list. Most days she'd have the whole thing done by ten-thirty but here it was, lunch time, and she'd barely been able to finish the most menial of tasks.

She hadn't lied to Janet. She did have trouble sleeping last night. Not for lack of trying. Nora couldn't manage to shut off her brain. Here she was, twenty-five years old, and it felt as if she were just drifting through her life, as if something bigger was coming over the horizon and all she had to do was wait for it. In the meantime, people around her were being promoted, getting married, having kids, living life all while she waited. Something tugged at a small portion of her brain, somewhere in the back, on the left. An epic adventure, a great experience, was coming for her. She had no idea what prompted these feelings or even if they were true. Could just be wishful thinking.

Nora loved her job though. She was a great secretary, or 'Administrative Assistant', depending on who you asked. Titles meant nothing to her. As long as someone needed her and she delivered her best performance, she was happy. She lived for creating expense reports, booking travel, building presentations complete with flow charts and graphs, organizing schedules and meeting calendars. She even adored filing. Nora always put one hundred and ten percent into everything she did, except today.

As much as she did love her work, her personal and social life were lacking in the excitement department. Her days consisted of getting up, going to work, coming home, watching television, walking the dog, and going to bed. Then she'd start the routine all over again the next day.

She did have friends. She wasn't a complete social outcast. A few people from work, three girls she kept in touch with from high school, one being her best friend of twenty years. But she preferred quiet time on the couch with Jethro, her slobbering howling bloodhound, to the meat parades disguised as bars that were filled with the smell of whiskey, stale sweat, and desperation. Just as Nora flashed back on an evening when a man, easily twice her age and triple her weight, staggered over to her and began to slobber on the bar, a piercing screech broke through her reverie.

"Attention. Attention. This is a fire drill. All employees, please head to your designated escape routes in a calm and orderly fashion. Again, this is just a drill. Please proceed to the designated escape routes."

Nora sighed. Great, another fire drill. Didn't they just have one last week? As she stood up, Janet rushed in and grabbed her arm.

"C'mon, Nora. Let's go!"

For some reason Janet loved fire drills. The thrill of potential third degree burns or death by smoke inhalation got her adrenalin pumping. More than likely it was because work was suspended for twenty minutes and everyone had to move outside to wait until it was complete. And on a day like this, Nora couldn't blame her. In fact, Janet's enthusiasm infected Nora's mood and she smiled as they walked down the hall.

They headed toward the east stairwell and waited outside the door until their Floor Captain arrived. It seemed ridiculous to assign some random employee with the task to ensure everyone left the building. If there really was a fire right now, it would be everyone for himself. Nora knew that Ed, the FC, would sooner trample over Miriam, the eighty-year old file clerk volunteer, than make sure she got out of the building safely. Hell, he'd probably push her down the stairs to clear a path for himself.

The jingle of keys alerted Nora to Ed's approach. He always carried an oversized ring, holding dozens of keys, on a belt loop at his left hip. For some reason Ed thought the more keys one possessed, the more important one appeared. Or maybe it was some kind of penis metaphor but whatever the case, Ed touted those keys like a prize fighter showing off his championship belt. Unfortunately, most everybody knew that only three of those keys were of any use – house, car, and office. The rest were copies of, or original, ancient keys that were just for show, sad and useless.

Ed pushed his beach ball girth through the waiting crowd and stood at the entrance to the stairwell.

"All right. Everyone here?"

"Isn't it your job to make sure we're all here, Ed?"

Nora turned around and looked at Phil, the source of the question. He was smirking and nudging the people around him.

While he did get a slight reaction from a couple people, most of the gathered employees rolled their eyes and turned back to Ed, whose face was beginning to darken as his blood pressure rose.

Ed cleared his throat.

"Remember, descend the stairs in a calm and orderly fashion. This is just a drill. We don't want anyone to get hurt, right?"

Ed lowered his head and stared at Phil as he asked the question. Nora coughed to cover a giggle but Janet blew out one single laugh as she turned to stare at Phil. Janet also loved employee conflicts so she was more than happy to do anything she could to encourage dissidence.

"Right, let's go," Ed announced. He opened the door and led the way down the steps. Nora wanted to say that Ed should remain at the door and make sure everyone went through it. You know, Captain going down with the ship and all. But confronting him would prolong the exodus and probably increase his irritation right now. Besides, the further down the steps she progressed the more excited she became. Sure it would be nice to be outside on this gorgeous spring day but was it more than that? The fog that had surrounded her mind all morning seemed to lift as she approached street level.

Maybe what she had been waiting for was just outside.

Janet reached the exit ahead of Nora and pushed it open. The clang of the metal spring handle reverberated in the stairwell. Nora stepped out into the breezeway between the office building and the parking structure next door then followed the rest of the group. They would need to wait on the south sidewalk until another random person announced the 'all-clear' signal.

As they all made their way forward, the hairs on the back of Nora's neck bristled. The sensation didn't come from the cooler air in the shaded breezeway but from something else, a haunted feeling of being watched. She looked around but saw nothing or no one out of place. Still, goose pimples popped up across her skin.

Nora heard Janet call for her to hurry up but instead Nora stopped walking. The tugging at the left side of her brain intensified and she turned. In a recessed doorway to the parking garage stood a man. His grey slacks and black jacket fit perfectly in synch with every other business man in the vicinity. The dark sleek sunglasses he wore sat evenly on his face. Nothing appeared strange or unusual at all.

But something in his manner, or the long delicate lines of his fingers, made him special. Maybe it was the pale golden hue of his skin. His presence was commanding and unobtrusive at the same time. The straight black hair, pulled into a ponytail at the nape of his neck, shone even in the shade. He was looking away from her when she first spotted him and as she watched, he turned his head toward her.

He still wore the glasses so she couldn't be sure his gaze was directed at her. He hadn't made any motion to catch her attention or acknowledge her in any way but Nora's heart skipped and she held her breath. Before she could recover, Janet grabbed her arm and pulled her toward the sunlit sidewalk next to their building.

"C'mon. Phil and Ed are getting pissy with each other.

Twenty bucks says they get in a fist fight in the next five minutes."

Nora allowed herself to be led away but she continued to look back at the peculiar man.

CHAPTER TWO

Fā Xīn stood with his back pressed against the metal door. Despite the mild weather, he could feel the cold steel through his clothes. Minute scratches in the paint irritated his skin as he adjusted his stance. He looked to his left and caught the eye of one of his team members, Mǐn. She had her long black hair pulled into a tight bun at the top of her head and wore similar clothing and sunglasses as Fā Xīn. She nodded back at him. He turned to his right to acknowledge his second in command. A young man, Taelin, who didn't look any older than eighteen, also in similar attire, stood behind the corner of the office building on its north side.

Fā Xīn turned back to studying the target. He and his team had been tracking Líng Pò for days as he worked his way through the city. Victim after victim had washed ashore of various rivers and lakes throughout the area over the past several weeks. No physical signs of trauma, no history of health problems or genetic disorders. Each victim simply dropped dead, their hearts or brains ceasing to function. The police remained baffled.

But Xīn knew better. All the pì rén, or Enforcers of the línghún, knew exactly what was happening. What looked like an unmarked body to a mortal was a roadmap of clues to the línghún. Their powers of sight increased exponentially when turned so what appeared to simply be pale skin showed a highway of broken cell walls and leaking fluids deep within the tissues of each corpse.

The nail beds, bluish purple to humans, were deep crimson with stagnated blood. But for a victim of the línghún, the absolute absence of any electrical activity was the tell-tale sign.

When people die, a miniscule amount of energy is contained for hours, sometimes days, within their cells. The brain will hold a charge, even the tiniest of surges, for up to twelve hours. A body also processes energy in its degeneration. Mortals can't detect such finite signals but the línghún can. And when they drain their victims, all electrical signals are obliterated. Period. The body still decays but at a much slower pace, a pace only detectable to the línghún.

Just as Fā Xīn had turned to study the target again, he saw a young woman staring at him. He had heard the commotion as a large group of people exited the stairwell of the office building in front of him. He had become accustomed to tuning out the various disruptions and disturbances from the mortal world when necessary so he didn't pay the group much attention. Only when he turned back to find Líng Pò did the woman catch his eye.

She had stopped walking with the others and stared at him. Her dark brown wavy hair framed her face in stark contrast to the bright blue of her eyes and the soft golden paleness of her skin. A smattering of freckles dotted her nose and high cheek bones. Her eyes tilted up in a slight almond shape and were framed by long black eyelashes and dark eyebrows. The lavender cotton dress she wore framed her slim but shapely figure and ended just at her knees, showing off the delicate curves of her calves.

She seemed taken aback by his presence though he didn't

remember doing anything to attract her attention. Before she could speak, another woman grabbed her by her elbow and dragged her away. As she stepped into the sunlight, streaks of gold lit up her hair. They swirled around her face as the wind blew past the building. She continued to look back at him and something in her face jogged loose a memory, like the faded remnants of a dream he couldn't quite grasp onto upon awakening.

He shook his head. He didn't have time to think on old memories. A loud banging sounded in his ears and he turned to look at Mǐn. She was tapping her watch then pointing to a low bench a hundred yards away. Fā Xīn nodded and moved forward.

Taelin followed behind, keeping pace without appearing obvious. They needed to grab Líng Pò now before he was able to kill again. Master Héng was counting on them. Though this wasn't Fā Xīn's first assignment, it was by far the biggest and most important. Wú lài popped up all over the world from time to time and most were easy to capture and secure for punishment. Líng Pò was different. He was a step ahead of them every time, escaping just before they arrived, thwarting their plans at each step. Pò's resilience made him a worthy adversary.

Líng Pò looked up at Fā Xīn just as he stepped into the afternoon sun. Pò's mouth curled up into a feral grin and he licked his lips. Fā Xīn stopped as he realized Pò had already fed on another victim, and recently. The blush of fresh energy colored his face and was responsible for his gloating and wicked demeanor. Fā Xīn balled up his fist behind his back and his two team members stopped in place.

Xīn studied his surroundings. A busy street and the river lay on his left. To his right stood the office building and dozens of innocent bystanders. Pò could take either route –escape toward the river or through the crowd and nab another victim. Xīn motioned for Mǐn to stay put and Taelin to go back and circle the building.

To Fā Xīn's surprise, Pò stood and walked toward him. Xīn's eyes flicked to the crowd of people on his right as he heard a scuffle break out. A thin rodent faced man in a suit was pushing an older, overweight, balding man whose large ring of keys jingled with every move. Several spectators gathered around them, passing money back and forth as if betting on a cock fight.

The young woman he saw earlier held up her hands and turned away from the fight, separating herself from the group. She gazed at Xīn who then snapped his head back to look at Pò but it was too late. Pò had seen her and moved in. Though both Xīn and Pò reached the woman at the same time, Pò managed to grab her arm. She pulled back in surprise then began to relax and her eyelids drooped. Pò was going to drain her right here.

Xīn grabbed Pò's hand and wrenched it away. As he did, Taelin and Mǐn swooped in and grabbed the rogue on either side. Most of this happened as the group of humans shouted and laughed, too involved in their entertainment to even realize the línghún were there. As his team escorted Pò away, the young woman's knees buckled and Xīn grabbed her by her shoulders before she fell to the ground. As he eased her to the sidewalk, he jerked his chin at his two teammates, indicating they should take

Pò back to the elders. They nodded and dragged their quarry away.

The young woman's friend gasped as she knelt next to Xīn, surprise and worry lining her face.

"Nora? Nora!"

She looked at Xīn, accusation darkening her expression.

"What happened?"

He didn't answer. Instead, he looked down at Nora as she sighed. She shook her head, as if to clear it from a fog then looked up at him. She smiled and her face flushed as he helped her to sit up.

"Are you all right?"

She rubbed her forehead. "Uh, yeah. I'm fine. I must have fainted or something. Wow, this isn't at all embarrassing."

She looked around, her brow furrowing. "Where'd he go?"

Xīn frowned as her friend answered. "Where'd who go, Nora?"

"That guy. I saw him run up to me. Well, he didn't really run but he was moving fast. I don't know. He grabbed my arm and that's the last thing I remember."

Xīn leaned back in surprise, his second one in the past few minutes. Most humans weren't even aware of a línghún's presence unless they became a victim. This woman had not only noticed Pò but also realized that he had come after her. This could mean great danger in the future for her and all the línghún.

She smiled and looked at Xīn. "Could you help me up?"

Xīn nodded and held out his hand. She took it and a flash of surprise lit across her face.

"Whoa. Did you feel that?"

He frowned and she continued. "Like an electric shock or something. You didn't feel that?"

Xīn pulled her to her feet. "No."

"Huh. Must have been me then. Thanks for your help. I'm…"

Xīn gave Nora a curt nod then turned on his heel. He needed to get back to Mǐn and Taelin as soon as possible.

"…Nora."

Nora finished introducing herself to the stranger's back. He held his spine straight and stiff as he walked, almost as if he were trying to keep himself from running away at high speed. Geez, was she that horrible to be near? Sighing, she turned to look at Janet.

"So, who won?"

"Huh?"

"The fight. Who won, Phil or Ed?"

Janet laughed. "Oh, I don't know. Let's find out."

They walked back to the gathered crowd. No one had noticed her fainting spell. She mentally thanked every god she could think of. She said an extra prayer when she smiled at seeing Phil on his ass, a small smear of blood coloring his upper lip. As much of a poseur as Ed was, Phil had always been cruel when he was trying to be funny, moronic when he tried to show off his intellectual prowess, and cutthroat in his ambition. Plus his pointy nose and small beady eyes made him look like a rat.

Janet nudged Nora in the ribs as she laughed.

"Sweet! Hey, Carl. You owe me money, dude!"

Janet walked off to talk to the accounting director and Nora smiled. She leaned her head back and closed her eyes, soaking up the afternoon sun. It felt fabulous on her skin. The image of the strange man kneeling over her flicked through her mind. She could feel her brow crinkle. The same feeling she had the first time she saw him swirled through her stomach.

Nora looked down the street, in the direction the man had left. A dark shape hovered near the far corner of the parking garage but disappeared almost as soon as she spotted it so she chalked it up to her imagination. The disappointment she felt surprised her. After all, she didn't even know who he was. It had been like a dream, first seeing him next to the garage and then waking up to his face so close as he knelt over her. What *had* happened?

Already the memory of her fainting spell was fading. Had somebody grabbed her? Her befuddled mind refused to grasp the details but then Janet was at her side, smiling and counting a stack of bills.

"Look at this! I made a hundred bucks off that fight. I knew ol' Ed had it in him."

She stopped prattling and stared into Nora's face. A frown creased her brow.

"Hey, are you all right?"

Nora shook her head. "Huh?"

"You look like your dog just died. What's up?"

Nora smiled to help ease her friend's worry. "Nothing. I just feel a little foggy, I guess. Is it time to go back in yet?"

"Yeah," Janet said. "C'mon. You can help me figure out what to do with my winnings."

As they followed the rest of the employees back into the building, Nora took one last look down the street. No strange man. No nothing. She sighed and followed Janet through the revolving doors.

****

Fā Xīn ducked back behind the corner wall of the garage just as the woman saw him. Why had he stayed? Despite the strange interest he was developing in her, he had no time to think on it now. He had to get back to the others and assist in securing Líng Pò. When he looked back around the corner at the office building, he could just glimpse the woman's lavender dress flap against her legs as she moved through the front doors. Fā Xīn nodded in satisfaction then retreated.

CHAPTER THREE

Fā Xīn pushed open the darkened glass doors of the Asian specialty food shop. As a línghún, he had no interest or need for human food. His presence here was not for culinary purposes. He nodded to the old woman standing behind the cash register at the front counter. She bowed deeply but Fā Xīn couldn't help but notice the trace of fear that tightened her mouth.

As he strode through the aisles, many of the older customers moved out of his way, clutching whatever talismans they had as he passed by. Most of the younger humans dismissed him, as if he were nothing more than another regular customer. It was logical. As each generation came to pass, the next one knew less and less of the ancient beliefs, myths, and monsters.

Fā Xīn stepped behind the meat and seafood counter and passed through the strips of heavy plastic that separated the main store from the refrigerated storage room in the back. The temperature was twenty degrees cooler here so many of the employees wore flannel shirts or medium weight coats to protect themselves. The temperature difference barely registered in Fā Xīn's mind.

At the far end of the storage area sat the steel door to the walk-in freezer. More employees bowed to him or simply moved out of his way. It didn't matter to him what they did. Worrying about showing proper respect or even wanting it was beyond his ability to care.

Xīn pulled open the silver door then closed it behind him.

Another steel door, heavy and pitted with dents and rusty holes, opened on the far side of the freezer. It screeched into a space hollowed out in the wall. He remembered one rogue línghún making a quip about some television show called 'Star Trek' but Xīn didn't understand the joke.

He strode through the door then after taking two steps down a long stone staircase, the steel door slid shut behind him, leaving him in thick blackness. He needed no light source to guide him. Even if he wasn't a vampire, Xīn was familiar enough with these stairs to navigate them with his eyes closed.

Out of habit he ran his hand along the stone wall to his right. When he first started coming to this building, he needed the extra help his light touch would give him to negotiate the stairwell. Now these stones felt like what he imagined old friends would be, if he had any.

He stopped his descent. Where had that thought come from? Since he had been transformed into a línghún, he'd felt neither desire nor need for friendship, family, or any kind of companionship. So why was he thinking about friends now? The young woman's face popped into his head. What did she have to do with any of this? He cleared her image from his mind and continued down the steps and made a mental note to speak with Master Héng about it later.

After exactly three hundred steps, Fā Xīn reached the bottom. What would have taken a mortal several minutes to complete took him seconds. Ahead of him lay three long corridors, one straight ahead and one off to each side. Every thirty feet a small torch marked the entry to over 200 individual chambers built to accommodate visiting pì rén or to help injured ones recuperate until they could get back out in the world.

At the end of the main corridor stood a large oak door inscribed with ancient hanzi characters. They spelled out an incantation of protection and restriction. Behind this door lay the main chamber where Master Héng, or whichever elder happened to be in residence, spent most of his days. Beyond that lay dozens of holding cells for any rogue línghún the Enforcers captured. Anyone without the proper ritual phrase could not escape the confines of the inner sanctuary or cells beyond.

Fā Xīn pulled a long rope to the right. A soft chime rang from a hidden niche in the wall above. Mǐn opened the door. Her normally placid face was crinkled with a frown. She stepped aside to let him into the chamber. When he entered, he noticed Taelin held the same expression. Those telltale signs, along with the missing presence of Líng Pò, told him they had failed in bringing the criminal back.

He stepped over to Master Héng who sat behind a large wooden desk set off to the left side of the room. Xīn removed his sunglasses and bowed to his master.

"Is it safe for me to assume we lost the target?" Xīn asked.

Master Héng stood up then walked around the desk to stand next to Fā Xīn.

"Yes," he nodded as he spoke. "Líng Pò is even more clever than we expected. We continue to underestimate him."

"The main problem we have is he is a former pì rén," Xīn

said. "He knows all of our rules, our regulations, even our tactics to apprehend the wú lài. He will always be one step ahead of us unless we change those measures."

"It's not only that," Mǐn added. "He has followers, too. They provide him with security, intelligence, as well as killing. Some are línghún but many are human and we don't know any of their identities."

"I think it's time we secured several línghún into the mortal world in order to ferret out Pò's spies," Taelin spoke.

The Master agreed. "Fā Xīn, coordinate the efforts. There are many Enforcers here at your disposal. Use whomever you need."

Fā Xīn bowed. He looked over at Taelin and then Mǐn, indicating he would like a few moments to speak with the Master alone. They both bowed to Xīn. After kneeling and then bowing to the Master, they exited out into the hall and shut the door behind them.

Fā Xīn wasn't sure how to begin and the Master waited patiently for him to speak first.

"Master, I encountered a human today. I don't know why but I can't shake her image from my mind."

"Did you speak to this mortal?"

"No," Xīn continued. "Mǐn, Taelin and I were tracking Pò. We were all in position, ready to capture him when a group of humans exited the building in front of me. She stared at me. No one else seemed to notice, as is usually the case but she continued to watch me, even as she was pulled away."

"Is that all?" the Master asked.

Fā Xīn shook his head and described the rest of the incident, from Pò picking the woman out of the crowd to Xīn's continuing thoughts with her, even as he approached this chamber. Logic and reasoning eluded him as much as his fascination clouded his thoughts. It was almost as if he felt eagerness.

Master Héng curled his hand into a fist and pressed it to his lips. He paced around the room as he contemplated Fā Xīn's story. Xīn only hoped the Master would have an answer to this somewhat troubling development. He hadn't felt anything in centuries. Why now? And why with this woman?

The Master coughed, not out of any need to clear his throat or to ease his breathing. Línghún had no need to breathe. He was trying to get Fā Xīn's attention. Another out of character development for Xīn: getting lost in his own thoughts. He turned to Master Héng, who almost smiled.

"I do have a theory, my son. I have only witnessed such an occurrence once before, a few centuries after my transformation. I will explain it to you as my master explained it to me."

He motioned for Fā Xīn to sit down on one of the chairs across from the large desk. Once he did, Master Héng continued.

"Once every ten centuries or so, a soul is born into a mortal that is so complete, so perfect, that it contains all the souls ever created before it. It bears a light, a power that can entrance, attract, and enthrall, even the likes of us.

"Usually the mortal himself is completely unaware of his special energy," Master Héng spoke as he continued to pace the chamber. "They think themselves ordinary, common but somewhere deep inside them they are aware. They always look to the horizon, waiting for something to come into their lives, though they know not what."

Fā Xīn nodded but in his heart, he didn't really understand. He knew the Master wasn't finished explaining and so he sat, patient and quiet.

"This woman you saw could very well be one of these souls. You say she appeared to stop, as if taken by a chill, before she turned toward you?" Master Héng asked.

"Yes, that's correct."

"She could feel your presence even before she saw you. Most mortals see us as no different from the rest of the world, just more cattle for the herd or lemmings following the crowd. But these special souls, these cǎi jí shén, truly see how we are different from mortals. They may not be able to know or understand what they see but they are linked to us none the less."

Fā Xīn stood to face Master Héng. "So you believe this woman may be one of these souls? But how does that explain these…"

"Feelings?"

Xīn nodded. The Master seemed to smile again.

"It is said that because they have so many souls gathered within them that merely being close to them will allow us to access their emotions. It would not be at the same level as if we were to feed on them but it can give us a jolt, for lack of a better word."

Understanding finally broke through for Xīn. It all followed a logical path. It would also explain why Pò was able to lock on her so quickly.

"Master, Líng Pò must have sensed the same thing in her. It only took him a moment to pick her out of the crowd."

"Or perhaps he noticed you noticing her?" Master Héng asked.

Xīn hadn't considered that possibility. Was he responsible for putting her in the path of the most dangerous línghún he'd ever encountered? The next logical step popped into his head.

"Master, I must be one of the spies we place in the mortal world. I must get close to this woman. I can't allow her to pay for what could have been my mistake."

"A very sound reason, Fā Xīn. I will gather the elders and convene the council to discuss this mortal. You will have your orders soon. In the meantime, take a rest. Think on what went wrong with Pò today and how you can improve our tactics."

"Of course, Master. Thank you for your insight. It has been most helpful."

Master Héng nodded and left the chamber by the far door. As it opened, Fā Xīn could hear the screams of the rogue línghún that had been captured and were being processed for their crimes. Fā Xīn thought on how many times throughout history that groups tortured, maimed, or killed those they considered criminals for the betterment of the entire society but always referred to it as processing or cleansing or some other euphemism so as to ease their burden of guilt.

Since the línghún didn't feel guilt, or any emotion, he wondered why they continued to carry on such a tradition.

CHAPTER FOUR

Nora packed up her computer bag and purse. She tried to stuff an over-sized accordion folder in with the laptop without much success. As she worked it from another angle, Janet poked Nora in the ribs and yelled 'boo' in her ear. Nora screamed and the entire contents of the folder exploded out of her hands. Pages and pages of graphs, notes, outlines, and hand-scribbled ideas rained down around them. As Nora tried to still the rush of adrenaline racing through her heart, Janet bit her bottom lip. Not out of guilt for making this entire mess but to keep from laughing.

She failed to contain her amusement for long, though. Nora blew a strand of hair from her eyes in exasperation. No matter how many times Janet pulled this trick, Nora always ended up to her elbows in scattered papers, or pencils, legal pads, binder clips, whatever she happened to be holding at the time. And each time Janet was entertained. As much as Nora liked her friend, from time to time she really had a talent for pissing people off.

"I'm sorry," Janet breathed through laughs. "Really, I am."

"Uh huh. You always are," Nora muttered.

"What?"

"Nothing. What's up? You heading out of here?"

Janet nodded. "Yep. How about an after work drink?"

Nora looked around at the scattered papers then looked back up at Janet.

"You're not skating out of here without helping me are you?"

Just then Janet's cell phone beeped in her purse. She smiled.

"Hold that thought."

Nora rolled her eyes and bent down to start picking up the mess of papers. She could hear Janet's end of the conversation, despite the fact that she was whispering, and Nora's agitation grew. She knew Janet was talking to some random guy she had picked up on one of her many 'after work drink' excursions. Nora also knew that Janet was about to rescind her invitation and that suited her just fine.

Janet snapped her phone closed once the conversation ended and walked to stand over Nora as she knelt on the floor. Nora had to crane her neck to look up at her.

"I'm so sorry, Nora. That was Jim. I was expecting him to call a couple days ago but, well, you know how men are."

"Uh, huh. Have a good time, Janet."

"Oh, no. I can help you first. But I've got to be quick because he's at the bar right down the street and if I don't get over there lickity-split, well, some bimbo is sure to get her claws in him."

"Yeah. Like I said, have a good time. I can handle this. Don't worry about it."

"Are you sure?" Janet asked. The eagerness in her eyes belied the guilty tone of her voice. Nora nodded and went back to cleaning up.

"No sweat. Now get over there before some other bimbo gets a hold of John."

"Jim. Oh, thanks, Nora. You really are a gem."

Nora waved a hand over her head and snickered once Janet was out of earshot. She had been able to slip in a small zinger without Janet ever picking up on. Honestly she was glad to be rid of her. Nora had no intention or desire to go trolling for guys with Janet. All she wanted to do was go home, pour herself a large glass of Mountain Dew, snuggle with Jethro and catch up on a few episodes of *Dr. Who* before tackling this presentation. After she put it back in order, of course, which would be after she picked it up off the floor.

Once she was able to get it all back in the folder, then secured into the computer bag, she threw it and her purse over her shoulder and headed out to the elevators. She peeked around the entry to the lobby just to be sure Janet was gone and not slobbering over another random guy she would have had the luck to encounter on her way *to* the bar.

Finding the coast clear, she sighed in relief and took the elevators down to the main floor. She pushed her way through the revolving door and crossed the breezeway toward the parking garage. Remembering the strange man she encountered earlier today, the hairs on the back of her neck rose again with the memory. She created a fantasy world in her mind about him. Maybe he was a spy. Maybe he was a private detective hired to get some dirt on a straying spouse. If she were lucky, maybe she'd get to see him again.

That thought surprised her. She was not easily distracted by men. Sure she was attracted to them but the ones she liked never liked her. Or if they did, they turned out to be weirdoes, momma's boys, or pervs. She also couldn't separate herself from an emotional connection with men, as Janet seemed to do with every one that entered her life and her bed. Janet didn't care one lick about these men personally. They could be Jeffrey Dahmer acolytes with Ted Bundy tendencies but if they were good in bed, that's all that mattered.

Nora hadn't realized she reached her car until she cracked her knee against the rear bumper. Startled, she dropped her purse. Its contents scattered across the cement in a flattering imitation of the great presentation incident just minutes earlier. She dropped her shoulders in defeat and the laptop bag slid to the floor. She resisted the urge to kick it, more out of concern for her toes than the computer itself.

As she knelt down, she cursed Janet for making her drop the presentation, Jim for being too manly for Janet to resist, the strange man for distracting her thoughts, and whatever god existed for creating the pantyhose she was about to ruin. She pressed her knee against a loose piece of gravel and yelped. Adjusting her legs, she was able to pick up her scattered belongings bit by bit.

When her hand closed on her cell phone she heard several shuffling steps behind her. Or thought she had. She straightened up to look around but didn't see anyone. She stuffed her phone in a side pocket then checked through her purse to make sure she had everything. With growing fear she realized she couldn't find her keys.

She didn't see them nearby so she bent down to look under the car. There they lay, halfway underneath and out of reach. She pressed her forehead against the concrete and slapped her palms against it in frustration.

"Why, why, why, why?" she mumbled over and over.

Nora clenched her hands into fists and sat up. She counted to ten through clenched teeth, banging her fists against her legs with each number. After counting to twenty, then thirty, she felt her pulse slowing and her anger abating. As she took a cleansing breath she heard the footsteps again. A dark flash of movement passed between two cars several rows away then disappeared.

Nora held her breath as she listened for further movement. When she heard the scuff of a hard-soled shoe, she jumped to her feet as she dug for the retractable baton tucked away at the bottom of her purse. Chiding herself for not clipping it to the strap of her bag she finally closed her fingers around its holding case. Two thick straps held the baton against a stiff woven fabric and she knew she'd never unsnap them in time to defend herself from whoever was running around the garage.

She felt more than heard the steps approach and stop behind her. The back of her neck exploded in goose bumps as she felt cold breath wash over her skin. Nora dared to turn her head and face whatever stood behind her. She blinked and whipped all the way around. Nothing.

Confused, she spun around several times, scanning the parking structure but seeing nothing. Nora ran a hand across her face. Her dedication to her job must be taking its toll and exhausting her mind into imagining things. She turned to open the driver's door, her empty hand reminding her that her keys were still underneath the car.

She threw her head back and screeched at the ceiling in frustration. When she finished she lowered her head and stood face to face with a young Asian man. She jumped back and dropped her purse, again spilling its contents on the cement. Before she could recover he grabbed her arms and pulled her close, their faces so near they could have brushed lips. He sneered.

"Who are you?"

Nora didn't expect the question. Fear choked off her voice and she couldn't answer him even if she wanted to. She tried to pull back but his hands were steel bands around her arms. Her fingers tingled as she lost the circulation to her hands. Even her knees began to weaken as if all her energy was seeping away. Again he pressed with his question.

"Who are you? What does Fā Xīn want with you?"

As she felt her legs fold, the foggy recollection of the earlier attack flashed across her brain. He wasn't the man that had caught her attention as he stood against the parking structure. This one had rushed up to her while Ed and Phil fought. He had grabbed her and the next thing she knew she had fainted.

Nora was powerless to fight. Even if she had been able to retrieve the baton from her bag, she would never have the ability to swing it. He moved too fast and was too strong. And now that she felt as if she was losing strength, she could only wait for whatever was to come.

But what came was unexpected. His vise grip released and she crumpled to the parking garage floor, smacking her head against the concrete. In the instant he let go she felt her energy returning but not fast enough to block her fall and prevent the lump that was forming on the back of her head. She managed to sit up and lean against the side of her car just as a dark blur of motion flew past her face.

Nora tried to track it and could only catch hints of the indistinct form. As she rubbed her head, trying to ease the pain building up into a monster headache behind her eyes, a loud crash of breaking glass echoed through the structure. A car alarm sounded nearby and she twisted her neck to locate it, causing her pain to deepen. Gripping the car door handle, she pulled herself up so she could get a better look.

A charcoal grey Jaguar convertible sat a few rows down, all the windows shattered. They had broken because the Jaguar was not built on the factory assembly line as a convertible. Its roof had been sheared off during the fight between her attacker and someone else. From the look of the car it had to be Godzilla. Perhaps a knight in shining armor? But when did knights have the ability to move faster than the eye could see or have the strength to convert your basic automobile into a kayak?

She'd lost track of the dark shapes and the garage fell silent. Perhaps they had taken the fight outside the structure. She ventured forward to inspect the destroyed car, wondering if she should leave a note. Not that it was her fault but she still felt responsible. A chill, like a centipede dipped in liquid nitrogen, crawled up her spine. She spun around.

A man in sunglasses, the one she had seen earlier this afternoon, stood before her. She inhaled and bit her bottom lip, not sure at this point if he was friend or foe. What she could see of his face was handsome: strong jaw line, wide but well defined nose, broad forehead, and sharp high cheekbones. His slick black hair reminded her of an Asian gang member from a movie she'd watched recently, as did his dark grey and black clothing. She took a small step away from him.

He reached up and removed his glasses, revealing eyes the color of bittersweet chocolate. Why did she always think of food when presented with a cute guy? Love and attraction always brought the sensation of being satiated after a good meal. And she could picture the beautiful complimentary color palate of his skin and melted chocolate…She shook her head to derail this train of thought.

He bent his head down in a small bow.

"My name is Fā Xīn."

She waited for him to continue. When he didn't, she barked out a clipped laugh. He frowned and she explained.

"I'm sorry. Usually when a guy introduces himself he also tells me where he's from, what he does for a living, and why the hell did that guy just attack me?"

Her question ended on a high shaky note. Though the attack was over, adrenaline still surged through her body. She saw her hands shaking and felt her breath come in heavy gasps. Fā Xīn guided her to a low bench a few yards away near the elevator.

"Here. Sit down. Try to take deep slow breaths."

Nora obliged. When her breathing didn't slow down like she wanted, she bent over and put her head near her feet. This only gave her a better view of her scraped knees and shredded pantyhose. She ground her teeth, willing herself to calm down.

She sat up again and her breathing felt better. Fā Xīn waited for her to recover as he stood off to the side, looking down at her. She gave him a half smile and a thumbs-up gesture.

"I'm cool. It's all good now."

He seemed satisfied with that answer then motioned to the bench.

"May I sit down?"

"Of course, please do," Nora replied.

He sat then turned to face her. He hadn't replaced his glasses so she studied his face. Yep, he was cute, all right. As she inspected him, she realized that he was doing the same to her. His eyes roved over her face as if he were trying to memorize every line or sear some deep secret from her freckles. He locked eyes with her and she looked away, embarrassed. When she looked back up at him, he was still staring at her, unfazed by her scrutiny.

"Um, I'm Nora, by the way."

As she held out her hand he stared at it. She realized that maybe she was supposed to bow instead. So she withdrew her hand and bent slightly at the waist, just as he reached forward. She bent further than she had anticipated and bumped her chin against his hand.

Fā Xīn recoiled and clutched his hand to his chest. Nora feared she insulted him and felt her face flush with heat.

"I, I'm so sorry. I didn't mean to offend you."

He relaxed and shook his head.

"No, don't apologize. I am not used to –"

"Having strange women try to bite your hand?" Nora offered as a backward joke. She hoped it would lighten his mood.

He frowned. Oh boy, she thought. Now I've really done it.

"I mean, I wasn't really trying to bite you. I was just making a joke, kinda lighten the mood a little."

"Oh, I see."

Nora pursed her lips and started tapping her feet. She'd never felt so uncomfortable or nervous around anyone before.

"So. So, I suppose I should thank you for saving my life, huh?"

"No need. I just happened to be in the right place at the right time. If anyone else had passed by, I'm sure they would have done the same."

Nora snorted. "You're not from around here, are you?"

Fā Xīn frowned again and she blew out a breath of exasperation.

"Never mind. Do you know who that guy was?"

"I…not personally. But he has been a source of trouble around the city before."

"Uh huh. So then why did he ask me who I was and what *you* wanted with me?"

Fā Xīn's eyes widened in surprise. "He said that to you?"

"Yuh-huh."

He stood, moving so fast that Nora had to lean back to avoid his jacket snapping against her face. He paced away from her then returned and repeated this pattern several times before she rose from the bench to walk behind him. When he turned he almost knocked her over.

She grabbed his arms to steady herself just as he grabbed hers. A second passed. Then two. Then ten. It felt as if time had stopped, like in that *Twilight Zone* episode. Someone else had clicked the magic stopwatch and everything stood still. She and Fā Xīn seemed to be locked in this position, unable to move, until the magic stopwatch was clicked again and time marched forward once more.

Nora knew she was standing in the parking garage. She knew her car was somewhere behind her and that she must look like she got in a fight with a paper shredder. But all was out of focus except Fā Xīn's face. His golden skin glowed and deepened in color. His eyes transformed from dark brown to amber to gold in smooth waves of rich color. She reached up with her hand and traced the contours of his brow, cheekbones, and jaw. Just as she began to outline the edges of his lips, his face contorted and he pushed her away.

Once released, her head spun. She felt dizzy, weak, and confused. She stumbled to the bench before collapsing onto it. Pushing her hand against her head, she groaned.

"What the hell?"

Fā Xīn's face pinched, as if horrified or disgusted. He took several steps away from her as he fumbled over words.

"Forgive me. I didn't mean to do that."

He bowed then turned on his heel. He ran out of the garage, and away from her, at high speed. The edges of his silhouette blurred as he moved like a VHS tape set on fast forward. She wondered if, beneath his visage of horror, she saw the same thing in his eyes that she felt when she touched him – desire.

****

Fā Xīn entered the parking garage behind the woman. He lingered just out of sight so he could observe her without her knowledge. He needed to find a way into her life to find out if she truly was this cǎi jí shén. Perhaps a security detail in her building might be the perfect cover.

As he tried to formulate a plan he heard a bang and a crash. Then he heard a female voice mumbling curses about someone named Janet. He moved to a concrete pillar a few yards away and saw her kneeling next to a car. She straightened and checked her surroundings. Xīn pressed himself against the pillar until he heard her mumbling again. When he looked over, she was resting her head against the floor and pounding it with her hands.

If he was capable of being amused now would be the time to find humor in her situation. Then suddenly she was standing, clutching her bag, and looking around the garage. He hadn't moved so she must be reacting to something else.

He closed his eyes and reached out with his mind. He could touch on any línghún within a two hundred mile radius and most mortals within a few miles. He hadn't expected to feel Líng Pò. Fā Xīn snapped his eyes open and saw Pò clutching the young woman. Why hadn't he sensed the rogue earlier?

Chastising himself for allowing his mind to become distracted, he launched himself toward the struggling pair. He could see she was already weakening from Pò's touch. Fā Xīn needed to get her away from him and fast.

Pò concentrated on the woman and didn't notice Xīn's approach. Just before he reached them, Pò released her and grabbed Xīn by the throat. Pò flung Xīn off to the side but Xīn recovered and was at Pò's back in an instant. They grabbed, struggled, flew, and smashed each other around the garage. Xīn had Pò by his feet and swung his body around, crushing Pò into a car and destroying its top half.

Once the screeching car alarm blasted their sensitive hearing, Pò stumbled away. He gave Xīn one last hate-filled look then disappeared out onto the street. Xīn struggled with the choice of going after him or seeing to the woman. As she was mortal, the woman would need immediate assistance and so Xīn let Pò escape. He approached her and she spun around to face him, rubbing the back of her neck.

He removed his sunglasses out of respect. After introducing himself, her body went into panic mode. He could hear her heart pounding hard and fast and her breathing grow shallow. She was going into shock and he steered her toward a bench a few feet away.

After she was able to calm down, she introduced herself and tried to make small talk. When she bumped against his hand, he pulled it back. He didn't want to run the risk of leeching any more energy from her. Her face flushed with embarrassment so she began to ask questions. When Nora asked about Líng Pò, his mind swirled with various deflections and cover stories.

But when she said Pò mentioned his name, in regards to her, Xīn was stunned. He leaped to his feet and began to pace. What was he to do now? It was clear that Pò had taken an interest in her because of Fā Xīn. How could he not have anticipated this course? He never considered Líng Pò an easy adversary and he never wanted to underestimate him but he never could have imagined this boldness in Pò's attack.

He turned and came face to face with Nora. Surprised, he slammed into her with enough force to make her stumble. She reached out for him just as he grabbed her arms. Instantly, her energy began to transfer into his body. It wasn't the same sensation as feeding on her. It was almost as if she was pushing her energy into him.

He watched her face. Her hand flew to her mouth as he felt himself change. Xīn knew how his eyes shifted colors before and during a feeding. He'd seen the fear in many mortals over the years but Nora was different. She didn't look nervous or afraid. She almost seemed eager.

Nora reached out her hand and touched his face. He should have stopped her. He should have released her immediately but something wouldn't allow it. Her curiosity, her interest in him, was intriguing, almost intoxicating. Xīn let Nora's emotions wash over him and he didn't want them to stop. Only when she touched his mouth did he finally pull away.

Her face paled to the color of ashes from a long dead fire and she swayed on her feet. She stumbled over to the bench and collapsed onto it, pressing her hand to her head. Appalled with his actions, he could only bow and remove himself from the situation. He regretted leaving like this but the situation could progress far beyond his control if he stayed.

CHAPTER FIVE

Fā Xīn's frustration pounded against his skull. He'd left the parking garage to protect Nora but realized he also left her there alone and in a frazzled state. He couldn't risk going back in there though. It had been a while since he had fed on anyone, and when he did, the participant was usually calm, accepting, and perhaps a little excited. But with Nora, who had a plethora of scattered and unorganized feelings rushing through her, he had trouble focusing. Agitated, he paced the sidewalk as he tried to think of a way to help her.

It dawned on him to contact the security office of her building. He needed a way into her mortal world and here lay his opportunity. Xīn rushed over to the revolving doors and pushed his way through. Approaching the security guard at the front desk, he tried to keep his face and voice calm.

"Excuse me, you must help. A woman was just attacked in the parking garage next door."

The man, dressed in a navy blue blazer, sporting neatly buzzed blonde hair that gave him a military air, looked down his nose at Fā Xīn. Straightening his jacket, he spoke in a low slow manner that reminded Xīn of a teacher trying to explain the basics of tying one's shoes to a dimwitted child.

"Sir, I don't have time for games. Please step away from the desk."

Fā Xīn frowned. "Why do you assume I am lying? I'm telling

you there's a woman in the parking garage-"

"Sir, you're going to have to calm down or I'll escort you out of the building."

Fā Xīn slammed his fist onto the marble desk top. "Are you listening to me or are you incapable of any competent and intellectual brain function?"

The man's brow furrowed and his face flushed red. Fā Xīn angered him which was what he hoped to do. He'd encountered many men like this one, so full of their own importance and abilities when all they could do was play dress up and pretend to be someone able to contribute to the welfare of society.

When the guard came around from behind the desk, Xīn backed up, feigning fear and insecurity. He wanted the man to think he was calling Xīn's bluff.

"Sir, I'm going to have to ask you to leave."

"Why don't you make me?" Xīn offered up the most juvenile response he could recall learning over the centuries.

As expected, the man took the bait. He stepped to Xīn's side and grabbed his arm. Within seconds, Xīn twisted free, kicked the guard in the kidney and the big man went down like a sack of rocks. Xīn grabbed his hand and pulled, placing his foot into the guard's shoulder. The man howled in pain.

Xīn gritted his teeth and pushed harder. "I demand you send someone over to the garage to help that woman."

"Wait, stop!"

Nora's voice echoed through the lobby and Xīn looked up to see her standing near the entrance. She had dropped her purse and computer bag as she rushed over. She moved to place a hand on Xīn's arm but stopped herself. He didn't feel disgust from her but something more akin to excitement and he dropped the security guard's hand.

She smiled up at Xīn. "It's okay. I'm all right."

A handful of large men, all dressed in navy blue suit coats, rushed into the lobby from the side hallway. Xīn assumed these were more security personnel. One of them, the oldest looking man of the group, stepped forward to speak.

"My name is Charlie Michaels and I'm the head of security in the building. I'm going to have to ask you to step away from Mr. Hutchins, sir."

Xīn raised his hands and backed away. Nora put herself between him and the security team.

"It's all right, Mr. Michaels. I'm sure there's an explanation for all of this."

"There is," Xīn interrupted. "I came in here to get some help for this woman and your man refused to listen."

"You did?" Nora looked up at Xīn, a small smile curling her mouth.

Xīn smiled back down at her. "I'm sorry I left you alone in there."

He stared over at Hutchins, who was now standing and rubbing his shoulder. Xīn turned to Mr. Michaels.

"*Your* man refused to listen to me about the situation. Just look at her."

Nora stared down at her shredded pantyhose and the

smudges of dirt and oil all over her lavender dress. She ran a hand through her mussed hair.

"Some man attacked me in the garage. Lucky for me my friend here," she motioned to Xīn, "came along and ran the guy off. But neither of us could be sure he was gone so I guess my friend came here to get help."

Nora smiled at Xīn and turned back to the head of security. "Seems to me you need to enhance your team's skills, Mr. Michaels."

"I am so sorry, Miss, uh…?"

"Nora Hudspeth. I work up on ten for the Walters Group."

"Miss Hudspeth. Please accept my sincerest apologies. Rest assured Mr. Hutchins will receive a steep reprimand for his behavior here today."

Michaels jerked his head to the side hallway as he glared at Hutchins, who grimaced and slunk away. Fā Xīn held out his hand.

"Mr. Michaels, my name is Héng Fā Xīn. I'm an expert in security training and enhancement. Perhaps I can be of service to your team? I can provide all my company information and training techniques. Would you care to discuss it in more detail?"

"I think that would be a good idea, Mr. Héng."

Xīn smiled. "Thank you for addressing me by my family name, Mr. Michaels. Most people don't know my culture well enough to realize which name is which."

"Vietnam taught me a few things, Mr. Héng. If you'll just follow me," Michaels directed Fā Xīn toward the hallway. Xīn turned to Nora.

"Will you be all right?"

Nora nodded. "I'm sure Mr. Michaels will spare one of his guards to walk me to my car. I'll be fine. Thank you, Fā Xīn."

Xīn bowed and followed Mr. Michaels to the security office. He turned one last time to watch Nora as she gathered her things while two large men stood on either side, ready to escort her to safety.

An hour later, Fā Xīn left the security office, smiling. He'd found the perfect operation to set up his spy ring. He could implement several línghún into the security enhancement team and at the same time keep a close eye on Nora. He had to get back to Master Héng and let him know.

As he passed the front desk, the guard now working there called out to him.

"Excuse me, Mr. Héng? There's a message here for you."

Frowning, Xīn walked over to the desk and took the plain white envelope the man offered. He looked down at it and then back up at the guard, waiting for an explanation.

"The young woman left it for you. She was very adamant that you get it before you left."

"Thank you," Xīn said.

He tore open the envelope as he headed out the door. All it contained was a small slip of paper with Nora's name and what he assumed was her address. He felt himself smiling, still energized with her emotions. First he must speak with Master Héng. Then he would find her.

After speaking with the Master and coordinating Mǐn, Taelin, Bō, and Zàn to be security team members, Fā Xīn stepped into the evening air outside the Asian food shop and closed his eyes. Taking a deep breath he concentrated on Nora. The address she left for him showed she lived in Madison Heights, the same small town where the shop was located.

What were the odds of that? When the línghún came to the New World a century ago, they spread throughout the vast land and established underground strongholds. Not in the bustling and growing metropolises but in the outlying communities and empty acres of land. It was easier to keep secrets with fewer prying eyes upon them. Even though Madison Heights grew around them through the decades, it remained small enough to keep their presence hidden and safe. The fact that Nora chose to live in the same city as a línghún fortress could not be considered a small coincidence.

As soon as he pictured her face, he could feel her energy flow into him. He could see a small brick house with a red front door set on a street with many similar homes. 1208 Edward Street. He opened his eyes and took to the air to find her.

Within minutes he was standing outside the same house he saw in his vision. The small porch was framed with purple, yellow, and pink flowers in shiny white flower boxes. The black iron railing lined either side of the two concrete steps that led to the red front door. He walked across the front lawn and up the steps. His finger sat poised over the doorbell but before he could press it, the door opened.

Nora stood before him, smiling. She had changed out of her ruined clothes and into red sweat pants and a black long sleeved t-shirt. Her wet hair hung to her shoulders and he could smell a hint of lavender and vanilla drifting off her skin. The bright yellow and orange chicken feet slippers threw a hint of lighthearted abandon to a night that could have been her last. The more he learned about her the more she impressed him.

He bowed in greeting and she returned it.

"Mr. Héng. I see you got my note. Please, come in."

He stepped into a small foyer that opened up into the main living room. The beige carpeting and cinnamon colored walls were warm and inviting. Xīn slipped off his black loafers and placed them near the door. She smiled at this and he wondered if he'd done something foolish. She raised her hand as if she knew what he was thinking.

"No, that's fine. Most people just come right in, tracking mud and god knows what else without thinking twice about my floors. I appreciate your thoughtfulness."

He nodded, though removing his shoes was a courtesy to all homes he visited, not just hers. He turned to take a seat but she held up her hand.

"Although it might be better if I put them in the closet."

Before he could ask why, a large brown dog lumbered into the living room. When it looked up at Xīn it stopped and stared. Xīn moved his feet to secure his stance in case the overgrown beast decided to attack him. To his surprise it looked down at the floor, spotted Xīn's shoes then darted forward. Nora scooped them up and held them above her head.

The dog sat back and barked, raising its paw and swatting at her legs.

"Ah, ah, ah. No. No shoes, Jethro. No."

She opened the closet behind her and placed Xīn's shoes inside. After closing it, she walked over to the dog, grabbed its muzzle under the chin, and leaned in close.

"No. Shoes."

It chuffed at her but accepted her decision to deny him his prize. She patted it on the head then turned to Xīn.

"Xīn, this is Jethro. Jethro, this is our new friend, Xīn."

What was Xīn supposed to do? Would the dog accept his outstretched hand in greeting or simply slobber on it? It could bite him but its disinterested demeanor suggested it was harmless. In the end Xīn just looked down at the dog as Jethro turned away and lay down in the middle of the floor.

"Come in and sit," Nora offered.

He moved to an overstuffed chair on his right. As he sat, his body sank backwards making it feel like he was falling. Unsettled by this sensation, he sat on the edge of the chair instead, keeping his back stiff and straight.

"I know," she said. "The chair seemed like a really comfy piece of furniture at the time. But now I just feel like it's trying to swallow me whole every time I sit in it. Would you prefer the couch? It's much more stable."

Xīn opened his mouth to protest but decided against it. He smiled and stood. Once he was up, Jethro sprang into action and jumped up on the chair. Nora laughed.

"Only Jethro likes that damn thing now."

Xīn looked back at the monstrosity as he walked over to the couch, a tan leather sofa which felt sturdy and comfortable as he sat. He shifted his weight back and forth just to be sure of its stability. When he was satisfied he would be neither injured nor 'swallowed' as she put it, he relaxed.

Nora laughed then sat beside him. "See?"

He smiled in return. It occurred to him that he hadn't felt this much emotion in over a hundred years. Her enthusiasm was contagious. How much more would his emotional state be altered if he fed off her?

"So," she continued. "You going to tell me what the heck is going on?"

Xīn wanted to feign ignorance to try and spare her the ugly truth. But she would need to know everything if they were going to survive Líng Pò.

"I do know the man that attacked you this evening, as well as this afternoon."

"You don't say?"

Her sarcasm was hard to miss. He shook his head and smiled again.

"What I'm wondering is this: did you cause the damage in the garage?" Nora asked.

Xīn nodded.

"So you move faster than most normal people?"

Before he could respond, Nora interrupted with another

question.

"And when that man attacked me this afternoon, he did something to me, didn't he? It felt like he was sapping all my energy."

"His name is Líng Pò," Xīn said. "He is a very dangerous man. I believe, as do my colleagues, that he has murdered dozens of people, several in this city alone."

Nora frowned. "How? By draining their energy until they die?"

"Yes," Xīn said and Nora snorted.

"Yeah, right. He's like a vampire but instead of blood he takes the 'life force' of mortals, huh?"

She held up her fingers to create air quotes when she spoke. When she saw Fā Xīn wasn't smiling, her jovial mood evaporated.

"Wait, I'm right? He's an energy vampire?"

"We are known as línghún, or soul feeders. The more popular term is vampire but unlike the monsters of your modern films, we do not feed on blood. Not unless we plan to transform a human into one of our kind."

"Wait, wait, wait. What do you mean, 'we'? *You* are a ling…ling…"

"Línghún."

"Yeah, that."

Fā Xīn studied his hands then looked up at her as he concentrated his immortal power. He felt the change in his eyes as he called upon his powers. They would remain like this as long as he needed them to or if he fed. If he was to transform a mortal into a línghún, his eyes would change from gold to red and his fangs would descend.

Nora jumped up from the couch and backed away.

"Holy shit!"

Jethro barked and stood on the chair but didn't move closer. Xīn willed his eyes to change back to their normal color.

"Nora, I won't hurt you," he explained as he stood.

"Yeah, you're damn right you won't. Stay away from me!"

"Please, Nora. I don't want to hurt you. I want to help you."

"Help me?" she yelled. "What the hell could you possibly help me with?"

"I can help keep you alive."

She snapped her mouth closed before her next outburst. Doubtful of his intentions she squinted her eyes at him. He sat back down on the sofa to show he was telling her the truth. She relaxed a bit but moved closer to the dog and it licked her hand. He continued.

"Nora, Líng Pò knows that you're special. It's my fault, really. If I hadn't paid attention to you, if I hadn't locked in on your energy, he may not have given you a second thought."

Nora frowned. "What do you mean, 'I'm special'? What the hell are you talking about?"

"Please, Nora, sit. I promise to tell you everything but you have to trust me, just a little."

She chewed on her bottom lip for a moment as she considered it. Instead of returning to the sofa with him she sat on the edge of the man-eating chair, her back straight and fists clenched against her knees. Jethro put his chin on her shoulder, staring at Xīn from behind the safety of his owner.

"Okay. Let's say I believe you for a minute. What exactly is going on?"

By midnight, Xīn had told Nora everything he knew, about the línghún, his own transformation, Líng Pò, and the other wú lài vampires. In addition, he explained Master Héng's theory about the cǎi jí shén.

"So your Master thinks I'm one of these mortals with, like, a thousand souls?"

"More like billions."

"Whoa."

Xīn nodded. "It would explain why, without feeding on you, I can absorb some of your emotional energy. You radiate it with a power beyond anything you could understand. Or myself, for that matter."

"So what does this mean? That I'm just extra tasty or something?"

"I'm sure there's more to it than that," he said around a smile, "but Master Héng didn't tell me anymore than what I shared with you. Perhaps there is a prophecy that you fulfill. And what happens if you fall into the wrong hands."

"At this point, I don't think I'd feel safe in anyone's hands but yours, Xīn." Nora blushed as soon as the words left her mouth.

Xīn cleared his throat. "I'm sure if I do a little digging I can find some more information. In the meantime, I think you would be safer to stay put for a while."

"What, you mean not go into work? I can't do that."

"Nora-"

"No way. I am not changing my life around because this Pò guy wants to come after me. I can't lock myself up at home. Besides, who's to say he won't attack me here? He is a vampire, after all. And from what you've told me, the 'movie rules' don't apply. No crosses, garlic, he doesn't need an invite to enter."

"But at least in a controlled environment we might have a better chance to protect you."

"No, and that's final. I'm not talking about this anymore."

Jethro barked his agreement. Xīn sighed. Mortal stubbornness was a difficult trait to break. He could post a couple of his team as sentries while she was gone and he could watch over her at the office. Maybe he was being overly cautious but it felt like the prudent thing to do, at least until he had more information on Pò's whereabouts and his operations, and on Nora.

"So it's settled then?" she asked.

"Yes. For now."

"Good. I was just about to make something to eat. Would you like anything?"

She stopped short and chewed on her fingernail. "Do you actually eat, I mean, like real food?"

"No, we don't require food for our nourishment but thank you for the offer."

She seemed to want to ask something more but nodded

instead and headed to the kitchen.

"Fair enough. I won't be long."

Fā Xīn stood. "I am intruding on your evening. I should go."

She stopped at the entryway to the kitchen then turned around. A scowl darkened her features.

"Mr. Héng, I invited you here, remember? You are not intruding. I would really like it if you stayed."

The dog remained standing and growled. Nora shushed him and he lay back down but never took his eyes off Xīn.

Xīn sat and felt his mouth curving up into a smile. He liked the sensation of it, as well as the warmth spreading through his stomach. It had been so long since he'd felt genuine happiness and desire. The last sacrifice a mortal made to him was six months ago and the man had been happy but it was a happiness that came with death, as he was dying of cancer and wanted to end the pain as soon as possible.

What he felt from Nora was pure unadulterated joy at being able to get up each morning, facing another day of possibilities and endless adventures that may be on the horizon. She looked forward to her job, her friends, even the commute to work. Some might think she was too perky or possibly on drugs but Xīn could feel the honesty in her heart and it was refreshing, if not intoxicating.

He could hear her banging pots and dishes in the kitchen. At one point, a loud crash echoed out to him, followed by a feeble "I'm all right" proclamation. When he heard her wince in pain, he was on his feet and at her side in seconds. She gasped when he appeared next to her.

"Shit! Oh, man. Don't do that. Give a girl some warning when you're going to magically materialize at her side."

"I'm sorry. I forget sometimes," he began but stopped when he saw blood on her finger.

He grasped her hand and pulled it close to inspect it. She snatched it away and reached for a paper towel.

"It's all right. Just a little cut. I'll be fine."

She sounded frightened and he understood why. He tried to allay her fears.

"Nora, I wasn't going to drink blood from your wound."

"No, no. Yeah, I know that. Phhssh, I know."

He arched an eyebrow at her and she hung her head.

"Okay. Yeah, I was freaked for a second. Sorry."

He smiled as he reached for her hand again. This time she allowed him to take it without hesitation.

"It is true that we drink blood. But it is a," he paused for dramatic effect and stared into her eyes, "delicacy reserved for special occasions. Like Arbor Day."

She blinked then laughed. He could see the tension ease from her shoulders. As she relaxed he inspected the wound. It was deeper than she claimed.

"This is a serious cut, Nora. You may require a trip to the hospital for stitches."

Her face turned pasty grey. Her eyes widened in fear and she shook her head back and forth. He didn't need to be a vampire to read her thoughts. Though he could, Xīn kept that small detail to himself for now. He pressed the paper towel back on the wound and pulled her close. Laying a hand against the back of her head, Xīn tried to reassure her.

"It's all right, Nora. I won't make you go. I'll think of something else. Don't worry."

She pressed her face against his chest and wrapped her free arm around his waist. He could feel her trembling and the rushing beat of her heart. He pressed her injured hand against his shoulder and held her close while her fear dissipated. She began to relax again but instead of pulling away she clutched him tighter.

Xīn pressed his face against her hair and smelled her shampoo, the scent mingling with the lavender and vanilla he smelled earlier. Her skin was warm through her t-shirt and he could feel the definition of the muscles on her back. He inhaled her aroma and squeezed her body close to his. When she winced, Xīn released her.

"I'm so sorry."

She smiled up at him. "It's all right. You're forgiven."

They stared into each other's eyes. She leaned in closer as if to kiss him but he stepped away and held up her hand, indicating a more pressing issue.

"I do have an idea to help you with this. Not sure if you'll agree to it, though."

She frowned. "What is it?"

"Well, I could put a little of my blood," he started.

"Uh, I am *not* drinking your blood."

"No, it is not required for you to ingest any. All I would need to do it put a few drops directly on the wound and it will heal."

She pulled her head back and arched an eyebrow at him. "That won't make me a vampire, will it?"

He couldn't help but smile. "No. You would need to be drained of your blood first then feed off a vampire's blood to be transformed. This will only affect the few centimeters of flesh where I put it."

"Oh. Well that doesn't sound too bad. All right. If this keeps me away from the hospital, have at it."

He motioned to a chair at the kitchen table. "Sit down."

As she sat, he walked to the sink and grabbed a dish towel, threw it over his shoulder, then grabbed a handful of paper towels and wet them from the faucet. He returned to the table and sat across from Nora, placing the clean dry towel to the side.

Xīn held out his hand and waited for her to offer her injured hand. He cleaned off the blood with the wet paper towels. When he could see the exact contours of the wound he could determine how much of his own blood was needed to heal it. Once it was clean he brought his free hand to his mouth. His fangs descended and he bit into one of his fingers, tearing a small gash in it.

Before the wound healed, he held his finger over her cut and let several drops of his blood fall on it. He then pressed his open wound against hers to seal it. Within moments, he removed his finger then grabbed the dry towel to wipe away the remaining blood. Her finger showed no trace of the wound or any kind of scar or mark. Her finger appeared exactly as it had before she cut it.

He put his own finger in his mouth, not just to clean it off but to savor what blood of hers had mingled with his own. It was only a trace amount but it was there. The entire room had filled with her blood smell and he simply could not resist a taste. The temptation overpowered him and the flavors melted onto his tongue: copper, salt, and fresh flowers.

Nora held her finger up to the light to inspect it. She turned her hand over and over as if looking for the wound to have transferred to another digit instead of it having healed and disappeared. She smiled in amazement then looked at him.

"Wow, thanks. How'd you do that?"

He lowered his chin and looked up at her from beneath his eyelashes. She blushed and began to babble, her words spilling out like water rushing over a cliff.

"I mean, I know how. Well, actually, no I don't. I don't understand the mechanics of it all or maybe the magic. Not sure what you'd call it. And I was expecting my finger to feel all weird and maybe vampirey. Is that a word? Vampirey? But it doesn't, my finger that is. And…"

She stopped talking when she saw the smile on his face. He picked out the thoughts of embarrassment and hurt from her mind as she moved to the sink to fuss with the few dishes there. Xīn didn't want her to think he believed her to be dimwitted or foolish. He picked up the bloody towel and handed it to her.

"You're welcome, Nora."

She sighed and threw the towel into the sink.

"I'll deal with that later. Guess I'd better clean up this mess."

"I have a better idea," he offered. "Why don't I clean it up and then take you out to eat, all right?"

She nodded. "That sounds perfect. I'll go change."

Xīn turned to the mess before him. For someone with the power of countless souls inside her, she seemed to be a magnet for disaster. He'd only seen her for the first time this afternoon and already she'd been attacked, fainted, dropped her belongings all over the garage floor, tore up and dirtied her dress, been attacked again, and almost sliced off her finger in a crockery incident. Maybe he should introduce her to the Master and he could evaluate her for himself.

As he threw out the last of the broken shards, Nora entered the kitchen.

"Okay, all set. Where do you want to go?"

He turned to see she had changed into an off-white cashmere sweater and dark blue jeans. She'd swept her hair into a sleek ponytail that exposed her long neck. Even though she wore no makeup, her skin glowed with a shimmery softness. He smiled.

"How do you feel about Chinese?"

CHAPTER SIX

Nora stood outside the Asian market squinting at the entrance.

"When you said Chinese, I assumed you meant a restaurant. And isn't the guy supposed to drive on a date?"

Fā Xīn raised his eyebrows and Nora felt her face burn.

"Not that this is a date, of course. I mean, really, we just met so why would we be on a date? It's not like you eat either so it would be kinda awkward if I ate while you sat there staring at me. Not that you'd be staring!"

Fā Xīn held the front door open and ushered her inside. Though she felt like smacking herself across the face, Nora shrugged then walked into the most jumbled, brightly colored mess of Asian goods she had ever seen. Boxes and bags, stacks of cellophane wrapped goods, bottles of colorful liquids, cases and shelves filled from top to bottom with every Asian foodstuff and product she had ever known, and more she never knew existed.

As Nora entered she turned to smile at the cashier, an old woman with salt and pepper hair and a deeply lined but friendly face. The woman stared at her. Feeling a bit foolish, Nora turned away and studied the nearest display. What at first had appeared to be unorganized chaos was an intricate tower of different teas and tea accoutrements. Each piece supported the next. Even if she was to remove a box of tea or one of the delicate china cups, the entire tower would remain stable.

She turned to Fā Xīn to comment on the feat of engineering and saw the old woman bow to him, bending so far forward that Nora tensed, ready to catch the woman in case she fell over. This act of respect, as well as the calm smile on the woman's face, proved she knew what Fā Xīn was and had probably served him and his kind for years. Fā Xīn turned to Nora and motioned for her to move to the back of the store. Before she walked away, Nora looked at the woman, thinking she should bow and smile just to be polite. Bu the bright speck of fear lighting the woman's eyes told Nora to walk away instead.

Fā Xīn and Nora moved through the store to an opening covered with thick plastic. Once they passed beyond that, Nora felt the drop in temperature and shivered. She wrapped her arms around her ribs and saw that Fā Xīn didn't notice the difference. He moved steadily ahead to a large steel door at the back of the storage area.

Once they walked through and into the freezer, Nora saw the dented steel door at the far side. When it rolled up into the wall, she whistled.

"Wow. This is straight out of Star Trek."

Fā Xīn turned to look at her with a puzzled expression on his face. She stammered an explanation, embarrassed she may have made a faux pas.

"You know, like the TV show, *Star Trek*?"

Fā Xīn continued to stare at her as if she had just spoken a language he had never heard before. She sighed.

"Let me guess, you don't want much TV or go to the movies

or anything, right?"

Xīn shook his head.

"Yeah, figures. Look, Star Trek was this show, created in the sixties - that's the nineteen sixties - about the future. In it, our world is a peaceful planet whose people are more interested in bettering their minds and intellects than gaining money and possessions. We flit about the galaxies, looking for other intelligent life. You with me so far, Xīn?"

He nodded, the same perplexed look on his face.

"Uh, huh. So anyway, there's a space ship, the Starship Enterprise. It's the flagship of what's known as the Federation of Planets. And on this ship, all the doors open like this one," she pointed to the door that just opened in front of them. "Actually, I'm pretty sure all of the doors on all of the worlds in this show open like that, unless it's a society that looks like it's still back at the beginning of the Industrial Revolution and they all live outside and farm and…"

She looked up to see him staring at her. Not perplexed anymore but almost as if he felt sorry for her, for becoming so involved in something that was make-believe. She snapped her mouth closed, feeling humiliated. He finally gave her a curt nod.

"That explains a joke I never understood. Thank you, Nora."

He turned on his heel and headed through the opening. She shook her head then followed behind. As they took the first few steps the door closed behind them. Without thinking she clutched his arm as the darkness enfolded them.

"Uh, Xīn, I have a confession to make. I'm a little afraid of the dark."

"Don't worry, Nora. I know this stairway as well as my own hand. I'll make sure you get through without injury."

"That's not exactly what I mean. Sure, I hate it when I can't see where I'm going but just the dark itself creeps me out."

"Creeps you out?" he asked.

"Yeah. Like, I can't see so I don't know what's hiding there."

"I assure you, Nora, nothing is hiding."

"That's not the point, Xīn," her voice began to take on a hysterical edge. "It's not a rational emotion, it makes no sense, I know, but it's still there."

She could barely make out his nod as he digested this information.

"I think I can help with this. Do you trust me?"

"Yes," she answered without hesitation. Did she really trust him already? He'd done nothing but help her since they first saw each other. He even healed her earlier tonight. So what was there not to trust?

Before she could answer that internal question, Fā Xīn wrapped her in his arms and picked her up. A small squeak of surprise slipped out of her throat and before she knew it, they were descending the steps.

Within seconds they reached the bottom. The torchlight here made it easier to see and she stared up at his face. Although his eyes were dark, she could just make out a shining ring of gold. He seemed reluctant to let her go, as she was to be let go. But they couldn't stand here forever so she shifted her weight and he took the hint. He eased her to her feet.

She turned to look down the long hallway ahead of them.

"Uh, I suppose it's a bit late to be asking this but where the hell are we and what are doing here?"

Xīn pointed to the end of the hallway. "At the end of this corridor lies a chamber where my Master awaits."

"Your master?" Nora asked.

"Yes. He is the one responsible for my transformation. You might say he is my father."

Nora felt her face slacken. "You brought me here to meet your dad? If I had known that, I would have dressed nicer."

She looked down at the casual sweater and jeans combo. "I mean, it's a little early in our relationship to be meeting your folks but I guess this isn't your typical boy-meets-girl kinda situation, huh?"

Her lame attempt at a joke to lighten the anxiety in her heart failed. Fā Xīn stared at her.

"Sorry. I make lame attempts at humor when I'm nervous. Please, lead the way"

Fā Xīn nodded and walked ahead of her. She followed, taking a quick peek down each of the auxiliary corridors as well as studying the doors they passed. Before Nora could ask if they were there yet, they arrived at the end of the hallway at a large wooden door. She could make out a few of the Chinese symbols but had no idea what they represented.

Nora hadn't noticed the rope to the side of the door until Fā Xīn pulled it and a small bell chimed somewhere above them. A moment later the large door swung open and they came face to face with a small ancient man, dressed in traditional black silk clothing. Nora leaned back in surprise, expecting Xīn's Master to be a bit more impressive.

When he bowed to Fā Xīn, Nora suppressed a laugh. This wasn't his Master but probably the Chinese version of an English butler. The little man stepped back, never making eye contact with either of them. As Nora followed Fā Xīn through the door, she looked around the room and though simple, the surroundings dazzled her.

Xīn moved to the center and knelt on the floor. He prostrated himself before a man sitting behind a large wooden desk. Nora gulped but stood frozen in place. She wasn't sure what she was supposed to do. Should she bow and scrape or just stay put? What would be the worse offense?

She would stand her ground until Fā Xīn or the man made a move to include her. After a moment of showing the proper respect, Fā Xīn rose and walked over to Nora. He held out his hand for her and she accepted it with a smile. Leading her to the center of the room, Nora's eyes fell on Master Héng as he stood.

He was a tall man, exceptionally tall for being Chinese. As he moved around the desk, his slim graceful frame appeared to glide. He clasped his hands behind his back as he circled Nora, as if he were a saloon owner sizing up his new whore. She prickled at his scrutiny but kept her mouth shut. Not only was she afraid of making this imposing man angry, she didn't want Fā Xīn to incur any wrath on her behalf.

After a few minutes, Nora began to squirm under his gaze. She looked to Fā Xīn for help but he stood off the side, awaiting his master's command, like a good and dutiful son. She looked down at herself from time to time, just to be sure her sweater was neat, her fly wasn't open, or no toilet paper was stuck to her shoe. Granted, she'd hadn't been near a bathroom for a few hours but with her luck, she would have picked some up on the trip over and trailed it all the way down here just so Master Héng could tsk at her for being unkempt and inappropriate.

Why was she so nervous? It's not like this was a job interview. She wasn't here to win some beauty contest. Hell, she wasn't engaged to Fā Xīn and need approval from his family. So what's with the inspection? Why did Fā Xīn even bring her here? And who the hell were they to 'approve' her anyway? She had a good mind to…

Nora had been so tuned in to her internal monologue she didn't notice that Master Héng stopped circling her. She turned around to face him, ready to let fly any defensive comment she could conjure at the first negative word out of his mouth. She never could have anticipated what he did.

Nora's mouth fell open in surprise as Master Héng knelt before her. She managed a quick peek at Fā Xīn who stepped away from his secluded quiet spot and stood behind Master Héng. He surprised Nora when he knelt as well, hands on his thighs and head down. When she looked back at the Master, he had folded forward at the waist so his forehead touched the floor in front of her.

When he moved to stand, she reached out to help him. She had forgotten he was a vampire, centuries old for sure, and didn't need her help but he was not offended by her gesture. He seemed almost grateful for her touch. Smiling, he patted her hand and turned to Fā Xīn, who was just standing.

"This is indeed as I suspected. She has the power of an almost infinite number of souls. It's most intoxicating."

Master Héng stumbled and Xīn quickly moved to his side to support him. He helped the Master sit down behind the desk. Nora remained in the center of the room, even more unsure of how to act now, and fumbled with the edge of her sweater while looking down at her shoes. She heard a low chuckle and looked up to see Master Héng smiling at her.

"Fā Xīn, please find a chair for our esteemed guest."

Xīn grabbed a high backed chair from the corner. It looked more like a torture device than a place for someone to take a rest. The back was solid wood painted with the image of a dragon. The design appeared three dimensional, its scales and horns ready to pierce flesh. The cushion, cracked red leather, looked like it had lost most of its stuffing. Nora grimaced but didn't want to be rude by refusing it.

She smiled at Master Héng then nodded to Xīn. She sat down, shifting and adjusting her weight so it would be as comfortable as possible. After a few moments she got it to the point where it felt like she was sitting on a hay-filled gunny sack while someone jammed a pitchfork in her back. Probably as good as it will ever get. She tried to hide her discomfort but it was obvious from Master Héng's smile that she failed

"I'm sorry, my dear. I'm afraid we don't usually have mortal guests down here. Most of the furnishings are for show. I promise next time we will have more appropriate accommodations for you."

Nora swallowed. Next time? She wasn't sure if she should be honored or frightened. Despite her trepidation she heard words tumble out of her mouth before she could consider whether or not it was rude to speak unless asked a question.

"What exactly am I doing here, sir?"

Master Héng raised an eyebrow and she feared she had overstepped the line. Even if she was important, she was still a guest. He looked at Fā Xīn.

"You didn't inform her that you were bringing her here, Fā Xīn?"

Xīn opened his mouth to explain but the Master held up his hand. "No, I suppose you didn't. Tsk tsk tsk."

He scolded Xīn like a teacher would a student who'd been acting up in class. Or like a father who has caught his son in a lie.

"I believe Fā Xīn wanted to bring you here to evaluate your authenticity, as it were. I told him of the legend of a mortal born with all the souls created before it. He suspected you might be this mortal and brought you here to get my opinion."

"And I guess he was right?"

Master Héng smiled. "Yes."

Nora blew out a long breath and stood. As she began to pace, she felt a great weight pressing down on her shoulders. The urge to sit down again overwhelmed her. She plopped down to the floor and crossed her legs. By the time she hit the carpet, Xīn was at her side.

“Nora, are you all right?”

“Uh, sure. Yeah. Just give me a minute, okay? I need to process.”

He knelt beside her as she tried not to hyperventilate. His cool skin brushed against her arm and she fumbled for his hand, gripping it in a panicked vise. Nora stared up into his eyes and their simple dark brown color reflected the worry creasing his brow.

She smiled. “I’m all right. I just, I just felt a little overwhelmed, you know?”

Fā Xīn nodded but didn’t release her hand. Despite the flutter in her belly at this news of her extra soulness she forced herself to calm down with several slow deep breaths. The Master sat behind the desk, hands pressed together in front of his face. She glanced at him from the corner of her eye and recognized a smirk of amusement, his eyebrow arched high and his eyes flicking between her and Xīn.

Nora patted Xīn’s hand then pulled it off. She couldn’t continue sitting in the middle of the floor like a child with Xīn fussing over her and the Master looking on. After folding her legs beneath her, Nora stood and brushed some imaginary dirt or carpet fuzz from her jeans. She glanced at Xīn who still frowned with worry, oblivious to his Master’s stare. She cleared her throat and rolled her eyes toward the desk. Xīn frowned and she jerked her head in the same direction, trying to indicate his Master was watching them.

Xīn looked at Master Héng and was immediately cowed. He bowed his head in contrition. Nora wasn't sure what he had to be sorry about but she said nothing. Still smiling, Master Héng approached them both. First he stood before Xīn. He reached out his hand and lifted Fā Xīn's face to make direct eye contact.

"My son, you are the perfect candidate to watch over our treasure. I can see how much you already," he paused and looked over at Nora, "feel for her. I have full confidence that you will protect her with your life."

The tension in Xīn's shoulders released. Master Héng then stood before Nora. He put a hand on her shoulder and she could see a small shiver pass through him. Her gut clenched in fear, the same reaction she felt in the garage when Líng Pò attacked her for the second time. Though part of her was fascinated by the línghún, Master Héng gave her the heebie jeebies.

"You have no need to fear me, child. I would sooner cut off my own hand than see anything terrible happen to you. And with Fā Xīn as your protector, you are assured to remain safe for a long time."

Nora nodded but still couldn't shake this feeling in the pit of her stomach. Maybe she'd talk to Xīn about it later, once they were away from here. The Master looked to Xīn who then walked to the chamber door. Nora regarded Master Héng when he held out his arm, indicating she should leave.

"Oh, right. Thank you," she said as she bowed then almost

ran out of the chamber.

On the walk back to the stairs, Nora looked sideways at Fā Xīn. She opened her mouth to speak but snapped it closed. Any questions she had might be better if asked out of earshot of Master Héng. How far could that guy hear, anyway? She hoped it wasn't all the way out to the 'burbs.

When they reached the steps, Xīn didn't even ask before picking her up. It was still disconcerting to be whisked up a few hundred steps in only seconds but at least she didn't squeak this time. After reaching the top, they moved through the storage area and exited to the main store. As they walked toward the front, the old woman sat behind the register. When she saw them, again she bowed to Xīn who returned it with a curt nod.

Nora expected the woman to stare at her again, like an intruder or outsider. But to her surprise, the woman smiled and scuttled out from behind the counter. She held a small black box covered in a design of pink cherry blossoms and green leaves. She bowed and held it out to Nora.

Surprised at this change in demeanor, Nora felt herself smiling. She bowed and took the box. The woman said something in Chinese and Nora looked at Xīn for the translation. He clasped his hands together and bowed to the woman.

"Xiè xie," he replied to her.

"Wha…" Nora began but the woman smiled and moved back to the counter. Fā Xīn motioned Nora toward the door. Blowing a lock of hair from her eyes in frustration, she'd have to find out what was said later. She nodded to the woman as Xīn pulled Nora out the door.

On the drive back to home, Nora kept silent. He volunteered to drive, offering her the opportunity to reflect on the night's meeting. She hoped Xīn would explain everything that had happened tonight, starting with why he took her to that place without telling her first. But his stoic manner as he concentrated on driving left her unsatisfied. Sighing, she looked down at the box the old woman had given her. She pried it open and found two metal spheres nestled in red velvet indentations.

Delighted, she picked one up to inspect it. The three inch diameter ball was gold plated metal with a green bamboo motif and the other was green metal decorated with a gold design. As she turned it over, a soft ring sounded from inside it. She held the sphere up to her ear and shook it. Whatever was inside clanged against the metal casing and the chime echoed through the car.

"Baoding."

Nora stared at Xīn. "Huh?"

Xīn pointed at the metal balls. "Baoding. Also known as Chinese Health Balls," he sniffed at the modern terminology. "They're good for aligning your Qì."

"Huh?"

Quicker than she could see, Xīn had the spheres in his hand. He rotated them around and around in one palm, almost as if by magic. The two spheres blurred together as he moved them faster and faster. When he stopped spinning them, he held them out to Nora. She grabbed one and put it back in the box. When she reached for the other, the car dipped as it passed over a pothole and the sphere popped out of both their grasps and fell to the floor at Xīn's feet.

"Oh, crap. The ball."

Xīn looked down and shook his head. "I can't see it. Don't worry. We're almost home. We can look for it then."

"Are you kidding? What if it's behind the brake pedal? If you need to stop in a hurry, we might be screwed."

"And why would we have to stop in a hurry?" he asked.

"Gee, Xīn, I don't know. A deer jumps out in front of the car."

"In the middle of the suburbs?"

"A small child runs out between two cars."

"At nine o'clock at night?"

"Aliens try to abduct us and the only way of avoiding their tractor beam is to slam on the brakes and take a hard left."

Xīn opened his mouth to reply but seemed to think better of it. Before she could come up with another reason, she laid the box on the floor at her feet and unbuckled her seatbelt.

"What are you doing?" Xīn asked.

She scooched up in her seat then bent forward, placing her left arm against the headrest on Xīn's seat and her right hand on the dashboard.

"I'm going to look for that ball, dammit. Master Héng said you have to protect me. How are you supposed to do that with a rogue Baoding ball on the loose?"

"But," he tried to protest but since he was driving he could do nothing to stop her. She grumbled and sat back.

"I can't see anything. I wonder if I have a flashlight in here."

She opened the glove compartment. Empty. She checked the back seat but couldn't find anything there either.

"Dammit. I didn't realize I was such a serious neat freak. I might have something useful in the trunk but what good does that do us now? Ah!"

She remembered a penlight she'd received as a free promotion for some new prescription drug. Why the hell did she have that anyway? She dug it out of her purse and clicked the end to make sure it was working. A small bright light lit up a small round circle of the car interior. Good enough.

She got back on her knees on her seat and leaned over Xīn again. She passed the light back and forth across the floor and saw the small sphere resting in between the gas and brake pedals.

"I see it. I can probably reach it if I just-"

She inadvertently grabbed the steering wheel and put her weight on it, pulling it to the right and the car veered. Xīn yanked on the wheel to correct its course and Nora flew forward into his lap. She'd been able to use her left arm to protect her face from hitting the driver's side door handle. Her elbow landed in a spot which, on a mortal man, would have resulted in excruciating pain but Xīn never flinched.

He lifted his foot off the gas pedal and eased it onto the brake. He steered the car to the side of the road and brought it to a complete stop. The Baoding ball didn't interfere. He threw the gear into 'park' then eased his hands beneath Nora's prone body and lifted her back up and over into her own seat.

She rubbed the top of her head where she'd smacked it against the door but the embarrassment was worse than any pain. She could feel her face, as well as every inch of her body, burning with indignation. Nora sat still in the passenger seat, waiting for a reprimand.

"Are you all right, Nora?"

She continued to rub her head, though it wasn't helping the pain. It was probably making it worse but she felt like such a fool that she didn't trust herself to speak in a steady voice. She nodded, hoping he would be able to see that in the dark.

He reached out to her. "Hold out your hand."

She obeyed and he dropped the single ball into her palm. He pressed her fingers around it then gave her hand a soft squeeze. She stopped rubbing her head and put the sphere in the box. Nora felt her mouth curl up into a grin as he put the car back into gear and continued driving.

CHAPTER SEVEN

WǔDá Kuí's father, Han, was a soldier in the Emperor's army in 685AD. Soon after securing himself in the Emperor's personal guard, WǔDá was born. The Emperor himself bestowed several gifts of silver and jade to WǔDá and his mother, showing favoritism over the other guards' children. It was rumored that the Emperor had slept with WǔDá's mother and that he was a direct heir to the throne. Someone in the royal household even attempted to kill WǔDá and his mother by poisoning their food.

But as WǔDá grew, his long fingers and thin face exact copies of Han's, the rumors died and life went on in the palace. Lucky for him, for when he was five years old, Wǔ Zétiān, the Emperor's concubine-turned-wife, took the throne after the Emperor's death. And if WǔDá had been a secret heir, he would have been dead within the hour of her coronation.

Under Empress Wǔ, China waged continuous wars with the barbarians to the northwest, the nomads in the north, and the Goguryeo remnants to the east. WǔDá's father was more absent than present so his mother mostly raised him alone. A few of the other soldiers dispensed advice every now and again, as did some of the palace advisors, physicians, and politicians.

It was an old hermit outside the palace, however, that gave WǔDá the most wonderful gift of all – information about the línghún chī.

When he was twelve, WǔDá snuck out into the world by the gate near the kitchen at the south end of the Palace. Daily deliveries arrived there because those fated in life to be servers were forbidden to mingle with the royal family or the high ministers housed at the north end and so were relegated as far as possible from the aristocracy. During one of the fresh meat and produce deliveries, WǔDá slipped out in the commotion.

Within minutes, he was perusing the sights of the city outside the palace. After an hour, he was in the hills overlooking everything. As long as he kept the palace in his sights he wouldn't get lost. But somehow he managed to get turned around and when night fell, he was still wandering the hills, scared and hungry.

An orange glow shone ahead to his right. It appeared to be the light of a fire coming from a cave in the hillside. Hopeful that whoever built it might allow him to rest and eat, WǔDá crept up to the entrance.

Looking inside, he saw a fire burning in the middle of the cave and an old crusty man sitting beside it. A messy pile of grey matted hair sat atop his head and his beard fell to the middle of his chest. His clothes were ratted and torn and WǔDá thought there was more dirt on the man's face and hands than on the entire floor of the cave.

Though he was thin, WǔDá could see the wiry strength of defined muscles underneath the rough clothing. Scrabbling and working hard for every meal, every moment of life, the old man was probably tougher than steel. WǔDá made this mental note in case he ever had to fight him.

"Do you plan to come in or just make eyes at me all night?" the man asked.

Surprised, WǔDá cleared this throat before he spoke. "I'm sorry to disturb you, Uncle," he started but the old man waved his hand.

"Bah. Come in and rest. I was just making supper. Would you like some?"

WǔDá licked his lips. "Yes, thank you, Uncle."

The old man grunted and continued to stir the contents of a metal pot suspended over the fire. As WǔDá sat across from him, the old man picked up several strips of dried fish and broke them up over the pot. Within moments of hitting the hot stew, the smell of cooking fish wafted over to WǔDá and his stomach growled. He clamped a hand over it, embarrassed, while the old man laughed.

"Been a long time since I've had anyone's stomach but my own to worry about. What are you doing out here, boy?"

WǔDá ruffled a little at being called 'boy' but he didn't want to be rude so he swallowed his retort.

"I was exploring the land outside the palace but somehow I got lost."

The old man stopped stirring and looked at WǔDá for the first time.

"The palace? You live there?"

WǔDá clenched his teeth at his stupidity. He wracked his brain to come up with a convincing lie but the old man only smiled.

"You'll be in a lot of trouble when you get back, boy. The palace doesn't take too kindly to those who escape."

"I wasn't trying to escape. I just wanted," WŭDá couldn't finish his thought. He wasn't trying to escape, was he? Yes, he felt stifled there. The strictures of palace life suffocated him most of the time. His mother forced him to study medicine and his father's friends required him to learn fighting, swordplay, and military tactics. But he didn't want to leave the palace forever, did he?

The hermit laughed. He studied WŭDá over the flames while he continued to stir the contents of the pot.

"You live there with your parents?"

WŭDá nodded.

"But you're not part of the royal family."

It was a statement, not a question, so WŭDá didn't bother to answer.

"Is Měi still working in the kitchen?"

"Yes. She oversees all the cooking for the royal family."

"Good. If you sneak back through there, just tell her I sent you and she'll make sure you don't get into too much trouble."

The old man scooped some stew into a bowl and held it out to WŭDá but he was too surprised to move. He stared at the hermit, unable to process that the filthy man sitting across from him was once a part of palace life.

"I thought you were hungry."

WŭDá shook himself and reached for the bowl.

"No. I mean, yes. Thank you. I'm sorry but I'm having trouble picturing you in the palace."

The old man filled another bowl with stew and began to eat. He spoke around the food in his mouth, bits of fish and rice slipped past his lips and stuck to his beard.

"Oh, it was long ago. I was never happy there. Too many rules, too many people always watching my every move. Everyone's moves."

"Hmm, yes," WǔDá agreed.

"I spent a lot of time in the kitchen where Měi was a novice cook. We became good friends, she and I."

The old man looked off in the distance, somewhere over WǔDá's shoulder. WǔDá sat in silence as he ate, waiting for the hermit to continue his story.

"Měi was just a slip of a girl when we met. Over the years she blossomed into a beautiful young woman. If you asked anyone, they would have said we were lovers, though I never touched her. Oh, I was in love, of course, but I would never have dreamed of soiling her before marriage.

"When I turned twenty and she was eighteen, I asked her to run away with me and get married. I was so sick of the palace by then. I had no interest in the military, wasn't smart enough to be a doctor or an advisor, and my parents were at a loss of what to do. So marrying Měi was my plan. I just never supposed she would say no."

The old man stopped talking and stared down at his bowl. WǔDá held his spoon an inch from his mouth, afraid he might slurp and ruin the solemn silence. When the hermit shrugged and began to eat again, WǔDá followed suit. After swallowing a spoonful, WŭDá cleared his throat.

"So how did you end up here?"

"I traveled for many years. I headed west where I encountered a band of barbarians. They took me in for over a year. Though I had no desire to fight, they taught me how important it would be as a survival skill, especially when several young men beat me daily as I tried to get a meal.

"I then went east, blended in with the Goguryeo people but after a few years, I became restless and headed north. There I encountered a nomadic tribe. I loved moving around the countryside, following the seasons and trade routes. I honed my sword fighting skills and learned knife throwing."

"How long were you with them?"

The old man looked at WŭDá, almost as if he'd forgotten he was there. He smiled.

"Almost twenty years. But even they couldn't keep me away from my home. I don't mean the palace. I mean this land, these people. My land, my people. So, home I came."

WŭDá could feel himself smirk. "And you came to live here?"

"I didn't start here so don't get smart, boy."

The old man stared at him over his bowl of stew, his left eye pinched closed. WŭDá mumbled an apology and asked the man to continue.

"I lived in various places, tried different professions but I always grew restless under the rules and regulations of others. As I moved from place to place, I found myself moving closer and closer to the palace, in an ever shrinking circle. Finally I settled here."

"How long have you been here?" WǔDá asked.

"Oh, I don't keep track of such things anymore. I was definitely younger than I am now."

That was the first of many nights and days to come that WǔDá would spend with the old hermit, Zhōng. And he had been right about Měi. She was always willing to help WǔDá sneak in and out of the palace, sometimes with a little snack or trinket for Zhōng. Though she hadn't run away to marry Zhōng, Měi still seemed to have feelings for him.

For the next six years, WǔDá was able to spend a lot of time with the hermit. He ended up being more of a father to WǔDá than his own. They spoke of philosophy, politics, life, love, war, the dangers and perks of living in the palace. Anything and everything WǔDá could think to discuss. Then one day, WǔDá brought up a topic he hoped might amuse the old man. He had no idea it would end up changing his life.

"Měi thinks there's a vampire in the palace. Isn't that ridiculous?"

Zhōng didn't laugh or even smile. He stared at WǔDá with an intensity he'd never seen.

"What is it?" WǔDá asked.

"If Měi believes there's a vampire among you, then it must be true."

WǔDá burst out laughing. Obviously the old man was pulling one over on him. But when Zhōng didn't share in the humor of it, WŭDá quieted and leaned closer to him.

"Are you saying vampires are real?"

"Of course they are. Oh, they're not the creatures of myth and folk tales. They don't take your blood with a single touch or sleep in the earth. They look much like anyone, maybe a bit paler, but it's not your blood they're after."

"Then what do they want?"

"Your life force, your energy. That's what sustains them. They take it from you, you die, and they live. Forever."

WŭDá swallowed, not in fear but in eagerness.

"How do you know all this?" he asked.

The old man merely shook his head and refused to answer. He grabbed WŭDá's arm and pulled him close. His eyes were bright with fear.

"You listen to Mĕi. And you do whatever you can to protect yourself. There are charms and spells you can use. Mĕi will know what they are. I don't want anything to happen to you."

Zhōng blinked and loosened his grip on WŭDá's arm. He'd never seen the old man look at him like this before.

"I know I'm not your father, WŭDá, but in these past years you've grown to be more like a son to me every day. I don't know what I'd do if you got hurt."

Zhōng's eyes welled with tears and WŭDá was shocked to see tears streak through the dirt on the old man's face. He gripped the man's hands in his own and made a promise, despite the growing excitement in his chest.

"Zhōng, I promise I will listen to Mĕi and do what I can to

protect myself. All right?"

The old man nodded, satisfied with WǔDá's vow. As Zhōng moved around the cave to make supper, WǔDá thought he could still keep his promise even if he sought out the identity of the vampire.

The next day, WǔDá peppered Měi with questions while she gathered ingredients from the store room.

"How often do you think the vampire is here?"

"What are the signs?"

"Do you know who it is?"

She studied him over a large canvas bag of uncooked rice. "Why are you asking me so many questions?"

"How else am I supposed to protect myself if I don't know what I'm protecting myself from?"

She squinted at him then nodded. "I suppose you're right. For now, that amulet I gave you will do the trick. Come back tonight, after the evening meal, and I'll tell you everything I know."

WǔDá smiled then kissed her on the cheek. "Thank you, Auntie."

She blushed and waved him off. WǔDá headed back to his room where he pretended to study medicine while he counted the hours until he could talk to Měi. He also practiced solemn and serious expressions to better hide his true intentions from her.

Later that night he snuck back to the kitchen where Měi was alone and cleaning up the last of the dirty dishes. He tried to sneak up on her.

"No point in trying to trick me, WǔDá. I heard you coming the moment you left the East wing."

He huffed his disappointment but smiled at Měi when he sat down on a bench against the wall.

"Ho do you always know, Auntie?"

She smiled. "I just do. Now, are you hungry? There's some rice and beef left over. The Empress wasn't feeling well tonight so she hardly ate a thing."

WǔDá sniffed at eating someone else's leftovers but when his stomach growled, he couldn't deny his hunger.

Měi laughed. "I knew you'd still be hungry. Here."

She carried a large clay bowl, heavy with food, over to him. WǔDá inhaled the rich delicious scents. As he grabbed a pair of chopsticks, he smiled at her.

"Auntie, how did you become such a wonderful cook?"

"Years of practice, boy. Is that why you came here? To talk about food?"

He chewed a large slice of beef and shook his head.

"I didn't think so," Měi said. "Well, you eat and I'll tell you everything I know about vampires."

Several hours later, full of food and information, WǔDá lay on his bed roll. He stared up at the ceiling as he replayed his conversation with Měi.

Měi had noticed that several of the kitchen staff girls had become listless, pale, and often went whole days without talking, smiling, or showing any emotion at all. One would recover just in time for another to fall under the same mysterious malady.

She couldn't be sure, since it's difficult to notice all newcomers, but Měi believed the vampire had to be inside the palace. There were too many people getting ill for it to be an outsider. And Měi had it narrowed down to two suspects: either the guard at the west gate, closest to the Royal Family's houses where her staff delivered meals, or the new assistant to the head physician.

WǔDá thought about these two men and while neither seemed suspicious to him, it might not be a bad idea to spy on them. After weeks of following them around, however, and taking notes on all their activities, both turned out to be plain mortal men.

Just when WǔDá had given up on finding the vampire, it found him.

CHAPTER EIGHT

Líng Pò crashed through the double doors of the empty building. He had just escaped from Mǐn and Taelin, two of Fā Xīn's best fǎ wǎng soldiers, after they'd accosted him downtown. If they hadn't been so overconfident in their abilities he might be stuck in one of those torture cells right now, beneath the bowels of that innocent little white trash community. Honestly, if those humans knew what lay below their streets, they'd have set fire to that market years ago and burned it into ash.

The doors swung closed behind him, the hinges screeching in protest. Abandoned buildings peppered the downtown Detroit area and because of their dilapidated states, no one was foolish enough to enter them, which suited Pò just fine. He could live or hide in any one he chose. If some homeless person, prostitute, or junkie wandered into his nest that was one less meal he had to hunt down.

He ran through what used to be the lobby of an old apartment building. Ragged remnants of a couch and two chairs huddled in one corner. Dirt, scattered bits of trash, and a variety of debris broke up the faded tile pattern of the floor. Discarded clothing from most of his 'meals' lay heaped in another corner, presumably making a warm home for the resident rats.

Skipping several steps at a time, he ascended the main staircase to the fifteenth floor. He could hear the vermin flee at his approach as well as the stirring of his many followers. So many of the wú lài línghún had been scattered across the world. When he arrived in this country many years ago, Líng Pò organized all of them into a cohesive unit. Even after the rogues had banded together, Pò recruited mortal devotees as well.

Pò frequented the underground clubs, goth hangouts, vampire wanna-be cultures, and found many helpful and willing humans to do his bidding. All he had to do was promise to turn them when they had sufficiently pleased him. He laughed to himself, as if any of these sub creatures were worthy of such an honor.

Once he reached the top floor of the apartment building, he ran down to the end of the hall and pushed through the last door. Pò had converted three separate apartments into one large living area. He left an adjoining apartment wall intact. There he could keep his food until he was ready.

When he entered, his right hand man, Gàn, stood waiting for him.

"Pò, are you all right?"

Líng Pò collapsed into an overstuffed worn chair under a cracked window. "I will be. Give me a moment."

Gàn stood silent and waiting. It's not like Pò needed to catch his breath or rest strained muscles, but his mind still raced from his encounter with that human woman.

Where had she come from? How is it he didn't notice her immediately? He saw the large group of humans as they exited the building. He was always aware of mortals on some level, and he'd been in contact with one from that structure. His spy would tell

Pò when the companies inside would perform these 'fire drills' requiring everyone to evacuate outside for a short period of time. It would create a perfect environment for Pò to skim the waters for his next meal.

He'd already tasted the energy of a feisty old man just hours before. But as much as he delighted in the fight still left in a man that age, his bitter taste soured Pò's palate, as most pedophiles and perverts did. He needed something to cleanse the tainted residue from his tongue.

He sat outside the building for thirty minutes before the horde of mortals spilled out into the afternoon air. As he looked them over, he felt the presence of another línghún but not one of his own. He scanned the area and saw Fā Xīn as he stepped into the sun. Pò grinned, baring his teeth at his one-time friend but now enemy.

Had it really been so long ago that they were friends? Pò had been brought into the línghún fold much later than Xīn but they bonded instantly. Xīn was a stickler for the rules and regulations, and hated to go against The Master. Pò brought a nice sense of balance, good and bad, into Xīn's life by constantly getting his friend to push the boundaries of acceptable behavior.

He had no time to reminisce. Once Xīn spotted Pò sitting on that bench, he could see his old friend tense into fight mode. As Pò prepared to escape, he saw Xīn's eyes, behind the sunglasses, flick toward the group of humans. Pò turned to look at what caught Xīn's interest and that's when he saw her.

A young woman with dark brown hair and pale smooth skin

stood out amongst the crowd. Not just because of her lavender dress or her singular beauty but because she glowed. She radiated power and energy that shocked Pò. He hesitated for a fraction of a second as he burned her visage into his memory.

Pò had to act fast. He sprang toward the woman, reached out and grabbed her arm. She tried to pull away but almost instantly she relaxed. Pò hadn't intended to drain her energy but something inside him clicked against his will. He'd only siphoned off a small amount when Xīn reached them and pried Pò's hand away.

Pò was vaguely aware that the woman fainted and that Xīn attended to her. As he stood, stunned and overwhelmed by the power he had tasted, Mǐn and Taelin swooped in from either side to restrain him. They dragged him away, no doubt to stand him before the council of elders to be tortured, judged, and sentenced for his 'crimes' against the línghún and mortals. He looked over his shoulder, trying to catch one last glimpse of the woman before he was pulled out of sight.

Once he acclimated to the power transfer, what he had absorbed from her energized him. He felt stronger, his head more clear than it ever felt before. It was an easy task to escape from Mǐn and Taelin. He pulled his arms toward his chest and bashed their skulls together. For a human, that would have been fatal. For the línghún, it merely stunned them long enough for him to escape.

Now here he sat, recovering from his experience and trying to organize his thoughts so he could share all he knew with the others.

"Gàn?"

"Yes, Pò?"

"Gather everyone in the main hall."

"Of course."

Gàn moved out of the room and down the hall. He banged his fists on every door he passed, ordering everyone to move downstairs. Pò could hear Gàn's voice fade as he moved farther away. When Gàn reached the main floor, even Pò couldn't hear him anymore but he could feel his second in command as he flitted through the entire building.

Once he sensed everyone in place, Pò moved from his chair and walked down the hall. He prepared his mind for the talk he planned to have with his wú lài. Only the línghún were here now. Most of his human helpers had their own homes and various lives to attend to. Besides, he didn't want them to dirty up his living quarters.

The main hall was a conference or meeting room when this building had been functioning. It was smaller than the lobby but it had an air of importance around it and Pò liked to use it for any important gatherings. All thirty of his group had crammed into the small space. They looked at him with varying degrees of expectancy.

"My brothers, I believe the time has come for us to take the next step in our evolution."

Many of the línghún shook their heads. They'd heard Pò speak of how the línghún were capable of more than this, that they should be evolving leaps and bounds beyond mortals.

"Yes, I know. Many of you are skeptical of my theories. You've all heard me talk about how the more souls we consume, the further along in our evolution we will grow."

Pò moved through the group, laying a hand on a few shoulders, nodding to others. Some met his gaze, their mouths curled into bold disbelieving smirks. They'd never earned his wrath before. Those who had kept their heads low, staring at their feet or the floor - he knew what they were thinking, but to their credit they kept their opinions to themselves.

For the others, he needed an example. Pò locked on a young wú lài, no more than fifty years in the fold. His cocky smile and arrogance smelled like weakness and he grabbed the boy by his throat. Lifting him off the floor, he squeezed his hand and twisted, crushing the boy's neck. His head popped off and rolled several feet away. Pò dropped the body with no more thought than he would give an old rag. Within minutes, the corpse dried into a brittle pile of skin and bone. Pò stomped his foot on it and bits of grit floated on the air.

Those that had been smiling stopped. They cowed their heads now and Pò smiled, satisfied that the lesson had been learned. He moved back to the front of the room.

"You all have heard the myths and legends that have been passed down by our ancestors for generations. Those stories are what led me to believe in our evolution. Well, my brothers, I had an encounter today that not only proves those stories are real but that our evolution is right at our fingertips."

Pò explained what had happened this afternoon. He

instructed his men to lay low and not draw attention to themselves. He ordered Gàn to research the old myths and legends, to find out as much information as possible that would help them on this quest. Pò himself would keep an eye on the woman. With any luck, she would be his for the taking within hours.

****

After weaving his way through the back streets of the city, Líng Pò arrived back at the office building where he first encountered the young woman. The sun had set and most of the humans had departed for their safe reliable lives in the suburbs. He could feel their energy trails fading away but hers was strong, almost at the same force he'd felt this afternoon. That meant she was still near.

Pò ducked inside the parking garage. He scanned the lot and found almost every corner well-lit and marked with security cameras. That could be a problem but not an insurmountable one. He walked through the lot, pretending to dig through his pockets as if looking for keys. While he did that, Pò reached out with his mind to find the woman's energy signature that would indicate which vehicle belonged to her.

It didn't take long. On the first level, in the third row of cars he passed, a flare of her essence leaped out to him from a small red car on his left. He walked over to it and laid his hand on the hood. Small prickles, like static electricity, tickled his fingers as he smoothed them over the surface. He walked around the car and when he approached the driver's side door, the energy increased and stabbed his hand with delicious power. He smiled.

Looking around, he saw two cameras aimed at this area of the lot. He walked to the concrete pillar where one was fastened, stood beneath it then jumped up and tore the power cord free. The red light on the machine blinked out. He ran to the other one, almost flying through the air now that the unplugged camera couldn't record his movements, and ripped it from its secured fastenings. Pò made a mental note to speak to his contact to destroy any tapes that recorded his image.

Pò smashed the bulbs of several nearby lights. He didn't want to destroy too many which could draw suspicions from anyone walking through the lot. Just enough to help him hide. He picked a dark corner near her car and hunkered down to wait.

Within the hour, he heard footsteps echo through the garage. He poked his head out from behind his hiding place and spotted her at the other end of the structure. She was fumbling with her bag and a large folder. Pò darted out of place and moved to a spot closer to her. She might end up seeing him before he had the chance to pounce but a reckless eagerness pushed him forward.

She looked lost in thought, though, and when she banged into her own car, surprising herself, he knew he was right. Her belongings tumbled to the floor and she let out a sigh of defeat. When she bent to pick them up, again he moved closer. He saw her straighten up and look around but Pò remained hidden. When he moved one more time, his shoe scuffed the concrete floor and she was immediately on her feet.

She spun this way and that, trying to find the source of the sound, but never saw him. Humans were so easy to confuse. When she leaned her head back and screamed in frustration, he used that opportunity to move in. Pò stood in front of her for several seconds before she lowered her head and looked him in the eye.

She gasped in surprise and he grabbed her arms.

"Who are you?"

She merely stared at him and offered no response. Either she was tougher than she looked or she honestly had no idea what to say. He repeated the question.

"Who are you? And what does Fā Xīn want with you?"

Her eyelids drooped and he could feel her body loosen. Against his will, he began to drain her. He tried to manage it this time, and had some success but just as he began to control it, something grabbed him from behind and pulled him away.

When he spun around to see who would dare touch him, he came face to face with Fā Xīn. Pò snarled.

"I might have known you'd be lurking around here somewhere, protecting your precious little qíng fù."

"Stay away from her, Pò," Fā Xīn warned.

"Why don't you try and keep me from her, then, if she's so special."

Líng Pò flew at Fā Xīn and they grappled with each other. They spun and kicked, throwing each other around like rag dolls. Xīn slammed Pò into one of the concrete pillars and Pò returned the favor by throwing Xīn against a wall. They continued like this for several minutes until Xīn got the upper hand.

He grabbed Pò by the collar of his jacket and swung him through the air several times. By the third rotation, Xīn had moved close to a dark grey BMW. Pò tried to throw Xīn off but Xīn had a superior position. Pò's legs slammed into the dark car and sliced through the roof, turning it into a convertible. Xīn released him and Pò flew through the air, landing with a thud against the floor, slid twenty feet then slammed into the far wall of the garage.

Pò realized he lost this fight and quickly retreated. He raced back to his hideout, crossing through several neighborhoods, always checking over his shoulder to make sure Xīn hadn't followed. Only when he could feel Xīn hadn't followed him, Pò entered his rundown apartment building. He stood in the empty lobby, frustrated, exhausted, and furious. He leaned his head back and screamed until the anger has dissipated.

He needed a snack. Pò ran up the stairs to his private chamber and kicked open the door. Thankfully none of his wú lài were here and he could have some private time. He approached the door to the separate room and pushed it open. A dozen humans were chained to the walls or hanging from long metal bars secured in the ceiling. Pò studied each one and decided on a middle aged woman in a sagging house dress who hung by her wrists from one of the metal bars.

Pò sauntered up to her, taking his time, drawing out her fear. He inhaled deeply of its peppery scent and licked his lips. She shook with every step he took and cringed away from his reaching hand, even though there was nowhere for her to escape. He placed his hands on her cheeks, caressing them like a lover. He lifted her face so she could look him in the eye.

"Relax, my dear. This will only take a moment. But I'm afraid it will be extremely painful."

She screamed in horror and Pò smiled.

CHAPTER NINE

Nora went to her bedroom to change into more comfortable clothing. She and Fā Xīn would be having a long talk tonight and wanted to make sure nothing distracted her. Maybe Fā Xīn didn't have to worry too much about comfort and pain but a good denim wedgie would drive her nuts. After changing into a pair of soft cotton lounge pants and an oversized t-shirt, Nora stepped into her chicken feet slippers and walked out into the hall.

As she entered the living room, she saw Xīn standing next to the overstuffed chair as he stared down at it and the snoring form of Jethro. Smiling, she tapped him on the shoulder. When he turned, she saw a frown had wrinkled his brow.

"Problem?" she asked.

"I was just considering whether or not to try the comfy chair again but it's been usurped."

She snorted as a Monty Python skit ran through her head. When she saw him smirk, she slapped his arm.

"You just made a pop culture reference, didn't you? And here I was beginning to think you were above such petty things as television and trashy romance novels."

Fā Xīn frowned. "Do you really think I'm such a snob?"

Nora cleared her throat to backtrack. If she didn't know any better, she'd say she'd hurt his feelings.

"Oh, no. You know, after that fancy underground lair and all this talk of souls and bowing to me, I just - I was just kidding. Bad joke, sorry."

Fā Xīn nodded but she saw the shadow of a smile curve his lips. She slapped at him again.

"You jerk. You were just playing with me, weren't you?"

"I'm sorry. I'm usually not like this but the more I'm around you, the more I pick up on your sense of whimsy."

"Uh huh. I'm going to make some tea. Do you want, oh, wait. No, you probably don't."

He shook his head and she scooted into the kitchen. Over the clanging of the tea kettle and cup, she called out to him.

"So, how old is Master Héng anyway?"

"He was turned at the time when the empress Wǔ Zétiān ruled over China. Just a little over twelve hundred years ago."

Nora dropped the porcelain tea cup she was holding. Within seconds, Xīn stepped into the kitchen. He looked down at the broken cup and back up at Nora. She could feel her jaw hanging slack and imagined she looked like she'd just had a stroke. She was having a little trouble wrapping her mind around the fact that the man who knelt at her feet tonight was alive during the Tang dynasty.

Xīn stooped down to pick up the broken pieces. He stood, holding the shards in his hands and looked at Nora, eyebrows up, as if expecting the answer to a question. She stared down at the remnants of the cup in his hands and shook her head.

"Oh, sorry. Uh, garbage is under the sink."

He gave her a half smile and pulled open the cabinet. He tossed the pieces of porcelain into a plastic bin then closed the cabinet door. After brushing his hands together he held them up.

"Done. I couldn't risk you cutting yourself again."

"Yeah," she sighed, surprised by how disappointed she sounded. "That would be just awful. Oh!"

She grabbed Xīn's hand. "Maybe I'm not the only klutz around here. Look."

Xīn looked down at his hand and saw a moderately deep gash in his index finger. He arched his eyebrows as if surprised.

"You didn't even feel it, did you?" Nora asked.

"No."

She tore several sheets of paper towels from a roll on the counter behind him. After moistening the towels under the faucet she turned back to Xīn. When she grabbed his hand, she saw that the gash had already healed. Only a small streak of blood painted his finger.

"Huh. I guess I've got to be quicker next time."

Xīn took the paper towels from her and wiped the smear of blood from his hand. After throwing them in the trash as well, he turned to her, smiling.

"Why don't you go sit down? You look a little shaky. *I'll* make the tea."

"You know how to make tea?"

"Nora," he looked at her from underneath long eyelashes. "I may be a man but I'm also eight hundred years old. I think I'm more than capable of making a decent cup of tea. Now go sit down."

Nodding she moved to the living room. Her limbs felt out of

her control, numb. She was still processing the whole 'vampires are real' concept and listening to Xīn talk about lives in terms of centuries was a bit disconcerting. She found herself standing in front of the overstuffed chair, Jethro still curled up against one armrest. Nora didn't care if the chair did end up sucking her into its overstuffed guts. She collapsed onto it and almost hoped she'd never be able to stand up again.

Xīn entered the living room carrying a tray. A small teapot steamed in the center kept company by a coffee mug. Various cookies, as well as containers of sugar and milk, sat alongside a canister of tea. He placed it on the coffee table in front of the couch.

"Would you like to stay there or move to the sofa?"

"I don't think I can move," Nora answered.

"Fair enough. I will serve you then. How do you take your tea?"

Nora stared at him, hoping to convey a look that said, 'who gives a shit'. He nodded then proceeded to fix her a cup of tea. Soon she became entranced by his movements. His hands deftly handled the cream and sugar, swishing them back and forth from the table to the cup. Putting two cookies on a napkin was a graceful dance. He cradled the mug in his hands and brought that to her first.

"Be careful. It's hot."

Nora nodded and took the mug, grateful for its warmth. She wrapped both hands around it and held it under her nose. She smelled a faint hint of orange and some kind of spice. Clove? She didn't remember having that kind of tea in the house but since she hadn't taken inventory of her pantry in five years, it was possible she had it and didn't even know it.

Nora sipped the tea. It was burning hot but she was happy to feel it scald her tongue and throat. She hadn't realized how cold she felt. Maybe she was in shock. As she took another sip, she looked over at Xīn. He was studying the curves of a Milano cookie. His fingers traced over the arch of it then he held it close to his nose and inhaled. Closing his eyes, he seemed to be savoring its taste through the smell. Nora felt herself smiling as she watched him.

"That's exactly how I feel about them, too."

His eyes snapped open and he looked at her, confused.

"The cookie. You almost look like you're eating it through your sense of smell. I assume you've never had one before."

"No," he answered. "I never saw one of these until I came to this country. Of course, I was already a línghún by that time."

Nora held out her hand. "Then I feel sorry for you, Xīn. Those cookies are probably the most perfectly delectable food on the planet."

He stood and walked over to her, placing the cookie in her palm. He watched as she took it, held it under her nose, and inhaled, much like he had done moments earlier. She dunked the sweet confection into her tea. Biting into it, she savored the melding of vanilla and dark chocolate as Xīn watched her, a smile curling his lips.

"I almost envy you, Nora."

She smiled at him. Without making a reply, she took another

bite and closed her eyes. She could hear him sit back down on the sofa and she cracked an eye open at him. He was still staring at her. She swallowed the bite and took a quick sip of tea. Sitting straighter, she turned to face him.

"I've got a lot of questions about tonight, Xīn."

"I thought you might," he replied.

"Do you mind if I just come out with them instead of tip-toeing around? You may be immortal but I don't really have the time to waste."

"Please, feel free to ask me anything you like."

"First thing I guess I'd like to know is can Master Héng read minds? In particular, my mind?"

"Of course. We all can."

"Uh, that was something you failed to mention earlier. Can you read my thoughts?" Nora asked.

"Yes."

"Have you read them before?"

"Honestly," he started.

"Crap. Look, you can't hold me responsible for any thoughts I might have had about you. It's not my fault if I think you're cute or mysterious or," she found herself babbling.

Xīn held up his hand. "I was going to say no, Nora."

Snapping her mouth closed, her face flushed with heat. She must look like a cherry lollipop or something equally embarrassing. She leaped up as well as she could from the chair then made a beeline for the bathroom. After slamming the door, Nora turned on the overhead fan to drown out any noise.

She put the cup of tea on the counter then turned on the cold water. She gripped the sides of the sink as she tried to push all her frustration through her hands and into the white marble. Would this night of unending humiliations never end? Nora blew out a breath and lowered her head. She splashed several handfuls of cold water on her face then looked into the mirror above the sink, hoping it wasn't as red as it felt.

She grabbed the nearest hand towel and dabbed the water off her face. Taking a deep breath, she picked up the mug as she left the bathroom and went back into the living room. Xīn still sat on the sofa but he had retrieved the entire bag of cookies from the kitchen. At her approach, he opened the bag and held it up to her.

Nora swiped it from him and handed the tea to him in exchange. She plopped back down onto the overstuffed chair. Cramming her hand in the bag and pulling out two cookies, she refused to look at him for several minutes. She crunched on one, then another, and as she pulled out the third she ventured a look at him. He smiled.

"You so better not be reading my mind right now."

"Don't worry, Nora. I try not to do that without someone's permission. Unless it's an emergency."

"Uh huh," she replied.

"If it makes you feel any better, the Master reads my mind all the time, whether or not I have conceded to it. He is my sire, after all."

She brightened at the change of topic. "Yeah, you mentioned that earlier but you didn't get into all the details about the ritual.

Are you allowed to tell me?"

Xīn rubbed his hands together. "No, I am not. It is a sacred event that even families are not allowed to witness. I can tell you that it is somewhat painful but if you are a willing participant, it is not difficult to bear."

"What if you're an unwilling participant?"

Xīn sat quietly, looking down at the tea kettle. Nora cleared her throat.

"I'm guessing it *is* rather difficult to bear in that case, eh?"

"The process of draining the energy alone can be made harsh, depending on the línghún. That's one reason why the rogue population is so troublesome. They cause unnecessary suffering of your kind."

"You mean what I felt when Pò attacked me tonight was only the tip of the iceberg?"

Xīn nodded. "It could have been so much worse for you, Nora. And to be honest, I don't think he meant to do it."

"Wait. You're telling me he was draining my energy without even trying?"

"Yes. It confounds me as well. I've never heard of such a thing. That's why I want to find out more about you."

Nora felt herself blush again but not from embarrassment this time. Xīn clarified.

"I mean, about you being this accumulation of past souls. I didn't mean to imply that I planned to stalk you or survey you or anything."

Nora nodded. "I got it, Xīn. No sweat."

It seemed her embarrassment had transferred to him and he was feeling its effects as well. That gave her a small bit of satisfaction. She didn't want to be the only one feeling like a complete idiot all night. But it was short lived. Her smile faltered as she thought about the implications of what Xīn said. How was he, or anyone else for that matter, supposed to protect her from something even the bad guy couldn't control?

Nora suddenly remembered the presentation she'd brought home with her from work and thought it might make a good distraction. She didn't think she could process all of this craziness anymore without her brain imploding. If the chair hadn't already enfolded her, she would have jumped out of it. She pushed and struggled to get up but only managed to scooch her legs forward and wedge the rest of her body further into the cushions.

"Uh, a little help here, Xīn?"

Smiling, Xīn stood and reached out to her extended hand. With one quick tug, she was off the chair and on her feet. She stumbled as she found her footing and leaned against him. He gripped her shoulders to help steady her. She looked up and saw his eyes change again from dark brown to amber. She wanted to stay against him like this. It felt safe. But he gently pushed her away.

She cleared her throat. "Uh, I forgot about some work I brought home that needs to be finished before tomorrow. I really should get to it."

"I understand. Nora?"

"Yes?" she could hear the hope in her voice and was surprised to know she wanted him to hear it, too.

"This may sound misogynistic but would it be all right if I stayed here to watch over you? I don't want to imply you can't take care of yourself but with Pò on the loose-"

"That's fine."

She laughed when she realized how quickly she interrupted him to answer. "I guess I really would like you to stay. I usually work out here on my laptop so if that won't be a bother, you're welcome to sit with me. The small room at the back of the house has a television if you'd prefer that."

"I don't suppose you know when that Star Trek show is on?"

She pointed her finger at him. "You just wait right there, mister."

Nora ran to the back room and returned a moment later with an armful of DVD cases. "I have the entire series on DVD; original and TNG."

"TNG?" he questioned.

"The Next Generation. The original series ended in 1969 and then they threw in a couple movies. But they basically reincarnated the series in 1987 with The Next Generation. Get it?"

"I see," he continued but she interrupted him with her babbling.

"There are a bunch of other series as well: Deep Space Nine, Voyager, Enterprise, but those kinda sucked. These two are the best. There's a great debate on who's the better captain, Kirk or Picard, but you can decide that for yourself."

Xīn tried to hide his smile but Nora saw it and clapped a hand against her forehead.

"I'm babbling, aren't I?"

"Maybe just a bit."

"Okay. Well, here you go," she handed him the tower of discs. "TV is in there. If you have any questions on how to work the DVD player just give me a shout, all right?"

He nodded then stared down at the stack of discs. She walked to her room to grab her computer and he headed to the back room. After settling onto the couch, she could hear a few clicks and bangs as Xīn fiddled with the DVD player. She smiled to herself as she booted up her computer and got to work.

By eleven that evening, Nora had finished the presentation. It had been quiet in the back room and the last time she checked on him, Xīn was in the middle of the third season of the original series. He was fast forwarding through the episodes and watching intently. She'd have to remember to ask him what that was all about.

She put away her laptop and snuck into the back room, wondering what she'd find. Apparently Xīn got through all of the original series and had moved on to TNG. Again, he was fast forwarding the episodes.

"Um, you know, it's a lot easier to understand the plot when you actually watch the shows."

He jerked when he heard her voice then hit the 'pause' button on the remote.

"The progress felt too slow. The faster each episode played, the better I could absorb their meanings."

"Uh huh. What about the dialogue?"

"To the human ear, there would seem to be no sound when I

forward through the show. But to me, I can hear it all even at its heightened speed."

"You're kidding?"

Xīn frowned. "Why would I be kidding?"

"Never mind. Well, I'm tired. I'm going to bed. Maybe when I get up in the morning, you'll have absorbed both series completely and we can have a nice philosophical discussion about them."

"I look forward to it."

Nora shook her head and smiled. "Good night, Xīn."

"Good night, Nora."

She went into her room and closed the door. Leaning against it, she sighed. For someone so old he could be pretty clueless. She couldn't believe he didn't jump on her comment earlier about thinking he was good looking. Maybe he was just trying to spare her the embarrassment she felt or maybe he didn't think about her that way. Well, duh, Nora, she scolded herself. He's a frickin' vampire. What could you possibly have in common?

She stepped out of her slippers and slipped off her lounge pants. Normally she only slept in her underwear but with the way things had been going lately, and having a guest vampire hanging out in the other room, wearing some kind of pajamas would be the better way to go. It would just be her luck if Pò showed up again to chase them out of the house and she'd be running for her life in nothing but a pair of Rainbow Brite undies.

Snuggling under her down comforter, she wondered what exciting new adventures tomorrow would bring. Please don't be werewolves, please don't be werewolves, please don't be werewolves.

****

Xīn turned off the DVD player. He walked to Nora's bedroom door and laid his head against it. He knew she would never hear him moving around but he wanted to make sure she was asleep. When he could hear her soft even breathing, he turned the knob and eased the door open.

Nora lay on her side, facing the door. Her face and body were relaxed in deep slumber. He stepped up to the bed and knelt beside it, now eye to closed eye with her. Leaning forward, Xīn inhaled her scent. He'd never been so preoccupied with a human before her. He knew there was something special about her, and not just because of the many-soul legend. She was a good person, smart and funny, especially when she wasn't trying. It was obvious that she was a beautiful person on the inside. She was lucky that her outside matched.

He stroked a lock of hair from her forehead and she groaned in her sleep. He stayed his hand, afraid he had woken her. When she spoke his name he pulled away. But when her next words were, 'I'd like some more cookies, please', he realized she was still asleep.

Smiling, he sat back against the closet door across from her bed. He settled in for the night, planning to watch over her until dawn. It was true that vampires could move about during the day. It was simply more comfortable at night and so he would guard her until morning. If he needed to he could sleep for a few hours tomorrow.

Nora mumbled a few more phrases, something about werewolves, before turning over onto her other side. Xīn smiled and continued his watch.

CHAPTER TEN

WǔDá awoke in a darkened room lit by a lone candle. The bed roll beneath him was plush and soft but when he turned onto his side, his ribs protested with a sharp pain that traveled down to his hip. What happened? How did he get here?

"I brought you here."

A voice, smooth as silk, hovered in the darkness and WǔDá squinted to find its source. The shadow in the far corner moved and stepped into the wan light of the candle. A man, tall and muscular, took shape. His long black hair was pulled back into a biàn, or queue, on his neck leaving his sharp angular features exposed. WǔDá thought he looked more Japanese than Chinese.

"I am," the man spoke, as if reading WǔDá's thoughts. "And yes, I am reading your thoughts. I've been reading your mind for years, my young friend. How do you think it was so easy for me to take you?"

WǔDá looked around but the only escape he could see was the door behind the stranger.

"Do not worry. I will not harm you, WǔDá. I have decided to give you what you want."

"What do you mean?"

"Do not play coy, WǔDá. It is not becoming. And you are not very good at it."

WǔDá huffed. "Fine. So are you going to make me a vampire or not?"

"All in due time, boy. All in due time. First you must study the ways of the vampire. You will be my pupil."

WǔDá narrowed his eyes. "What exactly does that mean?"

A low grumbling chuckle echoed through the room. "You will learn soon enough. Do you still want this or should I simply kill you now?"

WǔDá struggled to his feet, the ache in his ribs now throbbing up through the back of his skull.

"I want this. I will do as you say."

"Of course you will. Come, let us begin."

Over the next ten years, WǔDá learned everything there was to know about vampires: their strengths and weaknesses, abilities and powers, what to do when injured, what to do when trapped, their needs, wants, desires. Anything and everything required to live and die as a vampire became WǔDá's life, the learning passed down to him from his master, Shén Xiān Héng.

He'd also learned how to shield his thoughts from his master. As each year passed, WǔDá became more and more impatient as he waited to be turned. And each year he had to hide his frustration and growing hatred for his master. If he had failed to do so, WǔDá would have been killed long ago.

As he sat alone in his room, concentrating on how he could continue to hide his true feelings, Master Héng knocked on the door.

"WǔDá, may I enter?"

He stood and moved quickly to slide open the door.

"Of course, Master. Please."

His Master glided to the center of the room. When he turned around, WǔDá bowed.

"And what do I have to learn from you today, Master?"

"Today is the day you will be brought into the fold, my son."

WǔDá could hardly believe his ears. Would he finally become a vampire?

"Are you sure, Master? I've only been your apprentice for ten years."

Master Héng chuckled. "I know you have been frustrated. I put off turning you for the past few years to make sure the fire in your belly would be properly stoked when the day came. Is it?"

WǔDá nodded. "Oh, yes, Master. I am ready. I'm ready to join you!"

"I thought so. The ritual will proceed tomorrow night. Perhaps you might want to experience your world for the last time as a human. I fear you will not be getting much rest tonight anyway so you might as well 'live it up', as they say."

"Yes, Master. I will. Thank you, thank you."

He continued bowing even after Master Héng left the room. Part of him was still furious, though. Why couldn't he be turned tonight? Ten long years of prostrating and studying and being an errand boy was an insult to the greatness he knew lay within him.

But perhaps the Master was right. After tomorrow, WǔDá would no longer be human and would not be able to enjoy all the intricacies of mortal life: food, sex, love, hate. Although, who's to say he couldn't? Just because the cabal of elders followed an archaic set of rules and regulations didn't mean he had to.

Another thought he should keep hidden from Master Héng.

After a night and half-morning of debauchery, WǔDá stumbled into bed. Once the sun set he would become a vampire but even the thrilling prospect of attaining this most desired event could not keep him awake any longer. He fell into unconsciousness and didn't stir until an hour before sundown.

Master Héng came for him just before dark. The clouds still held the orange and pink hues of the setting sun though the sky's violet-black backdrop began to sparkle with the night's first stars. WǔDá bowed then followed his Master to the sacred space reserved for high rituals.

The incense assaulted his nostrils the moment he entered the room. He coughed into his hand and tried to ignore the cloying smoke. Master Héng pointed to a small red pillow in the center of the room.

"WǔDá, please kneel there."

WǔDá did as he was told and knelt in silence as Master Héng went about the various steps to ready the space for the ritual. It seemed to drag on for hours and WǔDá found his mind wandering but he had to stay in control, at least until the transformation was complete.

Once Master Héng was ready, the ritual itself blazed by in a fury. Barely able to keep up and answers questions when asked, WǔDá was at the Master's mercy, first with the soul extraction then the blood transfer. The pain and ecstasy melded into one long fiery blur until finally, WǔDá became vampire.

Master Héng pulled WǔDá to his feet and grasped his

shoulders.

"Now that you are no longer mortal, you will shed you mortal name. As your sire, I give you a new name, proper for a línghún chī. From now on, you will be Xīn Ài Héng."

He bowed to his Master and when he straightened, an old man stood before him. A mortal. Confused, he frowned at him.

"Who are you?"

"My name is not important. I am here for you to feed."

"Excuse me?"

"I am offering myself to you for your first meal as a línghún chī. Though you are immortal now, you must be weak from the transformation. Let my energy restore you."

WǔDá, or Xīn Ài, finally understood and bowed to the man.

"Thank you, uncle. But let me ask you, are you not afraid?"

The man shook his head. "I am old and have lived my life. I no longer fear death but rather welcome it."

Xīn Ài tsked. "You're lying, old man."

He shook his head again but Xīn Ài held up his hand. "I can smell it on you. You may be ready to die but you fear the pain."

Pulling the old man close, Xīn Ài sniffed his neck.

"Ah, I was right. Your fear is more seductive than your willing participation. And so I will terrify you until the end, for my pleasure."

By the time Master Héng returned to the ritual room, Xīn Ài had decimated the old man. Not only had he absorbed the life energy, he also drained the old man of every drop of blood. Limbs lay scattered across the floor, bits of flesh and bone stuck in Xīn

Ài's teeth and under his fingernails. He felt powerful and invincible.

"Xīn Ài! What have you done? This is not the way of the línghún chī!"

Xīn Ài wiped smears of blood from his chin and grinned.

"Maybe not for you, but for me it was glorious. The old man's fear was more delicious than any meat or grain I have ever tasted as a human."

He grabbed a heavy steel sword from the altar and brandished it at Master Héng. He knew his Master was old and powerful and could easily snap Xīn Ài in two. But he also taught his apprentice well in all matters of hurting or killing a vampire. The energy from the feeding helped make him strong.

Xīn Ài jumped into the air and sliced down with the sword, cutting off Master Héng's arm in one stroke. Spinning, he arced the sword again and severed his Master's leg. As he stumbled, Xīn Ài wasted no time and quickly dismembered Master Héng. He left his head for last. As his former Master struggled with the shock of this betrayal, Xīn Ài bared his new fangs.

"Just so you know I will give myself a new name. I will keep Héng in deference to you as you did give me a wonderful gift. But I will be more powerful than you ever were. I will be like a dragon on the mountain, ruler over all I survey and destroyer of those who oppose me. Lóng Wěi will be my name. Keep that with you for the rest of your life, all three seconds of it."

Lóng Wěi Héng swung the sword one final time and decapitated his sire. The world was now his for the taking.

CHAPTER ELEVEN

The following morning Nora woke to the sounds of a family of sparrows singing outside. Bright shafts of sunlight streamed in through the window, coloring her room in a soft yellow glow. She threw back the covers and growled. After stumbling to the window, she yanked down the shade, grumbling under her breath, wondering how the damn thing got open. She hated mornings.

The remnants of last night's dream lingered on her skin, like a dirty film of oil, and she had a hard time shaking the feeling. Nora couldn't remember everything that happened in it but the sinister shadow of Master Héng had darkened it for sure. And blood. There had been lots and lots of blood.

She slipped into her robe and shuffled out to the living room. When she heard dishes clanking in the kitchen she frowned. Confused, she moved forward and stared at a strange man making breakfast at her stove while Jethro wandered back and forth behind him. It took her several seconds to register the now familiar line of Xīn's shoulders, the gleam of his long black hair, and his smooth delicate fingers.

Before she could acknowledge the warm tingle in the pit of her stomach, her nose caught the scent of coffee. She pushed her way into the kitchen and headed straight for the cupboard where she kept the coffee mugs. Xīn turned upon hearing her bare feet slap against the tile floor. He opened his mouth to speak but she held up her hand.

"Nuh nuh nuh," she grumbled while grabbing a mug and then filling it with coffee. He watched her, a small smile tugging at the corners of his mouth, while she swallowed several gulps of the hot beverage. She clutched the mug to her chest and moved to one of the chairs at the table and sat down, facing him. After taking a few more sips she looked up at him. He was still smiling but she was not amused.

"I assume you were the one who left the window shade open?" she growled at him.

Xīn nodded and turned back to the stove and a pan filled with scrambled eggs. Nora frowned as she watched him.

"I thought you guys couldn't eat, or won't eat, or whatever."

"We don't. This is for you."

Nora raised her eyebrows. "Me? Why are you making me breakfast?"

He turned to look at her. "You don't want me to?"

"No, no, it's not that," she shook her head as she answered. "It's just that, well, I don't know."

He laughed and went back to cooking. "I wasn't sure if you ate breakfast but I thought I'd take a chance. I'm glad I guessed right on the coffee."

She smiled for the first time that morning. "Me, too."

Just then the front doorbell rang. Jethro barked once and ran out of the kitchen. Nora looked at Xīn, her eyebrows knit together.

"Who the hell could that be at this hour?"

Xīn shrugged but Nora saw his shoulders tense enough to

indicate he'd just gone on the defensive. She carried the mug of coffee with her and walked to the front door. She peeked through the view hole and didn't recognize the woman on the other side.

When she tiptoed back through the living room Xīn was standing in the kitchen entry.

"It's some woman. I have no idea who she is. She's probably collecting for the local paper or campaigning for some political candidate. I'll get rid of her."

Xīn nodded but moved further into the living room. Nora went back to the door and opened it. The woman stood there with a plastered smiled on her face, holding up a *Watchtower* pamphlet. Nora returned the smile, not wanting to be rude to a complete stranger, but secretly she could just have easily punched the woman in the face.

"Have you been saved?" the woman asked. Her golden blonde hair bounced as she tilted her head from side to side with the cadence of her question. Nora opened her mouth to answer but the woman interrupted.

"I'd love to come in and talk to you about our lord and savior, Jesus Christ."

With that the woman pushed her way through the front door and past the dog, despite his best efforts to remove her shoes from her feet.

"Hey!" Nora yelled after her and quickly shut the door before turning to chase the woman. When she caught up with her, she found Xīn and the woman in a quiet stand-off. Xīn's eyes were so dark they appeared black. The woman was snarling, her lips curled up to flash her teeth. Nora didn't see any fangs so she wondered what the hell was going on.

"You're one of his, aren't you?" Xīn asked through clenched teeth.

The woman growled and turned. She grabbed for Nora's t-shirt but Nora sidestepped her and the woman stumbled. She threw her hot coffee at the woman and she screamed in pain. Clutching her face, the woman staggered around the living room while Nora and Xīn circled her. Jethro continued nipping at her heels. Nora frowned.

"Xīn, what is…" but she couldn't finish her question. The woman lunged for Nora again and succeeded in grabbing her this time. She pulled Nora close and spat in her face.

"You're coming with me. He needs you."

"The hell I am!" Nora yelled and slammed her forearms down on the woman's hands. She broke her grip and then shoved with all her might. The woman flew backwards and tripped against the coffee table. She fell and crashed through the glass top. When she was down, Jethro stole one of her red pumps right off her foot and trotted out of the room with his prize. Nora thought that might slow the woman down but she got up again in seconds.

The woman looked between Nora and Xīn, who at this point put himself between the two women. Nora heard him growl and she peeked around his shoulder to see his fangs had descended and his eyes turn blood red. She gasped and retreated, pressing her face against his back. He wrapped one arm behind him to pull her close.

The woman screamed and took off for the front door. He spun to face Nora.

"Are you all right?"

Nora nodded and he grabbed his jacket and tossed it to her.

"I'm going after her. My cell phone is in the pocket. Hit speed dial number one, and you'll connect to Mĭn. Tell her what happened, where you live, and that I'm going after the woman. I want her and Taelin to get over here and stay until I get back. Understand?"

Nora nodded again and then he was gone. She did as instructed and by the time she changed into fresh clothes, Mĭn and Taelin were standing on her porch. She opened the door to let them in and they entered without a word. She'd have to find out if that myth regarding vampires and invitations was real or not. Nora didn't say the words, 'come in', but it was pretty much understood.

Mĭn moved through the house and opened every door to every room and closet. Taelin entered the basement and Nora heard him open the storage room and check the windows. Mĭn secured all the main floor windows as well. Nora lived in a ranch-style home so there was no upstairs to worry about but as Mĭn finished her sweep, Nora pointed to the ceiling.

"There's an attic, too, if you think," she began.

"Where's the access?" Mĭn asked.

"Follow me."

Nora led Mĭn down the hall into the spare bedroom. They both ignored Jethro as he lay on the bed, chewing on a red shoe. Opening the closet door, she pointed up at the ceiling. The edges of a recessed panel stood out against the smooth white paint. A long white string hung from it. Mĭn reached up and pulled, and a hinged ladder unfolded. Mĭn extended it and climbed up into the attic.

Nora waited in the bedroom while Mĭn investigated above. After several long minutes, Nora left the bedroom, feeling awkward and intrusive. She went to stand at the top of the basement steps but she could no longer hear Taelin moving around. She called down to him.

"Uh, excuse me? Hello?"

No response. She moved to the back door and opened it. Her screened-in porch faced the back yard where she saw movement to the left. There, back by the Rose of Sharon bush, was Taelin. Nora had no idea what he was up to and decided to go out and take a peek.

She stepped onto the porch and suddenly, Taelin was standing in front of her. She stepped back and gasped in surprise. Her hand flew to her chest as she tried to keep her heart from bursting through it.

"Dammit. You scared the shit out of me."

Taelin took a step back from her and bowed his head.

"I'm sorry. I didn't mean to frighten you."

"It's all right," she breathed. "I guess I'm just not used to you guys yet."

Taelin stared at her, neither agreeing nor disagreeing, his hands clasped behind his back. Nora cleared her throat.

"So, uh, what were you doing back there?"

"Just checking to make sure your perimeter was secure. Your fencing appears to be intact."

Nora frowned. "You really think that chain link monstrosity can keep out you guys?"

"I was thinking more along the lines of mortal enemies."

Gulping, Nora grimaced. "So you're saying that Líng Pò has humans working for him? Why?"

Taelin opened his mouth to answer but Mǐn walked outside before he could.

"Taelin. Xīn's on the phone. We need to talk to him. Excuse us."

Nora nodded at Mǐn's back. Damn that woman moved fast. Taelin bowed to Nora and she gave him a quick smile. He returned it but in a flash he was gone as quickly as he had appeared. Nora's mind was filling up with more and more questions without answers.

Why would humans be helping Pò? Did he promise them immortality? Power? Was the woman that came here today human? Even though she saw no fangs, Nora had assumed the woman was a línghún like the rest of them but now she wasn't so sure.

She walked into the kitchen and could hear Mǐn and Taelin on a conference call with Xīn in the next room. She glanced up at the clock. It was already eight in the morning. Damn, she had to be to work in an hour. Perhaps Xīn was right about her not going. Now that she knew humans would be working against her with Líng Pò, maybe she should call in sick.

That's ridiculous, she chided herself. Nora resolved to go to work. She was not going to hide here all day every day until this whole mess was finished. Who knew how long that would take? She still needed to shower, though, and get dressed. Since she was going to be late, Nora grabbed the phone and dialed her boss's number. After listening to his voice mail message, she spoke at the prompt.

"Hey, Mike. It's me, Nora. Look, I'm running a little late today but I'll be in as soon as I can. I've got the presentation ready so don't panic. I'll be in long before you have to meet with the board. So I'll see-"

Mǐn slammed her hand against the receiver and cut off the connection. Nora glared at her.

"Hey! What the hell?"

"No calls out or in. And you're not going anywhere today. Xīn's orders."

"I don't give a damn what Xīn said," Nora began but Mǐn held up her hand.

"After what happened this morning there is no way you are leaving this house. Xīn's on his way back and you will wait for him."

"I'll what, now? I told him yesterday that I'm not going to hide away in here like some scared little rabbit."

Mǐn stepped closer to Nora and leaned forward, pushing her face so close that they were almost nose to nose.

"Yesterday was yesterday. Today is today. And you will wait here even if I have to restrain you."

Nora swallowed, seeing the seriousness in Mǐn's expression. Though she couldn't win in a fight with this woman but she protested all the same.

"I've got the essential presentation my boss needs today. There's a really important meeting this morning."

Mǐn stepped back and removed her sunglasses. Her dark brown eyes narrowed as she studied Nora. After a moment, she seemed to relax, realizing Nora wasn't trying to scheme her way out of the house. She nodded.

"Once Xīn returns and can watch over you himself, I will take this file to your office. Where is it?"

"Well, there's an actual paper file, a CD, and electronic copy. If you could take the hard copy and the CD, I can email the back-up."

Mǐn accepted the proposal just as Xīn walked through the front door. She turned at his approach then explained that they had secured the house and that she needed to go to Nora's office, although Mǐn never said Nora's name. She kept referring to Nora as 'she' or 'her' or 'the human'. Nora wasn't sure if that was just Mǐn's style or she had some kind of problem with Nora.

Once Mǐn and Xīn finished conferring, she walked over to Nora and stared at her. After a few seconds, Nora felt uncomfortable.

"What?"

"The presentation?"

"Oh, right, right," Nora replied. "Sorry. I'll get it for you."

Nora moved to her bedroom and pulled out the laptop bag

from beneath her bed. It held the CD, and the accordion folder, where she'd stashed the hard copy. She walked back out into the hallway and ran smack into Mǐn. It was like running into a brick wall. Nora rubbed a hand against her chest.

"Ow."

Holding out her hands, Mǐn stared down at the CD and the folder. As Nora handed them over, she scowled.

"No, it's okay. I'm fine."

Mǐn arched an eyebrow at her then turned on her heel. She bowed to Xīn and then headed out the front door. Taelin appeared from the kitchen to stand at Xīn's side. Nora walked over to them.

"So, what's the plan for today? Little tactical surveillance? Maybe build a duck blind to spy on the enemy? What?"

Taelin frowned and then looked to Xīn, who only smiled and shook his head. He turned to Taelin.

"Double and triple secure all the windows and doors. Any way to get in or out of this house. Do you have any bā guà?

Taelin nodded. "Yes, I've already placed several at each window in the basement. Would you like me to place them at all the external access points to the house?"

"Yes. Call Bǎo, Lián, and Dì Shí as well. We can't have too much security here. We need to protect Nora at all costs."

Taelin bowed and moved away. He pulled several small amulets from a zipped pocket on the dark grey cargo pants he wore. He placed three on every window sill. When he finished with the living room, he moved on to the rest of the house. Nora turned to Xīn.

"What are those things?"

"Protection amulets," Xīn answered. "They'll give us a little extra power to help keep you safe. We're going to need every bit we can get."

"So, if you're going to be here watching my every move, how are you going to do research on the cǎi jí shén legend? I assume this kind of info isn't going to be something we can Google."

Xīn scratched his head. "No, I suppose it isn't. And yes," he interrupted himself when Nora scrunched up her face. "I do know what Google is."

She smiled and sat down on the sofa. "So what do you have in mind?"

****

Cora raced back to the abandoned apartment building downtown. She saw no trace of anyone following so she entered without hesitation. Once inside, she stooped over and braced her hands on her knees. Her breathing was still too rapid and ragged. She'd hyperventilate if she didn't calm down.

After several minutes her breathing slowed so she moved to the stairs and took them one at a time. No point in making her heart race again. She also wanted to delay meeting Líng Pò. When he found out she didn't get the woman, he would be angry.

She reached the top of the steps and walked down the long corridor. Doors opened as she passed each one as Líng Pò's brethren poked their heads out to watch her. Cora could see a few lick their lips as they tasted the fear radiating off her. At least they told her they could do that and she had no reason to disbelieve. Not after the things she had witnessed.

As she approached the door to Pò's room, she slowed her steps further. Faltering, fear now made her heart pound. She raised her hand to knock on the door and Pò called out to her.

"Come in, Cora. I've been waiting for you."

Gulping, Cora pushed open the door and saw Pò sitting in a low squat chair at the other side of the room. She closed the door behind her and leaned against it. Pò tsked at her.

"You've come back empty handed, I see. What did I tell you before you left?"

"You said that I should come back with the woman or not at all."

Pò nodded. "You were listening. So, you failed me not out of ignorance or incompetence. You *chose* to disobey me on purpose."

"No, no. I didn't!" Cora pleaded. "I tried to get her. I really tried."

"Seems you didn't try hard enough," Pò purred.

"It's not my fault! Fā Xīn was there helping her."

"What?"

"Fā Xīn," she started.

"I heard you, flesh puppet. That was my incredulous 'what' in response to learning that my old friend, Fā Xīn, assisted this woman. Again."

Cora shook with fear but said nothing more. Pò arose from his chair and paced. He mumbled to himself as if working out a plan. He called to his right hand man. When Gàn entered, Pò whispered something to him and Gàn nodded. They both looked at Cora and whispered some more. Gàn bowed.

"As you wish, Líng Pò."

Pò turned to Cora and waved. "Good bye, my dear."

Cora screamed just as Gàn grabbed her by her hair. She fell to the floor, kicking and screaming, trying her best to escape but deep down, she knew it was no use. As Gàn dragged her down the stairs and then turned toward the basement access, Cora's vocal chords froze. She was not just going to die. She was going to die in fiery, tortuous agony.

When Gàn pulled open the basement door, the foul stench that wafted up from its black depths gagged even the línghún. A low growl echoed up the steps just as an arm, grimy and bloodied, moved into the light shining down from behind them.

"Fā kuáng, I've got a little snack for you. Enjoy."

Cora screamed again as Gàn shoved her down the steps. As he slowly closed the door, and the small rectangle of light disappeared forever, Cora prayed for her death to be quick. When the beast tore her arm from its socket in one swift movement, she wept with hopelessness.

CHAPTER TWELVE

Xīn got on the phone to one of his trusted team members, Yong. They spoke briefly about the hall of records and access to it. Only a limited number of línghún were allowed to enter the room containing thousands of books on their history, legends, myths, and whatever other information had been collected over the millennia. Xīn was one of those precious few and so he gave his access information to the man at the other end of the phone. The elders may not permit it but he had to try.

After closing his cell phone he looked at Nora. "Where's your computer?"

"In my room. Why?"

"Maybe we can't Google this legend but perhaps we can find something floating out there in the internet ether. It's better than just sitting here."

Nora agreed and went to get her computer and a lap desk. When she returned, Xīn had cleared away the broken remnants of the coffee table. She sat on the sofa and booted up the computer. Xīn sat beside her just as she opened the browser. She held her fingers over the keyboard not knowing how to proceed.

"You're going to have to take the reins here, bud," she said to Xīn. "I wouldn't even know where to begin on a search for this stuff."

"May I?" he asked as he pointed at the computer.

"Have at it."

Nora handed the desk and computer to Xīn. He typed in a few key words: Chinese, lore, legend, myth, souls. Thousands of pages of information contained these words and Xīn began pouring through them all, page by page. After looking at a few of them, he asked Nora to get him a pad of paper and a pen so he could jot down a few notes.

At first he would delve into the entire site where he'd linked in. But after an hour, he stopped taking copious amounts of notes as it was tedious work and wasn't helping him make much progress. Instead he wrote down the site addresses that might contain the information he was looking for and said he would go back to them later after looking through the rest.

After several hours of an unrelenting search, Nora was exhausted. And she wasn't even the one doing the research. Just watching Xīn hunched over a computer was tiring and it made her back ache. Rubbing her eyes, she stood, getting some much needed blood flow to her ass. She walked a few tentative steps to make sure her lower body still worked then turned to Xīn.

"Aren't you tired? Don't you want to take a break or something?"

Xīn looked up at her for a second then turned back to the computer, shaking his head. Nora blew out a sigh.

"Well, I do."

Nora decided to switch out her winter clothes for her summer ones. True it was only early spring but she had to do something other than sit here and watch Xīn do all the work. It took her an hour to switch everything out and still Xīn hunched over her computer. She then did two loads of laundry. After that it was the dusting, vacuuming, cleaning the kitchen, shaking out the floor mats, organizing her underwear drawer, polishing her shoes, replacing the batteries in all her smoke detectors, and cleaning out the fridge.

Even after all that, Xīn still hadn't finished his on-line research. Nora looked down at the legal pad on the coffee table and noticed that many of the notes he had written earlier were crossed out. Apparently, the sites he wanted to go back and check out had been a waste of time. She sat down next to him.

"Xīn, this isn't working."

When he didn't respond, she reached forward and grabbed his hands, holding them still to keep him from typing. He snapped his head to look at her and he seemed almost surprised at her presence. She released one of his hands and waved hers in front of his face.

"Hello? Xīn? You in there?"

He shook his head. "I'm sorry, Nora. I guess I became engrossed in my research."

"And how's that going by the way?"

"Not well," he answered in defeat.

"I thought as much," she replied as she pointed at the legal pad. "C'mon. You need a break."

"We don't have time."

"Uh, yes we do. You've been sitting at this computer for hours, Xīn. Look outside. Most of the day is gone. I bet even vampires need a little R&R from time to time, right?"

Xīn stared out the window then hung his head. "I suppose a short diversion would do me some good."

She smiled at him and he returned it. She walked to the hallway where she opened a small closet and pulled out a long rectangular box. Carrying it to the living room, she called out to Xīn.

"You ever play Monopoly before?"

As she laid the game on the floor in front of the couch, Xīn frowned and shook his head. Nora rubbed her hands together and laughed.

"So, a Monopoly virgin, eh? Don't worry. I'll be gentle."

He frowned as the joke sailed over his head and she blew out a breath. "I guess some humor is a bit of an emotional stretch for you guys, too, huh?"

He opened his mouth to reply but she held up her hand. "Never mind. I'll explain the joke later. Right now, get down here on the floor and I'll tell you how the game is played."

What was supposed to be a short break turned into an hour and a half Monopoly marathon. By the end of the game, Nora had most of the money from the bank, the majority of the real estate buys, with homes and hotels, and Xīn had, well, Xīn had the shoe.

When the game was over, Nora stood and pumped her arms in the air. She shouted her victory cry to the ceiling.

"Woohoo! Nora's number one! Nora's number one!"

Xīn sat cross-legged on the floor, smiling up at her. Although he had lost the game, he was happy because Nora was happy. He liked to watch her revel in the simplicity of a game well played, and won. After yelling for a minute, Nora began to do a dance move that she called the 'cabbage patch'. He wasn't sure what dancing had to do with vegetables but he did laugh out loud as she chanted.

"Go Nora, it's your birthday, won the big game, beat the vampire."

He hadn't felt such mirth in years and was surprised when he laughed. Even Nora stopped celebrating and knelt down in front of him.

"Dude, did you just laugh?"

Xīn smiled and nodded. Nora jumped up and whooped with delight. She began her cabbage patch dance again but with a new chant.

"Go Fā Xīn, it's your birthday, made your first laugh, 'cause Nora's so cool."

Her giddiness was going to get the better of both of them if she didn't stop. So he grabbed her arm before she could get the full groove of 'the running man' and pulled her down to the floor. She hadn't expected it and fell, collapsing on top of him. He rolled backwards to absorb the blow of her body weight.

This made her laugh even harder. Xīn gripped her shoulders and tried to shake a little sense into her even though he was enjoying himself. He begged through his smile.

"Nora, please. You've got to calm down. You keep all this up and we'll both end up laughing until tomorrow morning."

As he pleaded with her she reached up and gave him a half salute but that only managed to stifle her laughter for a moment. He laid his head back on the floor, exasperated. That seemed to get through to her and she stopped. A small giggle popped out every few seconds but she was calming down.

When her chest stopped hitching Xīn lifted his head to look at her. She stared down at him, her eyes roaming over his entire face. He should have pushed her up and away at that point and continued with his research but something inside him wouldn't allow it.

He enjoyed the pressure of her weight against his body. The blue of her eyes matched the color of the sky after a strong rain. Her pale skin glowed underneath waves of reddish brown hair. He reached up a finger to trace the line of her jaw. She didn't flinch. She wasn't disgusted. Most humans, unless they were willing to sacrifice themselves, hated to be touched by anything dead.

Her energy was infectious and he couldn't resist it. Even she seemed to understand the shaky territory they were entering but she didn't stop him. She reached out to touch him and for what felt like hours, they simply explored the contours of the other's face. He was fascinated by her bone structure, the feathery texture of her eyelashes, the powdery smoothness of her skin. She ran her fingers through his hair, traced the lobes of his ears, and smoothed the back of her hand against his cheek.

Their eyes locked. He could feel the shift of color in his own. He'd had centuries to familiarize himself with the sensations. What amazed him, though, is that her eyes began to change as well. The blue shifted to green then hazel. Lastly, a golden amber light fell over her irises and he imagined that if they stood side by side before a mirror, their eyes would be identical.

His shock was mirrored in her face and that was what propelled them apart. She scuttled backwards until she reached the big chair. As he straightened, her hands flew to her cheeks as if making sure it was still her face attached to her head.

"Nora," he said but she jumped to her feet and ran to the bathroom. He followed then stood behind her as she stared at her reflection. She leaned in close to the mirror, running her fingers over the delicate skin beneath her eyes. The gold color was fading but still prominent enough to be obvious.

"My eyes," she whispered.

They both stood at the mirror and waited until the normal familiar blue of her eyes returned. She stared at Xīn in the mirror.

"Did you know that was going to happen?"

"No. I'm just as surprised as you," he answered.

"Oh, we *really* need to figure this out, Xīn."

"Agreed," Xīn nodded. "Perhaps Yong has discovered something useful. If not, I may have to check the records myself. Maybe speak with Master Héng."

Nora shivered and he placed a hand on her shoulder.

"What's wrong?"

Nora rubbed her arms. "No offense to your Master or anything but he gives me a bit of the creeps."

Xīn frowned with confusion.

"I don't understand."

She stammered over her reply. "Well, it's just that, I don't know. I can't pinpoint it. It's just a feeling. The way he looked at me."

"Nora, he honored you last evening. Do you think he kneels at the feet of just anyone?"

He could hear his voice rising in anger, an emotion he hadn't felt in centuries. Nora stepped back from him, fear shadowing her eyes.

"I'm sorry, I just," she began.

"No, please. Forgive me. You were only sharing how you feel. I have no right to get angry with you for that."

She nodded. Xīn thought maybe they'd crossed a line in their new relationship. A point where things of the línghún world lost a bit of their shiny splendor and showed her their darker, more stained side. He honestly felt sorry to see a taint of fear in Nora's eyes but perhaps it was for the best. For both of them.

Xīn pulled out his cell phone and called Yong. Nora walked into the kitchen to give him some privacy.

"Were you able to find anything, Yong?"

"Yes and no," he answered. "I was able to find several references to the cǎi jí shen but not much beyond that. Some of the text was an ancient form of Chinese and only the elders can interpret it. There were several scrolls that were supposed to contain information but I never got the chance to look at them."

"Why not?"

"They're not in the archives."

Xīn didn't understand. "What do you mean? Why wouldn't they be in the archives?"

"I don't know," Yong replied. "I was told I didn't have clearance to see them anyway. Only the holy men do. Maybe you can find something I didn't. Or ask for Master Héng's help."

"All right. Thank you, Yong."

Xīn closed his phone and walked to the kitchen. Nora stood at the sink, looking out the window that overlooked her driveway and garage. She didn't hear him approach so he took some time to study her posture. As he moved to her left, he saw that she held a coffee mug filled with hot water. A tea bag soaked inside it and she moved a small spoon back and forth.

He caught her profile as she stared outside. He didn't want to intrude on her thoughts and so couldn't imagine what might be going through her mind right now. After a few seconds, she released the spoon and looked down at her hand. She turned it over, palm up, and rubbed her thumb against her index finger, the one she'd cut yesterday. The one he had healed with his blood.

Her mouth curled up in a small smile and a dimple pierced her cheek. He hadn't noticed it before. Without thinking he reached out to touch it. When she turned she wasn't surprised to see him. It was as if she knew he was there the whole time, watching her.

They shared a long stare. In a moment she had thrown the mug in the sink and he had tangled his hands in her hair, pulling her close. He crushed his lips against hers, careful not to hurt her. As much as he felt himself spinning out of control he always kept in mind that he was a vampire and she was mortal. He could accidentally kill her with just one swift movement.

Nora had wrapped her arms around his waist and pressed her body against his. She opened her mouth to him and he hesitated. She felt it and broke the kiss to lean back and look up at him.

"What's wrong?"

Xīn looked down at her mouth, partially open with flushed red lips. It was so tempting to lean down and…no, he mustn't. He couldn't. He released her and backed away. Although he had no need to breathe, it felt like his chest was going to implode. She took a step forward, her face creased with concern. He held up his hands to stay her.

"Please, don't come any closer."

"Xīn? Tell me what's happening."

"I," he began but couldn't finish.

Her eyes widened as she understood what he was dealing with. "You want to feed on me, don't you?"

All he could manage to do was nod. As much as he didn't want her to see him like this, for her to even know he had to feed from time to time, she needed to understand how much power she had over him. Not just now but every time they were together. Gods, how was he supposed to protect her when all he wanted to do right now was consume her?

"What if," she started, "I let you?"

He stared at her, shocked. Yes, it was true, she was more open and acceptable of his kind from the first moment she understood they existed. And she was even honest about her feelings regarding Master Héng. But here she stood, telling him she would voluntarily allow him to feed off of her. He didn't know how to respond.

"I know. I think I just shocked myself with that offer. Here's how I see it. It seems to me that we're going to have to spend a lot of time together until this nightmare is resolved. I assume that, because of what or who I am, it's rather difficult for you to be around me all the time."

He started to protest but she stopped him. "I know I'm only human but I'm not an idiot, Xīn. Your kind is built to feed off mine. And I'm a gajillion times more savory than all the rest. You with me so far?"

Xīn nodded but wasn't sure where she was going with this.

"You ever hear the theory of forbidden fruit? You know, you want something more because you can't have it?"

He understood and said as much.

"All right. So what if I make myself unforbidden, just to you? You get a taste, swish it around in your mouth, and finally know what all the fuss is about. Then it's not so exotic or mysterious and maybe loses some of its power."

"I'm not sure that would be the best idea," Xīn answered.

"I know. We run the risk of, 'oh my God this is the best person I ever tasted and I can't stop' problem. But I think being side by side, all the time, close quarters and all, will just make it that much worse if we don't do this. What do you think?"

"I'm still not convinced you understand what you're saying."

"Then why don't you break it down for me," Nora replied.

"It's not that I don't appreciate the offer. I will only feed from someone who volunteers themselves of their own free will. And when I do, it is usually until they die. But if we follow your plan, and you still live, assuming I can control myself, you will always be in my flesh. I will forever be connected to you in every sense –

emotional, mental, physical."

Nora chewed on her lip as she thought about it. When she looked up at him, she was smiling.

"But wouldn't that be a good thing, especially now? If I'm ever in trouble, you'll always be able to find me."

Xīn opened his mouth to reply but snapped it shut. He had never thought of that though he shouldn't use that as an excuse. He always tried to follow the strictest of codes when it came to feeding off mortals. Was she truly ready for something like this? Was he? He looked into her eyes. Could he resist her offer, even if he wanted to?

Xīn took a step toward her but before he could do anything his cell phone rang. She laughed and hung her head. He apologized and pulled the phone from his pocket. Opening it, he snapped out a greeting.

"What? Yong, yes, what is it? He does? All right. Good. As soon as they arrive I will leave. Thank you."

He ended the call and put the phone back in his pocket. He reached out and caressed Nora's face. She pressed her hand against his.

"Master Héng?" Nora asked.

"Yes. Yong explained what we're doing and the Master said he would help. But I'll be going alone. Mǐn and Taelin are on their way to watch over you while I'm gone."

Despite her earlier confession about Master Héng, she appeared upset that he was leaving. When she leaned in and kissed him on the mouth, he could feel the disappointment pass into his skin.

He pulled her close and wrapped his arms around her. He kissed the top of her head then pressed his cheek against her hair.

"How did we get here, Nora? I never thought I'd ever feel anything like this for a human. Or anyone for that matter."

She laughed softly. "Neither did I."

He pushed her far enough away to stare at her face. She smiled up at him, so trusting, so full of hope and joy, despite having her world turned upside down. He kissed her forehead just as a knock sounded on the front door. Nora sighed.

"Damn, they're fast."

Xīn chuckled and moved to the living room. He opened the door and ushered Mǐn and Taelin inside. He gave each of them orders for protecting Nora and the house. He wasn't sure when he'd be able to return so they were not to leave for any reason until he got back.

After instructing them, Xīn turned to go back in the kitchen but Nora was already standing in the living room. He smiled and walked over to her. He gave her another hug and whispered in her ear.

"I'll return as soon as I can. Hopefully with some good news. Or at least just news."

She giggled and squeezed his waist. "All right. Hurry back. We have a discussion to finish."

He pulled away and brushed his fingers along her cheek. He turned to Mǐn and Taelin. Mǐn arched an eyebrow at him and Taelin tried to hide a smile. He glowered at them both until their expressions returned to something more neutral. Nodding, he moved to the front door. He stopped in the open doorway and turned to look at Nora one more time.

She gave him a small wave and then he moved out into the night.

CHAPTER THIRTEEN

Xīn entered the inner chamber to await Master Héng. As he did, he thought about what Nora said. While he couldn't imagine anything appalling about the Master, to a human he could be quite intimidating, perhaps even sinister. Although Master Héng was much better at controlling his emotions, when subjected to them, Xīn had to be sure there would be no misunderstandings. Nora may have to come back here and Xīn didn't want anyone to get hurt.

Funny. Even this far away from her, Nora's influence still colored his thoughts and motivations. He wondered how long it would last.

"I would say at least twenty four hours, my son."

Xīn turned, surprised at the Master's sudden entrance. He had been so deep in thought that he never realized Master Héng stood behind him. Xīn bowed deeply.

"Yes, I've been away from her for a few hours yet I still feel her influence."

Master Héng's eyes seemed to radiate with a fever. They were bright and fierce. For the first time since his transformation, Xīn felt a small tingle of fear at the base of his spine. Lucky for him the Master didn't notice. Or at least he didn't say otherwise.

"So, Xīn. Yong tells me you're trying to find information on the cǎi jí shén. How can I help you?"

"Yong says some of the texts he found are written in an ancient form of Chinese and he is unable to read it. Also, some scrolls are only accessible through the elders and the council or are missing altogether."

"I see," Master Héng said through laced fingers. "And what would be my reward for assisting you?"

The Master's voice sounded belittling, as a seasoned artist might mock an apprentice who has stepped above himself and his abilities. Master Héng laughed.

"Oh, Xīn. You misinterpret me. I was only playing a joke on you. Forgive me but her power lingers within my flesh as well and I feel good-humored today."

Xīn smiled and nodded but was not fully convinced so he changed the subject.

"Would you be willing to help me by translating the texts and perusing the scrolls for any information?"

"Of course I would, Xīn. I do ask one thing though. Maybe not a reward but perhaps a favor? Would you bring Nora to see me again?"

The way the Master's face lit up at her name chilled him. Nora was right. He cleared his mind of all such thoughts and bowed.

"Of course, Master. When you have had the chance to translate the documents, and I am sure neither Líng Pò nor any of his minions are near, I will bring her for a visit."

"Wonderful, wonderful," Master Héng replied.

He walked away, rubbing his hands like a child who has just been told he may have sweets before dinner. Xīn watched the Master exit the room and felt a dark sense of ruin take his place.

He shook his head and left through the opposite door to a hallway that led to the records room. As Master Héng retrieved the scrolls from the other elders, Xīn would look through the old records to see if there was anything Yong might have missed.

****

Nora laughed as she laid out four kings, three aces, and a low number run of Hearts on the table.

"Gin!" she exclaimed.

Taelin scratched his head. He hadn't quite caught on to the mechanics of the game yet and was still losing hand after hand. Nora stood up from the kitchen table and did her victory cabbage patch dance.

"Go Nora, it's your birthday, won the card game, beat Taelin the vamp."

Taelin stared up at her, his face a blank slate. She bounced in place a couple more times then sat down, defeated.

"Well, Xīn thought that was funny."

Mǐn entered the kitchen from the basement stairs. She checked all the windows and bā guà every fifteen minutes. She was nothing if not thorough and mule-headed in her consistency. Standing at the table she stared down at Taelin.

"We need a perimeter sweep. Take Guǒ Dān with you."

Taelin stood and then bowed. He stepped out through the back door, motioning to the middle-aged Asian man on the back porch. More than likely he was much older than he looked but Nora never asked. Mǐn sat down across from Nora then held up the stack of cards.

"What are you doing with these?"

"Um, playing Gin Rummy?"

"These are a distraction," Mǐn answered. "We are not here to be your friends. We are here to keep you safe from harm. Do you understand?"

Nora nodded then stared down at her fingers. She picked at a hangnail, afraid to look up at Mǐn lest she get scolded again. Why did Xīn have to leave her alone with Mǐn? She obviously didn't like Nora and would rather have been doing anything else but play babysitter.

When Nora braved a look back at Mǐn, the línghún was inspecting the cards, back and front. She gave Nora a sideways glance.

"So, how do you play this Gin Rummy?"

Nora smiled and held out her hand. Mǐn placed the cards on Nora's outstretched palm and offered her a small smile. It looked like Nora's energy was affecting Mǐn's state of mind. Nora shuffled and explained the rules.

"Okay. Now this might actually just be called Gin but I can never remember. My dad taught me a long time ago. The object of the game is to get ten cards to match up in sets of three, three, and four. For example…"

An hour later, Mǐn had won ten of the twelve games they had played. Nora slammed her head down against the table top as Mǐn turned her extra card over on the discard pile and exclaimed 'Gin'. She banged her head repeatedly as Mǐn stood and tried to mimic her cabbage patch dance from earlier.

"Go Mǐn, it's your birthday, won the card game, beat Nora the mort."

Nora lifted her head and watched the vampire as she danced. Then she threw her head back and howled with laughter. If Nora hadn't already known Mǐn was a vampire, she would have thought her as normal as any human performing a victory dance over something so silly and trivial as a card game. Mǐn stopped dancing and stared at Nora. Then her mouth twitched. The twitch turned to a grin then into a full smile. She laughed, a lilting musical sound that echoed throughout the kitchen.

Taelin stood in the doorway to the porch and tilted his head as he studied them. Nora jumped when she saw him and held one hand over her chest and wiped the tears spilling down her cheeks with the other.

"Oh, Taelin. You scared me. Is anything wrong?"

"No. I just wanted to inform you that Xīn has returned."

At the mention of Xīn's name, Mǐn immediately stopped laughing and walked to Taelin.

"Where is he?"

Taelin jerked a thumb over his shoulder. "Behind me."

Xīn stepped out from behind Taelin and Nora saw Mǐn pale under his gaze. His eyes were dark and his scowl, directed at Mǐn, was fearsome to behold. They stared at one another for several beats then Mǐn nodded at him and moved toward the living room. She managed to give Nora a sidelong glance before disappearing out the front door.

Xīn jerked his head toward the backyard and Taelin moved in

that direction. Xīn turned back to look at Nora and she felt like as small child who stood before a parent awaiting punishment. He took her by the elbow and escorted her to the back of the house, and into her room. He closed the door gently then made Nora sit down on the bed.

"I'm sorry, Xīn. I know I shouldn't have been distracting her like that," Nora started but Xīn shook his head.

"I didn't bring you back here to talk about that."

His voice was tight and Nora immediately felt afraid. "What is it? What's wrong?"

"Two things. One, I found out more about the legend of cǎi jí shén. We already know that once every millennia, a human is born with the power and energy of all the souls that ever existed before them."

"Uh huh," Nora said as she nodded.

"This mortal can take any form: man, woman, child, adult, genius, fool, rich, poor."

"Yeah, got it. Anything's possible. What else?"

"And more than likely, this human is completely unaware of her power."

Nora pointed at herself. "Obviously."

"But here's where it gets interesting. Apparently, if a línghún can harness that untapped power, get control of all that energy in its pure form, he will have the power to change the world."

Nora stared at him, waiting for more of an explanation. When none was forthcoming, she held out her hands.

"That's it? Change the world? Like what, the Young

Republicans, the ministry of television evangelists, what?"

"You don't understand, Nora. He can change the world into anything he wishes. If he wants the world to be brimming with vampires, he can do it. If he wants blood to run through the streets as humanity tears itself apart, he can do it. He can create and destroy at will, anything and everything he chooses."

Nora dropped her hands. She sat still as she absorbed the awesome implication of Xīn words. Even with this power in the right hands, even in the best case scenario, the world would belong to Chaos.

"I…I…" she stammered. She couldn't seem to form a complete sentence.

"I…"

"Don't worry, Nora. I won't let anything happen to you. I promise."

She looked up at him as one question popped into her head.

"What do you mean, 'in its purest form'?"

He frowned and she gestured wildly with her hands. "You said if a línghún got a hold of my mojo in its purest form. What does that mean?"

He rubbed a hand over his face. "For us, the purest form of human energy comes from the blood."

"Of course! Why would it be anything else?"

Nora stood up and paced. "Of course he'd need my blood. Heaven forbid it would be a strand of hair or my toenail clippings. Stuff I can live without. Gonna be a little hard to attend the company picnic without all my blood, though. 'Gee, Nora, you look a little pale. You okay?' 'Oh sure, I'm good. Just had some psycho vampire steal all my blood, no biggie!"

Her voice rose as hysteria began to take over her mind. "What exactly did I do in my past life to get handed this shit platter? Was I a baby-killing cannibal or did I strangle little puppies?"

Xīn grabbed her shoulders and made her stand still. She was breathing hard and could feel the panic rising up from her toes and collecting in her lungs. Before it could explode out of her chest, Xīn gripped her head in his hands and forced her to look at him.

"Nora, please, nothing will happen to you. I won't allow it. I won't. I'll die first!"

She held her breath as she looked into his eyes. Her heart still slammed against her ribs but as she stared at him, she felt herself calm down. She took slow breaths at his direction. When she took one long deep breath she threw her arms around him and buried her face against his chest.

Xīn wrapped his arms around her and held her close. She inhaled his scent, a cross between spices and earth. An odd combination but it fit him. A cool dampness pressed against her cheek. She pulled back and touched her face. Looking at the dark splotch on his shirt she realized she'd been crying. Great, first she had hysterics and now she's bawling like a baby.

"I'm sorry," she said as she wiped the tears from her cheek. She pinched the fabric of his shirt between her fingers and pulled it away from his skin. When she looked up at him to apologize again she saw a bright glistening trail on his face. Both of his eyes were brimming with tears.

She reached up and brushed away the one that ran down his cheek. "Xīn."

He stared down at her wet fingers, amazement lighting up his face. He touched her hand and then his cheek. At that moment several more tears broke free and fell across his hand. He stared at the moisture. His mouth curled up on one side in a small smile. Nora blinked in surprise.

"Xīn, why are you smiling?"

"Nora, I haven't cried since the day I was turned. The last time I did was the day before the ritual, when my mother and sister wept in the doorway of our home as I walked down the road to Master Héng's temple."

Nora wasn't sure what to say so she remained silent. Xīn stared off as he remembered that day.

"We had just completed the evening meal. My father was never an overly emotional man and so he left the common room as soon as he finished eating. I knew in his heart that he was sad to see me go, even though it was a great honor to be chosen for the transformation."

Nora gently guided Xīn to the bed so he could sit down. Once he did, he continued his story.

"My younger brothers had work to finish in the fields so they said their good byes in a quick and efficient manner. They were so much like my father. But my mother and sister were two different animals, as women usually are."

He turned to look at Nora. Maybe he was expecting an

accusatory look from her but she didn't oblige. Unlike most uber-feminists in the world, she did recognize the differences between men and women as just that. Neither one better nor worse, just different. He smiled at her.

"I was expecting you to contradict me."

"I figured as much. Sorry but I happen to agree with you. Go on."

He nodded. "My mother had made me a new set of clothes to wear for the ritual. I have no idea how she had the time or energy to do it after working in the fields all day. But she did, handing me the bundle wrapped in a modest but beautiful square of cloth. My sister made me this."

He pulled a black leather cord from beneath his shirt. At the end was a figurine of a dragon carved from green jade, the front half a dark forest green and the back half such a light pale green it appeared white in comparison. He held it up for Nora to inspect.

"She carved this herself? It's beautiful."

Xīn agreed. "Yes. She was very young at the time but had such a talent for this kind of craftsmanship. I always believed she would become a true artisan in her lifetime."

A memory slipped through Nora's mind.

"It was a long straight road, right?" Nora asked.

"What?"

"It had rained earlier that day. The road had been dry for so long that you almost forgot what it was like to struggle through the mud. So the journey to Master Héng took longer than you thought."

Xīn stared at her. "How could you possibly know that?"

"I don't know. For the past few days I've been getting flashes of places I've never been. Events I've never witnessed. But when you started talking about your family, the images popped in my head again."

Nora looked up at him. "I think I've been flashing on your life, Xīn. Or at least to places that are connected to you."

He tucked the charm back into his shirt and wiped the tears from his face.

"I'm sorry. I shouldn't have gone on like that. Right now we have more important things to worry about. In particular, this link you seem to have to me. Maybe we can find some information about it."

Nora shook her head. "Not right now we don't. There's not much else we can do today. Look, it's dinner time. I'll fix, uh, me, something to eat, we'll sit down, relax, and just hang out. All right?"

Xīn tensed like he did before he argued a point but shrugged his shoulders instead. Nora nodded in satisfaction.

"I'm sure you've got some orders to bark at your troops and you'll need to double and triple check the security. So when you're done come find me in the kitchen."

She darted out of the bedroom. She heard Xīn walk through the hallway behind her but instead of following, he went out the front door, calling to Taelin. After digging through her refrigerator, she decided the comfort of a three-cheese macaroni bake would be best.

Nora was glad to have this time away from Xīn. The more they were together, the harder it was to keep her distance. It would be smarter to keep a bodyguard/employee type of relationship between them but each hour brought more delights and surprises into her world, even if some of them were slightly dark and disturbing.

As she gathered the dishes she would need, she couldn't help thinking about Xīn's family. It was obviously an important memory to him and she felt she owed him something in return. Her family hadn't been all that close, except for her and her father. They were all gone now anyway so it's not like she could introduce them to Xīn . She did have something she could share though.

Within the hour, the kitchen smelled of baking cheese, homemade salad dressing, and a slight hint of cinnamon. While she prepared dinner she warmed up the leftover apple pie she'd made at the beginning of the week, before all this craziness began. Had it really only been a couple of days?

Xīn returned inside and sat at the table watching her as she flitted between the stove and the counter. She had set the table while he was still outside checking security. She had a bit of a monkey obsession - monkey napkin holder, placemat, and salt and pepper shakers. Soda bubbled away in a monkey glass. If she could find monkey plates that would the perfect complement to her table scheme. Xīn picked up the salt shaker, a small smile softening the worried crease on his forehead.

She brought her food to the table and sat down then looked up at Xīn.

"Are you sure this won't bother you?"

"No, not at all. While eating food would make me ill, the smell of it is not bothersome in the least."

"That's good because I'm starving."

Jethro sauntered into the kitchen. He took a cursory sniff at Xīn and when he was satisfied there was no food to be had from the línghún, he moved over to Nora. Sitting at her feet, the dog put a paw on her thigh. She pushed it away and poked a finger in Jethro's direction.

"No. Bad dog."

Undeterred, he did it again, this time adding a soft whine. Nora ignored him but saw Xīn staring at her.

"What?"

He nodded at the dog. Nora waved her hand.

"Just ignore him. He'll lie down eventually."

"That's how you discipline your dog?"

"No. Usually I give him a bite so he'll go away but I don't want him to look bad in front of company."

Xīn shook his head, covering his eyes with his hand. When he did, Nora plucked a gob of cheese from her plate and snuck it to the dog. She smiled and mouthed 'good dog' as he slurped it down. Satisfied, Jethro moved away and lay down in the corner, curling into a ball to sleep.

Nora picked up her fork and shoveled the mac and cheese into her mouth. She must look like a swine at the trough but didn't care. Xīn just looked amused so she didn't stop until almost half of the food was gone. She grabbed her glass and took a few sips of the soda. She gave Xīn a tight-lipped grin around a mouth full of food.

"Snoo bud uf cat eet," she mumbled, trying not to spew out any of the masticated food. He frowned at her, but still smiled, obviously not understanding a word she just said. She chewed a few more times and swallowed, then washed down any remnants of food with more soda. She spoke again.

"I said, it's too bad you can't eat. This is great, if I do say so myself."

"I'll just have to take your word for it."

She nodded and continued to eat. Once she finished, she stood up to clear the dishes but he stopped her.

"Why don't you go sit down and I'll take care of this."

She arched an eyebrow at him. "You want to clean the dishes?"

"I didn't say I was going to wash them. I'm just getting them off the table. So go."

"Huh, don't have to tell me twice," she called over her shoulder on her way to the living room.

She got to the couch and pulled a large Washington Redskins blanket over her legs, tucking it underneath her feet to keep them warm. Just as she settled back, she remembered the apple pie. She debated with herself whether or not she should get out from beneath the soft warmness of the blanket or just let the damn pie burn.

Before she had to choose, Xīn walked into the living room with a slice of pie on a plate in one hand and a hot cup of tea in the other. She smiled up at him and he set them both down on the

TV tray. He grabbed a coaster and put it under the hot mug.

"I figured you might want this now so I took the liberty of taking it out of the oven. Is tea all right?"

She nodded. "Of course. Thanks, Xīn."

He took a seat next to her and smiled. "You're welcome."

Nora leaned forward and picked up the pie. She put a small forkful in her mouth and closed her eyes. Dinner was all right to shovel in and devour as quickly as possible. Dessert, however, was a different story. Each flavor, texture, each nuance had to be savored and enjoyed, one small second at a time. She leaned back against the couch and moaned

"Mmmmmmmm. This is why I eat dinner in the first place. To get to the dessert."

Xīn laughed. "I can see that."

After she finished the pie, she grabbed the mug of tea and sat back. She inhaled the sweet cinnamon scent before she took a sip then looked over at Xīn.

"You know, besides being a really great house guest, I wanted to thank you for earlier."

He frowned at her. "What do you mean?"

"When you shared that story about your family with me. I could tell that they meant a lot to you and that the story was very personal. I feel like I owe you something similar in return."

"Nora, you don't owe me anything. And I shared that story with you because, well, because I feel very comfortable around you."

Her face warmed. "Well, thank you. I feel the same way. Which is another reason I think I should share something personal with you. It might be something you've been wondering about anyway."

Xīn studied her face for a moment before he answered. "Why you're afraid to go to the hospital?"

She nodded as she felt her smile weaken and disappear from her face. "Exactly."

He registered the change in her demeanor and placed a hand on her knee. "It's all right. You don't have to tell me now if it's too difficult."

"Xīn, it won't matter if I tell you now or twenty years from now. It'll still hurt just as much."

He nodded and sat back against the couch. Nora put the mug of tea back on the table and settled in her seat until she was comfortable. She took a deep breath as she tried to figure out where to begin.

"About ten years ago, my father started having trouble with his health. He used to go on daily walks, but for some reason he was having difficulty breathing after only a few blocks. He figured that wasn't normal and so went to the doctor.

"At first his doctor couldn't figure out what was wrong. He sent my father to several different specialists all around the area. They treated him for emphysema but that didn't make him feel any better. He was diagnosed with chronic bronchitis, enlarged heart problems, severe allergies, congestive heart failure, pneumonia, which he did have on several occasions but was not the permanent problem. He'd been in and out of the hospital so often that all the nurses knew both of us pretty well.

"Eventually, his doctor referred him to a lung specialist at Henry Ford Hospital, a Dr. Stelov, who was also the head of the pulmonary health board there. After putting my dad through a stress test…do you know what that is?"

Xīn frowned. "Is that where they make you run on a treadmill for hours to find out how your body reacts to the stress?"

Nora smiled. "Yeah, basically. After recording all his body's reactions, taking a few simple x-rays and having my dad perform some basic bodily functions, he was able to come up with a diagnosis. After months and months of tests, we finally had an answer: Pulmonary Fibrosis."

Xīn's expression didn't change and a small laugh burst out of her mouth. "Yeah, I didn't know what it was either. The quick and dirty explanation is the tissues of the lungs are slowly replaced with scar tissue, making it harder and harder for the patient to breathe and take in oxygen."

Xīn grimaced. "That doesn't sound pleasant."

"No, it wasn't. At first it wasn't so bad. It almost seemed that nothing was wrong. Just if he tried to walk a long distance or go up and down the stairs too many times during the day. By the second year he was on supplemental oxygen during the day. By the fourth year, he was on it twenty four hours.

"He had a winter home in Florida for several years. Funny thing was he bought it shortly before he was diagnosed. He was only able to enjoy it for a few years before he could no longer make the trip down. It became too stressful on his body to do all that traveling.

"In the last year, the April before he died, I went down to visit him. He knew it was close to the end. We never had a lot of serious or deep conversations during my lifetime. But this one afternoon, as we sat on the deck by the pool, he was quiet for a long time, staring off into the woods behind the house.

"Then he turned to me and said, 'I'm probably going to need some support in a few months. Maybe you could work part time and help me out.' Reading between the lines, of course, meant he knew he wouldn't be able to take care of himself soon.

"So in July, I would go to work until one o'clock then head over to his condo. I'd take care of the grocery shopping, cleaning, cooking, that sort of thing. I didn't live there with him or anything. He was very independent and still wanted some sense of control in his life, even though what was happening to him was far beyond anything he could ever fix."

She paused, taking a deep breath. The story tumbled out of her mouth so fast she almost forgot to breathe. Xīn reached over and took her hand in his own, giving it a soft squeeze. She gripped it in return, thankful for his presence and for not interrupting her with a bunch of questions. She continued.

"Just before Thanksgiving, we called in hospice. They basically just came in once a week to check his vital signs, ask how he was feeling, helped him bathe but for the most part, just he and I relied on each other to get through this. Well, we knew he wasn't going to survive it but you know what I mean.

"The week before Christmas, my company was having its annual Christmas party. Normally, I would have been gone by the afternoon to go over to my dad's but we decided that I wouldn't come over that day and should go to the party instead. So the evening before, I said good night at seven o'clock, grabbed up my stuff and left. I didn't know it would be the last time I would ever see him.

"I was at work the next day and I'd just finished eating a sandwich from a local deli when I got the call. My dad's neighbor had gone to visit him. She knew I wouldn't be there that day and wanted to make sure he was all right.

"She found him face down on the floor of his bedroom. She didn't know that with hospice, you need to call them first so she called the police instead. She explained his situation, clarifying there was no need to resuscitate him even though it is the law. Then she called me at work. It was the first time I'd ever felt the need to vomit after receiving bad news."

Nora could feel the tears welling up in her eyes. She wiped them away before they could spill down her cheeks. Xīn moved closer and put his arms around her. He leaned back and forced her to lie against his chest as he smoothed her hair.

"His doctor figured that the night before, when he shuffled off to bed around two in the morning, he sat on the edge of the bed to catch his breath. Just walking ten feet could wipe him out for a while. When he stood, his blood pressure plummeted, his heart stopped, and he fell over, dead almost instantaneously. And that was it. Just that fast. It was over and he was gone."

Nora began to weep. She'd never told anyone all the details regarding her dad's illness and death before. She kept most of her life private, especially from her coworkers. Nothing against them but she never really felt close enough to anyone to open up like this, not even Janet. But with Xīn it was different. Everything in her life since he came along was different.

To his credit, Xīn said nothing as she cried. He wrapped his arms tighter around her and just allowed her to release. She never noticed when Mǐn entered the room. She felt Xīn tense and Nora raised her head. Mǐn stood at the kitchen entry, her head down as she looked at her feet. Nora looked at Xīn.

"It's all right. Do what you have to do."

"I'll only be a moment."

Nora sat up and gave him room to move. He and Mǐn walked into the kitchen to talk. Nora went into the bathroom to get some tissues. She looked at her reflection in the mirror and cringed. Her eyes were swollen and bloodshot, her skin blotchy and red, like she had been used as a punching bag.

"Oh, nice. Lookin' good, Nora."

She turned on the cold water and splashed some on her face. As she reached for a towel, Xīn rapped on the open door.

"You all right?" he asked as he entered.

She nodded then patted her face dry. "I'm more embarrassed than anything. Sorry about that."

"What do you have to be embarrassed about?"

She pointed to the large wet splotch on his shirt. "Again, I have gotten you all wet. If this is going to become a pattern, maybe you should keep some clothes here."

The word were out of her mouth before she could stop them.

She made it sound like they'd been dating for a while and he needed to have a drawer in her dresser or something. She cleared her throat and pushed her way past him back into the living room. Mǐn stood next to the sofa and stared at Nora. Nora frowned.

"Everything okay, Mǐn?"

Mǐn stared at her for a beat and then rushed over. She threw her arms around Nora and gave her what she assumed was a hug. Awkward and stiff, but a hug none the less. Nora felt her mouth twitch with a smile.

"Uh, thanks, Mǐn."

Mǐn nodded, bowed to Xīn who by this time was standing behind Nora, and walked out the front door. Nora turned to look at Xīn.

"What the heck was that all about?"

Xīn scratched his head. "I attempted to convey some of the story about your father. I believe all the time she spent with you this afternoon has given her part of your energy and that was her attempt at a sympathetic hug. I think."

Nora laughed and stared at the front door. She shook her head. Guess the old soldier could be a big girlie after all. She turned back to Xīn who smiled.

"Mǐn, Taelin, and the other team members will stand guard outside. We'll have a few others in the house but they'll be in the basement or on the porch. I am at your disposal all night."

"I see," Nora said. What was she going to do with him all night? Well, she could think of quite a few things. She shook her head. Nope, let's not go there. Not the best of ideas. You remember what happened earlier, don't you, Nora? When your eyes went all vampy?

"Are you all right, Nora?" Xīn's brow was wrinkled as he laid a hand on her shoulder.

She felt a warm tingle start in her toes and work its way up to her thighs.

"Uh, yeah. Fine. Fine."

Okay. Think. It was just a few hours before she'd need to go to sleep. What could they do in the meantime to keep themselves preoccupied? Another board game? Cards? Maybe she could get Mǐn to come back in here and stand guard at the window instead of outside.

An hour later they were both sitting on the couch in the back room watching television. She pulled out her DVD sets of the television show *Supernatural* thinking it would be the perfect show to watch. Scary stuff, blood, terror, ghosts, demons, nothing that would make her think naughty things about the sexy vampire sitting at the other end of the couch.

She mentally slapped her face and looked back at the television. Concentrating on the show she realized the episode they were watching had a pretty decent sex scene in it. There was no full nudity or anything but for television it was hot.

Maybe now was a good time to excuse herself to get a pop.

"Uh, I need something to drink. Be right back."

"Should we pause it?"

"Oh, no. That's not necessary," Nora said as she shook her head. "I've seen this before. It's cool."

Nora ducked into the kitchen seconds before the scene began. She could still hear the TV though so she decided to turn on the faucet to drown out the noise. After taking a pop from the fridge, she got a glass from the cupboard above the dishwasher. She slammed the cupboard door closed then clanged a handful of ice into the glass.

By the time she poured the soda and drank half of it while standing at the counter, the sex scene was over and she could sit and enjoy the rest of the episode. She sat back down at the opposite end of the couch from Xīn and put her glass on the small wicker chest to her right.

She grabbed a small blanket off the back of the couch and threw it over her legs. Her eyes slid over to look at Xīn. He was concentrating on the television but it seemed like he was trying a little too hard, like he was avoiding looking at her. He fidgeted in his seat, he kept running his hand through his hair. She began to wonder if that last scene had made *him* uncomfortable.

She cleared her throat and took another drink. As she set the glass back down, she looked over at him again. He snapped his head back towards the TV, not wanting to get caught staring at her. She smiled a little and sat straighter. He shifted his body and legs, as if to get more comfortable. As he did, he moved his arms and his hand fell on top of her feet.

Nora tensed. She didn't move because she didn't want him to think she was disgusted by this touch, though she wasn't sure if she should be letting him touch her either. Her decision was made for her when his hand tightened on her foot and his thumb brushed across the blanket over her toes.

There was no way she was going to stop him from doing that. Besides, that was pretty harmless, wasn't it? The blanket, and her socks, prevented a skin on skin contact. Which was good. If she felt his cool skin on hers she wasn't sure she could control herself.

She shook her head and concentrated on the television. The episode was just wrapping up and one of the main characters had to kill his new girlfriend because she was a werewolf. Nora could feel tears building up in her eyes so she tried to break the sad moment.

"Are werewolves real, Xīn?"

Without taking his eyes off the screen, or his hand off her foot, he answered. "Of course."

Nora jerked at his cavalier attitude.

"Ah."

He turned away from the TV and looked at her. "What?"

"You say that like everyone should know, like it's common knowledge."

He laughed. "I'm sorry. Sometimes I forget how little the mortal world knows of ours."

She shivered. Apparently her fear of werewolves wasn't so goofy after all. He squeezed her foot.

"Are you afraid of werewolves? If you never knew they existed, how could you fear them?"

"People are afraid of all sorts of things they don't know are real. Weren't you ever afraid of anything when you were human?"

Xīn stared up at the ceiling for a moment then looked back at her. "Ants."

"Ants?" she asked.

"Yes. I hated the idea of these small bugs with antennae and pinchers that could just sneak up on me and crawl in my ears or my mouth."

"Eww. Now that you mention it, eww."

Xīn laughed and pushed his hands beneath her legs. He shifted to the middle of the couch and laid her legs over his lap.

"Here, I'll protect you. I'm make sure no ants or werewolves bother you."

"Or were-ants, right?" she laughed.

The tingle she felt earlier turned into a jolt that set her insides on fire. She gulped around a half-assed smile and reached for her pop. When she lifted the glass she found it empty. She tilted it back anyway and popped an ice cube into her mouth. She chewed on it, hoping it would distract the butterflies in her chest.

The episode ended and she grabbed the remote. Nora looked through the DVD cover and picked the funniest episode she could find. She hoped that would make for a less romantic or erotic mood that had fallen over the room. Although she wouldn't mind if it got a little warmer in here.

As the show progressed, she found herself leaning forward so she could be closer to Xīn. She wasn't sure if it was on purpose or if her subconscious was taking control. Didn't really matter either way. She felt better the closer she was to him, even if she did have trouble concentrating on the program.

By the end of the episode and the start of another one, she

found herself leaning on his shoulder, very relaxed and very warm. His arms had tightened around her legs as she bent them to sit closer to him. She took a deep breath and stretched her arm across his chest. He reached up one hand and stroked her forearm. She felt the goose bumps dance across her skin.

As the light from the TV flickered through the room she felt his head turn. His lips caressed the top of her head. She lifted her head and leaned back so she could look at his face. Half of it was lit by the television and the other was black in shadow. But she could still see his eyes, their golden amber color glowed in the darkness.

He reached a hand forward and touched her face. His thumb traced the curve of her cheekbone, the line of her jaw then moved to her mouth. As he traced her lips he looked into her eyes again. He pulled back, almost as if afraid.

She felt the strange sensation behind her eyes, almost as if they turned in their sockets but her vision remained clear. Nora remembered the feeling from before. It wasn't painful, just strange. She reached out and pressed Xīn's hand against her cheek. She needed him to know she wasn't afraid anymore.

Relieved, he moved his face closer, their noses almost touching.

"Nora," he breathed.

She pressed her lips to his. He surprised her by opening his mouth immediately to her kiss, pulling her as close as possible. When that didn't seem close enough he gripped her shoulders and lifted her up. She straddled his lap and reached behind his neck and untied the leather strap that kept his hair contained. Plunging her hands into the silky raven tresses, she leaned in and kissed him again.

He encircled her in his arms and drew her to him. She pushed her hips against his but still wanted him closer. Taking the initiative, she swung her body to the side and back, drawing Xīn on top of her. He straightened his arms to push his body away.

"I don't want to hurt you."

"You won't."

Nora pulled on his arms until their bodies pressed together. She lifted her legs and squeezed them against his hips. Xīn pushed against her, no longer afraid of putting his full weight on top of her. They melded their mouths together again and she could feel him tense again. She pulled back and looked into his eyes, which glowed amber.

"Please, Xīn. I want you to."

No longer in doubt of her resolve, he pushed off the couch then scooped her up in his arms and carried her to her bedroom. Kicking the door closed behind him, he kissed her neck as she tilted her head back. He walked her to the bed and gently lay her down on it.

She sat up and reached for his shirt. She smoothed her hands down the soft fabric then reached up toward the collar. Slowly she unhooked each button until she could push the garment off his shoulders and expose his bare chest.

He had no need to breathe but he gasped each time she touched his skin. His eyes changed color again, this time from amber to a warm deep orange and she wondered if hers had done the same.

She pulled off her own shirt and mentally thanked herself for going braless today. One less piece of clothing to fight with right now.

Xīn looked down and studied her flesh. He reached out to trace his fingers along her collar bone, bare arm, along the waistband of her pants, and smoothed his hand over her ribs. She inhaled when he cupped her breast and he leaned in to kiss her, not allowing her to exhale.

Nora lay back and pulled Xīn on top of her. Twisting and turning, they explored each other's bodies, any and all curves and lines, with their mouths and hands. Nothing about one was unknown to the other, down to the smallest freckle.

Xīn stared down at Nora and she could see the fevered hunger in his eyes. She arched her back to expose her neck but Xīn only chuckled. She straightened then looked at him in confusion.

"Don't you want to feed from me?"

"I do but I don't need your neck for that. At least, not for what I have in mind."

He leaned in close, his forehead touching hers. Every detail of his face came into sharp focus. His eyes were closed so she did the same. Within moments, she felt something building inside her. Almost like the feeling you get when riding a roller coaster but instead of waxing and waning, it continued to build.

Her chest felt heavy but she could breathe fine. Her hands and feet tingled and the sensation traveled up her arms and legs. It added to the pressure in her belly and chest and she felt warm all over, as if submerged in a hot bath. She needed to arch her back but wasn't sure she could with Xīn lying on top of her. Within moments, her body contracted and then pushed against him with barely any effort.

At that moment the need to exhale pushed the air out of her lungs and her eyes flew open, just before Xīn opened his. His eyes were a mix of colors: gold, amber, orange, yellow, and green. They were the most beautiful eyes she had ever seen. His hands gripped hers and she laced her fingers with his. Her mouth opened and a stream of glowing white light passed between her lips and into his mouth. As she exhaled, he inhaled, pulling the energy into himself.

When the flow waned, she inhaled and that same white energy flowed back out of his mouth and into hers. Only this time, the color was tinted with specks of red. It didn't frighten her. In fact, seeing it made her open her mouth wider and breathe deeper.

She looked up at Xīn as the energy passed into her and he looked surprised. Perhaps this wasn't a normal part of a línghún feeding. She tried to make a mental note to ask him about it later but when his eyes changed colors again, this time to yellow-white flecked with red, she forgot everything except their bodies and the flowing of energy between them.

After several hours, the energy exchange stopped and Xīn closed his eyes and mouth. Nora gasped, exhausted and exuberant at the same time. Xīn nuzzled his face against her neck and she entwined her fingers through his hair. He raised himself up on his arms to look at her.

His eyes were normal again and she was almost disappointed. He smiled and brushed his lips against her cheek. Then he crushed his mouth on hers and rolled them both onto their sides. He ran his hand down her bare skin. When he reached her thigh, he pulled up and draped her leg over his hip. He spoke into her open mouth.

"And now, my dear Nora, for Act Two."

Nora couldn't believe that regular sex would ever compare to what they had just experienced and shared together. She was wrong.

CHAPTER FOURTEEN

Líng Pò sat in the back seat of the dark sedan as Gàn drove. Five other cars followed, each filled with Pò's minions. They drove through the city streets toward the freeway. Once on it, it wouldn't be long before they reached the suburbs. Pò tapped on the back of Gàn's seat.

"Yes, Líng Pò?"

"You're sure everyone knows their roles tonight?" Pò asked.

"Of course, but we can run through the plan one more time before we enter the store if you'd like."

Pò mumbled an agreement and Gàn nodded. "As you wish."

Gàn pulled a walkie-talkie from his belt and contacted the leaders in each car. He instructed that once parked, they were to come to Pò's car to receive final confirmation of duties. After receiving their replies, Gàn clipped the radio back on his belt and spoke to Pò over his shoulder.

"All set. They will meet with you one last time before taking any action."

"Thank you, Gàn. I don't know what I'd do without you." Gàn merely nodded and continued to drive. After twenty minutes of silence, Gàn announced, "We're here."

He pulled the car over to the curb on the street opposite a small strip mall. An Asian market sat in the middle, its store front dim with wan light and one small light bulb above the door. As soon as the car came to a stop, Pò got out and walked around to the back. There he leaned against the trunk as he waited for his team leaders to approach.

When they had gathered, and Gàn stood to his right, Pò spoke. "All right. You know why we're here. We need information on the cǎi jí shén. Anything and everything written down must come with us. Any línghún that can assist, spare them. For now. The elders will be our best bet but don't discount anyone until you're sure."

They all nodded. As they went back to their vehicles, Pò turned to Gàn.

"Remember, Héng is mine."

Gàn nodded. "Of course."

Pò stepped away from the car and Gàn opened the trunk. He dug through several boxes and pulled out two large machetes and handed them to Pò. Gàn grabbed another one and a sawed off shotgun for himself. The guns wouldn't kill a línghún but it would do enough damage to slow them down long enough to decapitate them, which would be fatal.

After slinging two loops of shotgun shells over his shoulders, Gàn closed the trunk and waved to the assembled group. Pò took the lead and they followed him to the store. When he reached the front door, he motioned to Gàn who walked up and gave it a powerful kick, shattering it. Pò loved the sound of breaking glass.

Before they walked through, Pò held up his arm to stop Gàn. He'd noticed an 'open' sign in the front window so he pulled on the door handle. The now empty frame opened without protest. Pò threw back his head and laughed while Gàn grinned. Pò walked through the door first, followed by Gàn and then the remaining group. Several employees screamed and ran for the back of the store. Pò motioned for his group to follow them while Gàn stayed by Pò's side as he sauntered through the shop.

Pò turned to his left and saw an old woman behind the front counter. He could see the fear in her eyes but she stood her ground. She neither retreated nor flinched as Pò approached her but bowed instead. He looked over at Gàn who seemed as surprised as he. Pò returned her honor with a bow of his own.

"What is your name?"

"Lài," she replied.

"You honor me though I've done nothing to deserve it."

"You are línghún chī. That alone deserves respect, even if you are wú lài."

Gàn turned to look at him but Pò raised his hand. "And honest to boot. Hmmm, I may have to spare your life after all."

"That is not the only reason."

"No? Why else would you bow to me then, Madam Lài?"

She swallowed then moved out from behind the counter to stand before him.

"Do you not remember me, Líng Pò?"

"How do you know my name?"

"I suppose time has not been as kind to me as it has to you. It has been over sixty years now."

A spark of a memory flashed through Pò's mind: China, the end of World War II, communist victory over nationalism. Pò met a young woman caught in the turmoil between the two groups. She and her siblings had become targets for cleansing. The only thing he could do was get them on a boat and out of the country. As a quán pì rén, his duty left him no choice but to help.

He never thought of her again after that.

"Lài," he said as he brushed a hand over her cheek. "I remember now."

The woman blushed like a school girl and bowed again.

"I only wish my sisters had lived long enough to see you again."

Gàn laid a hand on Pò's shoulder.

"I'm sorry to interrupt, but we have work to do."

"Yes, you're right. Madam Lài, it has been a great pleasure to see you but I must be going. Perhaps we can talk another time?"

She bowed. "If you so wish it."

He turned to Gàn and nodded toward the rear of the store. "Let's get on with it."

The pair moved through to the back area. Pò's group stood around an open walk-in freezer, waiting for him. He pushed his way through the crowd and stood inside the freezer before a dented metal door. He wasn't sure if he needed a code or password to open it but when he moved close enough, it opened automatically.

"Tsk tsk, fellas. Might think of having tighter security next time."

He stepped through the doorway and stood at the top of a long flight of stairs. Gàn quickly moved in front of him.

"Let me go first, Pò."

Pò nodded and allowed Gàn to take the lead. Pò turned back to the others and pointed to five of them.

"You stay here and make sure no one goes in or out, understand?"

They nodded. Two of them moved back toward the front of the store and the others remained in storage, corralling the employees into the middle of the room. Pò called out to the two moving away.

"Make sure you don't harm the old woman."

They nodded then pushed their way through the plastic curtain and out into the main store. Pò turned back to the stairs and began to descend. As the rest of the group followed, he heard the metal door close behind them. Within seconds he stood at the bottom where Gàn had waited for further instructions.

"Gàn, you and I will proceed ahead. The rest of you split up and check the other corridors. When you're done, check the rooms along this main hallway. Gàn and I will go directly to the inner chamber."

Pò watched as they headed down each passage, their weapons glinting in the dim torch light. He smiled. Even if his men didn't find any useful information, at least they'd have a good time trying to get it. He nudged Gàn forward and they walked side by side down the main hall.

Pò could feel the línghún sheltered behind each door. Many were still injured and working through the healing processes. There would be time enough to 'talk' to them later. Right now he was more interested in getting to the inner chamber, the elders safely ensconced behind it, and the prison cells. He might even be able to find a few more wú lài to add to his collective.

He and Gàn encountered no resistance as they proceeded even though he could hear the screams of the línghún as his men slaughtered them. Surely that noise traveled to the perfect hearing of the elders but as was their custom, hide first, protect the tradition second, and fight last. Pò spit on the ground, disgusted that he ever blindly followed their ways at all.

Gàn stepped ahead of Pò as they reached a large wooden door at the end of the hallway. Gàn traced his fingers over it and muttered under his breath. He stared at the long rope to the right then turned to Pò.

"It's protected by a spell. Without the correct incantation, there's no way we can get inside."

Pò screamed in frustration. He hadn't planned on this. So much for his snide remark earlier about lax security. He pounded his fists on the door in a futile attempt to assuage his anger but it only made it worse. As he stared up at the monstrous entrance, two of his men came down the hall dragging an injured línghún with them.

"What is this?" Pò snarled at them.

"We heard this one yelling from his room that we'd never be able to penetrate the inner chamber," one of them replied.

The other finished. "So we dragged him out here, hoping you might motivate him to share what he knows."

Pò's mood lightened at the prospect of being able to torture someone. He stepped forward and grabbed the línghún by his jaw. He turned the man's face left and right, noting a series of bloody slashes that were just beginning to heal. Looks like his crew tried to motivate the man already but had no luck. Pò pulled one of his machetes from the scabbard at his back and held it up.

"See this, my friend? I know cutting you won't kill. Sure, it hurts like hell but wounds heal, right?"

The injured línghún stared at him without responding. Pò lifted him so his feet dangled off the floor.

"But I also know that over time, after many wounds have been inflicted, even we don't have the energy to heal anymore. Unless we feed. It can be a long, long, long and extremely painful process. And you have no idea how patient I am."

Pò pushed the tip of the machete into the man's stomach. He howled in pain as it entered and again as Pò dragged it back out.

"Now, you're already hurt. You might get lucky and die long before I have too much fun. But then again, you might not. So, feel like sharing any pertinent information with me right now?"

The vampire spat in Pò's face. Pò smiled and dropped him to the floor.

"I thought not."

Pò turned to the closest door and kicked it open. The injured línghún in there looked up from her bed. She reached out a trembling hand as Pò rushed in and decapitated her. After rolling the body to the floor, he motioned for Gàn and the others.

"Bring him to me."

They dragged their victim to the room and tossed him inside. He landed on his back and lay there, stunned.

"Wait outside."

Gàn nodded and pulled the door closed. Pò picked the línghún up off the floor and slammed him against the wall. He took his machete again and shoved it through the vampire's chest with such force it pinned him to the brick wall. He pulled out his second machete and held it up.

"You *will* tell me what I need to know. And when you do, I'll make sure you live a long time before I'm inclined to give you a merciful death."

Within minutes, the screams became music to Pò's ears. It had been a while since he'd had the pleasure of torturing a línghún and he didn't realize how much he'd missed it until now. With each slash and cut, stab and poke, his mood improved. Even after he got the information he wanted Pò continued the torture.

By the time he tired of the game, he was soaked in blood from head to toe. The room looked like it had been painted with the gore of a hundred victims. Pieces of the línghún were scattered across the floor, the walls, and even the ceiling. Skin and hair clung to the brick and stone. Pò pulled a scrap of flesh from his shirt and flung it to the floor.

"Ah, much better."

There was a soft knock at the cell door and Pò called out.

"Come in."

Gàn pushed the door open. He glanced around the room, nonplussed by the scene that confronted him. Then he turned to Pò.

"Did you get what you needed from him?"

"Oh yes," Pò replied. "And much more. He was very

therapeutic."

He picked up a torn piece of clothing from the now dead línghún and wiped his hands clean. Well, cleaner anyway. He dropped the rag to the floor and stepped over the shredded corpse without a second glance. Emerging from the cell he saw several of his men standing ready for his command. He smiled.

"I was able to secure the spell needed for us to enter the inner chamber. However, feel free to continue questioning anyone you find. Who knows what other little tidbits we might pick up during the course of the evening."

His men nodded and scattered, either running down the corridors or smashing their way into various rooms. When the screaming started to build, Pò nodded at Gàn and the two of them made their way to the Enclave. A handful of his minions followed to provide security.

Once at the large wooden door, Pò began to recite the spell needed to open it. At the proper time, he pulled on the long rope to his right. And just like magic, the door opened. Gàn stepped in front of Pò to survey the room for any potential threat.

After several moments, he turned to nod at Pò and then stepped aside. Pò moved into the inner chamber. No one occupied it at this moment but he knew the elders were close by. He could smell them.

Gàn moved through the room, checking the furniture, behind tapestries and testing the three doors that led from here to the records room, the prison cells, and the elders' personal chambers. All were locked, as Pò suspected they would be. They were nothing if not a paranoid bunch. Pò nodded to his men.

"Gàn, you take the records room and get as many of the books and scrolls as you can. You three, head down to the prison cells and start releasing any wú lài locked up in there. The rest of you follow me. We need to collect the elders."

As they all moved to their destinations, Pò held up his hand.

"Remember. When you come across any elders, do not kill them. I need all of them alive. If any happen to get seriously wounded, well, I can't fault you for that, now can I? Go!"

Gàn headed to the door on the left and gave it a swift solid kick. It splintered but didn't break. With a second kick, the door flew off its hinges and he headed to the records room. On the right, the three línghún ordered to the cells pounded on the door four times before they could get through. Pò shook his head and pulled back both his arms. With one good shove forward, the middle door exploded.

Pò looked to the man on his right. "See what I did there? No messing around. Just got right to the point. No time wasted. Remember that."

The man nodded and moved forward, followed by the other línghún. Pò stepped through his doorway and smiled. He called out, knowing the elders would hear him but never reply.

"Come out, come out, where ever you are!"

Within a half hour, Pò and all his men had returned to the Enclave. Gàn was still collecting ancient leather bound books as well as a substantial amount of paper scrolls. He had to be extra careful with them because they were delicate and aged, susceptible to major damage from the slightest bump or jostling. Pò ordered him to take his time and be as careful as possible.

The other men had gone into the prisoner area and released over thirty wú lài from their cages. Some had been there for years, starved and tortured. They would need to feed before they could be of any use to Pò. The others were weakened but stable. All of them wanted revenge on the council members.

As for the elders, all but Master Héng were accounted for. Twelve men, the youngest at two thousand years old to the oldest of all línghún, at four thousand years, knelt on the floor in the middle of the chamber. With that collected amount of age came enhanced and great power. Pò had prepared for that by commissioning an ingenious little weapon called "The Drainer".

He wasn't sure exactly how it worked but its purpose was to drain energy from various electronic devices and gadgets. It was a mortal invention but Pò had it modified to work against a línghún. It was a dangerous tool, especially if anyone stopped fearing him long enough to use it against him.

For those who had been able to hear or read Pò and his men coming, they'd hidden, as usual, when confronted with danger. He used it on each elder and it rendered all of them too weak to resist. All but Héng. He had simply vanished. Pò addressed the group of elders kneeling before him.

"You may all be wondering what I'm doing here, am I right?"

None of them answered, as he expected. It didn't mean he couldn't play mad and get a little rough though. He backhanded the elder closest to him and sent him sprawling to the floor. One of the others reached out to assist him, but Pò cracked him across the face as well. He then grabbed the Drainer from a holster at his hip and pressed it against the elder's shoulder. The man screamed then lay still.

Pò continued as if he hadn't been interrupted. "I'm looking for information on the cǎi jí shén legend. You notice I don't call it myth because, and I think we can all agree here, it is real. I know some of you have studied the stories and the ancient records. So I already know you know, you know? The question is will you help before or after I kill everyone tonight?"

The elders that remained conscious said nothing. Most of them jutted their chins out in defiance and a few stared at the floor. All avoided eye contact with him save one - Master Tsang. He knelt at the end of the line, farthest from Pò, and stared at him. Neither rebelliousness nor anger, nor any other emotion for that matter, colored his face. He simply watched Pò as he spoke to the elders.

Pò walked down to stand in front of him. Master Tsang had to crane his neck as Pò approached so he knelt down to be eye to eye with the elder.

"Do you have anything to say to me, Master Tsang?"

Master Tsang nodded. "I have one question, Líng Pò."

Pò arched an eyebrow at the man. "Do you now? And what would your question be?"

"What do you plan to do with the cǎi jí shén once you have her?"

Pò hadn't expected this question. Most elders were stoic and silent, uncooperative and a general pain the ass. He'd have to torture them all to get what he wanted. Well, he wouldn't *have* to but he wanted to. He really, really wanted to. But here was Master Tsang, all nonchalant and inquisitive. This intrigued Pò.

"I suppose that depends on what the story books say about her and her power. I hope to put her to good use."

Tsang pursed his lips, as if thinking over Pò's answer. Eventually he nodded.

"I can help you."

He could feel his face split into a wide smile at this surprising turn of events.

"You can? How wonderful. Can you tell me what the texts say about this woman?"

"No, I cannot," Tsang shook his head then offered nothing more.

Pò could feel his chest tighten in anger. "But you just said you could help me."

Tsang nodded. "I can."

Pò stared at the man then held out his hands, palms up. "Well?"

"I cannot translate the books and scrolls but I know who can."

Pò smirked. "You plan to rat out one of your brothers here?"

Tsang turned to look down the line of kneeling elders and pointed at two of them. "Master Hóng and Master Qín-Lo. They have studied the myths and legends of the cǎi jí shén for millennia. They are the ones you want."

Pò straightened then walked over the two elders. Grinning down at them, Pò swung his leg around in a wide arc and kicked Master Hóng in the jaw. The elder flew backwards, blood spurting from his mouth and nose. He did the same to Qín Lo and was satisfied when he heard the second elder's nose crunch under his foot.

As the two lay back and groaned in pain, Pò walked back to Master Tsang. He knelt down in front of the man again.

"Why did you do that, Master Tsang?"

Master Tsang stared at Pò for a fraction of a second before a sly smile crept across his face.

"I have followed your exploits for years, Líng Pò. I have always thought the elders' rules and regulations have been stilted, ridiculous, and hypocritical. If any of the other línghún knew even a fraction of what these men have done in their lifetimes, there would be a great upheaval within the kindred."

Pò sat back on his heels, amazed and delighted at Tsang's rant. The elder continued.

"I never understood why we should try to live alongside the mortals, why we should live in secret and restraint. I knew that real power lay within the council of elders and their scrolls. I bided my time among them until I could find the strength to rise against them myself or to follow another línghún who could."

Master Tsang bent forward at the waist to bow before Pò. When he straightened, his smiled faltered.

"There is just one thing I must ask of you, Líng Pò."

Pò slapped the man on the shoulder. "Tsang, all you need do is ask. I would give you anything after this wonderful revelation."

Tsang looked down the line at the elders. When he turned back, Pò could see the fire of hatred burning in the man's eyes. Tsang licked his lips.

"May I be allowed to participate in the questioning of the elders?"

Pò laughed. When he stood, he pulled Tsang by his shoulders to stand him up.

"Tsang, you may be the first to crack the whip."

Tsang smiled and bowed deeply to Pò several times before Pò stopped him. He turned Tsang toward the assembled elders and noted Hóng and Qín Lo had recovered and again knelt with the rest. He pointed at them.

"How would you like to begin the inquisition with these two?"

Tsang smiled then walked to stand before them. He reached down to his ankle and pulled out a long, slender, silver knife. Images of tigers adorned the white jade handle. He watched as Tsang held the knife to Hóng's ear. Tsang then looked back at Pò as if to waiting for permission. When Pò nodded, Tsang turned back to Hóng and deftly sliced off the kneeling elder's ear.

Before Hóng had a chance to begin healing, Tsang sliced off his other ear. He moved to the man's nose, lips, and eyelids then proceeded to rip off chunks of scalp and hair. Tsang sliced and tore at Hóng's clothes until the elder was naked. He swiftly slashed and cut at Hóng's flesh for many hours before Hóng was no longer able to heal himself without great difficulty.

Before Tsang could kill the elder, Pò laid a hand on his shoulder.

"Now, Tsang. Can't you see he's exhausted? Let's give him some time to rest and recuperate a bit."

The flash of pure joy at the prospect of extending Hóng's suffering that passed over Tsang's face was chilling, even to Pò. As Tsang stood over Hóng, arms folded to wait for the exact second he could continue his work, Pò moved over to Qín Lo. Master Qín Lo did not shake in fear, as was expected, but Pò was sure the man understood what was in store for him if he didn't cooperate.

"So, Master Qín, what do you say? Feel like talkin'?" Pò asked him.

When he didn't answer, Pò turned to Tsang. "Tsang, perhaps you can persuade our brother here to assist us in our quest tonight."

When Tsang moved, Master Qín held up his hands for mercy. Pò smiled down at him.

"I thought you might have a change of heart."

Before he could savor this triumph, Qín Lo reached out with lightening speed and plucked one of the machetes off Pò's back. He spun and kicked at any of Pò's men that came within range. Just as Gàn stepped into the room with yet another arm load of documents, Qín Lo moved to the far end of the room and held the machete to his own throat.

Pò screamed, "No!"

Qín Lo's expression never changed as he cut off his own head. His body slumped to one side and his head rolled to the other. Pò lurched forward and gripped the decapitated head in both hands then screamed at it in frustration. Seconds later, it crumpled to dust and scattered to the floor.

Once Gàn had deposited the books onto the desk, he ran to Pò's side.

"It's all right, Gàn. There was nothing any of us could have done to stop him."

"Shall we continue with our work, then?" Gàn asked.

Pò nodded and Gàn motioned to Pò's men.

"You. Get the prisoners from their cells and bring them here."

As they scuttled down into the prison area, Pò stood and motioned for Tsang. When he came over, Pò whispered in his ear, while pointing at Hóng.

"Get him to tell us what he knows or you will join Master Qín."

Tsang bowed and turned on Hóng, whose wounds had partially healed. Before he could begin more torture, the prisoners shuffled into the room, some helped by Pò's minions and some of their own volition. When they entered the room, they stared between Pò, Tsang, the remaining ashes of Master Qín, and the kneeling elders. Pò explained.

"My brothers, you have been wrongly imprisoned, tortured, beaten, and starved. While Tsang here works over Master Hóng, you are welcome to the other elders to do as you please. Retribution and dining come to mind but that's just me."

Seconds ticked by as they stood there, unsure if Pò was telling the truth. One of the prisoners, his swagger and demeanor showing him to be a leader, stepped to the closest elder kneeling on the floor. Frowning, he looked over at Pò. When Pò nodded, a small smile curled the prisoner's mouth.

He picked up the elder and threw him against the far wall. He then ran over to him and gripped him by the hair. The elder yelped in pain. The prisoner bent him in half, folding the elder like a cheap plastic chair. The light seemed to dim in the elder's eyes but he wasn't dead. As he lay in a heap on the floor, the prisoner sat atop him and forced his head and shoulders up. He shoved his face against the elder's and drew out his energy.

In minutes, the elder was dead, the prisoner having drained him completely dry. That didn't mean there wasn't anything worthwhile still left inside. With most of the older vampires, traces of energy would linger in the blood, even for a short while after death. Pò watched as the prisoner's fangs descended and he leaned over the elder's corpse. He sunk his teeth into the body and tore a large chunk of flesh away.

Blood didn't spray, as vampires' circulatory systems did not function like a human's but there was a lot of it and it gushed onto the prisoner who lapped at it like a dog at a water bowl. Once the flow slowed to a trickle, the prisoner nuzzled his mouth against the elder's neck and the slurping noises echoed through the chamber.

Pò had watched a mortal eat a crawfish once and suck out every last bit of flesh and fluid from the little creature. At the time, it made him sick to watch and listen to the whole process. But here, now, it brought a smile to his face. He swept his arm over the remaining elders on the floor.

"My brothers, vengeance is yours."

The remaining prisoners descended upon the elders, except for Hóng who prattled on and on like a parrot, tearing them apart.

CHAPTER FIFTEEN

As Nora and Xīn lay in bed, curled up against each other, the floorboards creaked. Even if she were awake, Nora never would have heard it but Xīn's eyes flew open and he saw Mǐn standing at the foot of the bed.

Xīn leaned up on one elbow, careful not to wake Nora.

"Mǐn, what is it?"

"You need to come with me, Fā Xīn."

Xīn tensed at the tone of her voice. He nodded and before he could move, Mǐn had left the room so he could dress in private. After slipping out of bed and back into his clothes, he couldn't resist placing a soft kiss on Nora's forehead before he stepped out of the bedroom.

As he walked into the living room he was jolted by the presence of Master Héng.

"Master Héng! What are you doing here? Is everything all right?"

"No, my son, it is not."

Xīn's heart dropped as he waited for him to continue.

"Líng Pò and his men have attacked the sanctuary."

Mǐn, Taelin, and the other línghún present exchanged looks. Some began to talk amongst themselves but Xīn silenced them.

"What do you mean? How could he possibly get in?"

Master Héng raised an eyebrow at Xīn. "You know as well as I do how treacherous that wú lài is. He's quite capable of almost anything, although I must admit his unmitigated gall displayed this evening was a surprise to me as well."

"What do you think he was after?"

"Information on the cǎi jí shén legend, of course. We know what will happen if he gets the information he wants. Where is Nora?"

Xīn jerked his head back toward the bedroom. "Asleep. Shall I wake her?"

"I'm afraid so," Master Héng nodded. "We'll need to move her immediately. Líng Pò knows where she lives now because of his spy."

"Do you have a safe house?"

"Yes, I do. Now fetch her and we'll all go together."

Xīn nodded and slipped back to the bedroom. He turned on the small lamp on the bedside table and leaned over Nora's sleeping form. He laid a hand on her shoulder and gently shook her.

"Nora? Nora, wake up."

She mumbled protests but did not awaken. Xīn couldn't help smiling as he tried again, more forcefully this time.

"Nora, you must get up now."

She jerked back and her eyes snapped open. She rubbed her eyes a few times and looked up at Xīn. It took her a few seconds to recognize him and when she did, a soft smile lit up her face.

"Xīn, it's not morning already, is it?"

"No, Nora. It's not."

"Then why," she started but he interrupted her.

"I'll explain everything but right now you've got to get up, get dressed, and come with me. We're in trouble."

Nora she sat up in bed, her mouth pinched in fear.

"It's Líng Pò, isn't it?"

Xīn nodded and Nora threw back the covers. Just as she stepped out of bed, her hand flew to her mouth and she tried to press herself against Xīn. Confused, he pushed her shoulders back to ask her what she was doing but she pointed to the space behind him and clutched his shirt.

Xīn turned around to see Master Héng standing in the bedroom doorway. He couldn't be sure but he thought he saw a gleam in Master Héng's eyes as he stared at Nora's naked form. He held up a hand.

"Oh, I am sorry. I didn't know you were unclothed. Please forgive me. I will wait out here."

With that he turned on his heel and headed back toward the living room. Xīn turned back to Nora who peeked around his shoulder to make sure Master Héng was gone. She blew out a breath and grabbed some clothes. Xīn quickly moved to the door and closed it. He watched Nora as she moved about her room getting dressed. He whispered, hoping none of the others could overhear.

"I agree with you."

Nora stopped with one leg held in the air before she slipped it through the leg of a pair of yoga pants.

"Huh?"

"What you said before, about Master Héng. I think you might be right. There's something predatory about him when he's near you."

Nora continued getting dressed as she nodded. "I was hoping you might see it. I didn't want to influence you because he's such an important part of your life."

"I'm sorry I didn't believe you before."

"Xīn, you are more than welcome to feel conciliatory later. And then make it up to me in any fashion I see fit. But for right now, grab me that little jacket over there and let's get the hell out of here. Where are we going, anyway?"

Xīn grabbed a lightweight zip up hoodie from the back of the rocking chair in the corner.

"Master Héng says he has a safe house in mind where we can hide you."

She arched an eyebrow at him and he held up his hands. "I know. Creep-o-meter is running high. Right now we don't have a choice."

She smiled. "Creep-o-meter? Did you just make that up yourself?"

He couldn't help but smile in return as he tossed her the jacket. "Let's go."

They found Master Héng and the others waiting in the living room. He was giving each of them specific instructions.

"Mǐn and Taelin will stay here along with a small contingent of línghún. If Líng Pò comes here looking for Nora, they're our best bet to stop him."

Xīn frowned. "Master, don't you think it would be better for our two best soldiers to come with us? What if Líng Pò doesn't come here?"

Master Héng stared down at Xīn and he hung his head. "Forgive me, Master."

Nora stared between the two of them as Master Héng continued. "The rest of you will come with us. I have twenty more men waiting for us at the safe house. I think they should be sufficient enough to replace Mǐn and Taelin, yes?"

Everyone nodded including Xīn. Master Héng looked to Nora. "Are you ready, my dear?"

She nodded and Xīn wrapped his arm around her shoulders. He hadn't realized he did it until Master Héng looked at him, disapproval tightening his mouth. But he couldn't bring himself to step away from her. After what they shared only hours before, Xīn was terrified of losing her now.

"Do you have a vehicle, Xīn?" Master Héng asked.

"Yes, of course. It's in the garage."

Nora grabbed the keys on the way out and opened the garage door. Master Héng turned to Mǐn and Taelin.

"Remember, you two must stay here and fight Pò with everything you have. We're counting on you."

They bowed deeply to Master Héng and he gave them a curt nod. He moved outside to the car and motioned at two of the soldiers.

"One of you sit up front with Xīn. The other will sit in the back with Nora between us."

Nora looked at Xīn and he nodded. "The Master is right, Nora. It's too vulnerable a position for you to sit up front."

"Please, my dear, we must hurry," Master Héng spoke as he put his arm around her shoulders to usher her into the car. A momentary pang of panic lit in Xīn's chest but he pushed it away. He had to get Nora out of here and fast. Once they were in the car and backing down the driveway, Xīn spoke to Master Héng.

"Where are we going?"

"Just get to the highway and head north. I'll instruct you along the way."

An hour later, they were still driving. Xīn questioned the Master several times about their destination but he would never give any instructions beyond immediate turns or exits. Throughout the car ride he spoke with Nora and the other línghún about any precautionary measures they might need to take against Líng Pò.

There were no more of the rapacious feelings or inappropriate signals coming from the Master. Maybe it was a fluke or just being near such a powerful presence. He didn't want to doubt his master and he did feel uncomfortable about his misgivings. Perhaps when the time was right, Xīn could speak to him about it.

After another long hour of driving, Master Héng spoke.

"Xīn, turn here. At the end of the ramp, turn left and drive until the road ends."

Xīn did as instructed and when a t-junction lay ahead, the Master told him to turn right and stop at a small cabin at the end of the road. Before they reached it, the road turned into a line of dirt and gravel, pockmarked with pits and holes that made the car bounce. After hitting a deep rut, Nora slammed into Master Héng.

"Oh, I'm so sorry. This road's a little rough, I guess."

"Don't worry, my dear. You honor me with your touch."

Nora looked into the rearview mirror and caught Xīn's stare. She looked scared and Xīn had to swallow a curse. She tried to inch away from Master Héng but being cramped between him and another línghún, she had nowhere to go. So she looked out the window instead and chewed on her bottom lip.

Before Xīn could say anything to reassure her, he spotted the cabin off to his left. It was a small wooden structure surrounded by acres of trees. He drove the car along the flattened patch of grass that passed for a driveway and threw the car into park. Staring through the windshield at the tiny structure and the expanse of land, a feeling of doom soured his stomach.

They piled out of the car and Master Héng nodded at the front door.

"I believe there is a key on top of the door frame, Xīn. Please be so kind as to retrieve it."

Xīn looked at Nora as Master Héng draped his arm around her. His expression was smug, as if to say it was his turn to be the protector, that Xīn had Nora to himself long enough and it was time to share. She swallowed but nodded to let Xīn know she was all right. He climbed the small steps and reached above the door. Sure enough, on the edge of the door frame, he felt the cool metallic surface of a key.

Taking it down, he slipped it into the door lock and heard the latch click as it turned. He looked back at the others and motioned for them to wait. He wanted to check the cabin before securing Nora inside. Master Héng nodded and held on to Nora as they waited. The soldier standing next to them turned slowly in a circle, scanning the immediate area for any intruders while the other moved around to the backyard.

Xīn made a quick sweep of the house. There wasn't much to check: the main room, a small kitchen to the left, one bathroom, and one bedroom in the back. All were empty. Where were the 20 línghún the Master said would be here? Xīn returned to the porch to see only Master Héng and Nora standing out front.

"Where the hell is Shun?"

Both Master Héng and Nora looked scared as they approached the cabin.

"I am unsure. He said he heard something and moved off into the woods," Master Héng answered.

"Hurry. We need to get Nora inside."

Master Héng ushered Nora up the stairs and up to the cabin door as quickly as she could move. Fā Xīn moved ahead of them to take another quick scan of the cabin. After a half minute passed and neither Nora nor the Master entered behind him, Xīn turned to see an empty doorway. Frowning, he moved forward, expecting to see the two of them just beyond the door. Whom he met instead was Líng Pò.

Xīn felt his mouth open in surprise. "What are you doing here?"

"The question is," Pò replied, "what are you doing lying there?"

Confused, Xīn cocked his head as if trying to interpret a puzzle he couldn't solve. He felt a sudden flash of white hot pain at the back of his neck. Darkness washed over him.

****

"Why the hell did you do that?" Nora screamed at Master Héng.

She struggled in the grip of one of Pò's men as Master Héng stood over the prone body of Fā Xīn. He stared down at his 'son' with what looked like a mixture of pity and hate darkening his eyes and curling his mouth. At the sound of Nora's voice, he looked up at her and the vague smile he wore fell sharply away. In a flicker of time, he moved from the doorway to the front yard where she stood and gripped a handful of her hair. He yanked it down and her neck cracked in protest. Master Héng pressed his body against hers as he towered over her. He leaned in close, pressing his lips to her ear.

"My dear, you should show a little more respect to your betters."

As he moved to look at her face, she saw his eyes turn from black to dark red. Tendrils of crimson spread out from the irises into the whites of his eyes and then penetrated the flesh of his brow and cheek bones. Nora held her breath as she waited for his next move. She watched him as his eyes roamed over the contours of her face and body. If she were to guess, she'd say he was lusting for her right now.

In a brief moment of defiance, she lifted her chin so her mouth was dangerously close to his. She gave him a coy smile as she whispered against his lips. Nora felt him shudder against her.

"I recognize you as my elder, Héng but you will never be my better."

Nora expected Master Héng to become enraged. He no longer hid the emotions he felt more often than he led everyone to believe, especially after she learned he was in league with Líng Pò. She waited for Master Héng to give one hard jerk to her hair, breaking her neck, and ending her life. Death would be a better fate than ending up his prisoner.

Instead he smiled, flashing a pair of sharp shiny fangs. He placed his hands on either side of her face, caressing her skin. He trailed his fingers over her jaw, down her neck, and onto her shoulders. There he tightened his grip as he dug his fingers into her flesh and she whimpered in pain. As if mocking her earlier defiance, he pushed out his chin and whispered into her mouth.

"I don't know why the gods deemed you a suitable vessel for the greatest power in the world and so I don't plan to kill you, my dear. Not yet. But you don't have to remain conscious, either."

All of Nora's bravado fled and she gulped in response. Master Héng chuckled deep in the back of his throat.

"As I thought. Líng Pò, you and your men will escort us back to the Enclave."

"That wasn't the arrangement. We agreed to go back to my building."

"You don't honestly believe I would ever set foot in that pestilence laden rodent morgue, do you?" Héng sneered at Pò.

"But we agreed-"

"Enough!" Master Héng screamed. "We will return to the Enclave to perform the ritual. No one is forcing you to accompany me, Pò."

Nora watched as Pò hung his head in defeat. Even a rogue recognized Master Héng's power.

"I will do as you say," he replied as he bowed.

"Of course you will. Now let's go."

Master Héng draped his arm around Nora's shoulders as he ushered her toward two cars parked several hundred yards away. She tried to squirm out from under him but he held firm. Craning her head around to see Xīn's body lying in the doorway to the cabin, she felt a tear slide down her face.

"Xīn," she whispered.

Nora turned back and saw Líng Pò studying her. She gave him the evilest eye she could muster. She imagined it wasn't much of one because Pò ignored her and looked back at the cabin.

"What about Fā Xīn?"

Master Héng twitched his head in the direction of the cabin before he answered.

"He's no longer a problem for either of us. Leave a few of your men behind to dispose of him."

Pò nodded and then instructed two of his men to deal with Xīn's body. Nora watched as Pò stared back at the cabin. His features twisted with regret and pain but when he saw Nora studying him, he snarled and turned back toward the car.

During the long car ride back, Nora stared out the window thinking about Fā Xīn and wishing she'd had more time to know him. She refused to wipe away the tears that spilled down her cheeks despite Master Héng's quiet snickering.

When she turned to glare at him, she caught Pò's stare. For a moment, he shared her pain. He held her gaze, his eyes glowing a soft green. Xīn hadn't shown that eye color before and she never saw it in any of the others either. Maybe it represented regret? Maybe Pò didn't hate Xīn like she assumed.

Nora opened her mouth to say something comforting. She didn't know why, especially after what Pò had done and planned to do. But she couldn't turn off that part of her brain that wanted to reach out and comfort the lost hurt puppies of the world, even if they were rabid and tried to chew her face off.

It really didn't matter though because Pò turned away and looked out the window next to him. Nora sighed and looked out the front of the car. The lights of the small strip mall shone up ahead on the left and they parked across the street. Her sympathy for Pò dissipated the instant he grabbed her wrist, dragged her across the back seat, and pulled her out of the car.

"Hey!" she yelped.

"Pò, please don't damage the vessel," Master Héng admonished.

Pò frowned. "You're the one who said she didn't need to be conscious. What's a little bruising going to hurt?"

Master Héng seemed to consider this then nodded.

"I suppose you're right. Continue."

Pò sneered and yanked on Nora's arm as he led her across the street. Two of his men led the way while Master Héng followed behind. Master Héng's arrogance would suggest he lead them into the store but it must be easier for him to keep an eye on them all from the back of the processional.

Nora could see the broken glass scattered over the sidewalk in front of the store. Jagged pieces clung to the door frame like the teeth of some giant creature waiting for its prey to slip inside. Pò jerked the door open, the sudden movement causing a few shards to pop loose and break on the sidewalk. He pulled on Nora's arm again then shoved her though the door.

She stumbled into the store and the scent of blood slapped her in the face. Nora covered her mouth as she stared at the carnage before her. Half a dozen men lay on the floor, their bodies torn and ravaged, their blood drying into sticky pools surrounding them. The old woman Nora met before stood over one of the bodies, holding sticks of burning incense. She mumbled something that Nora assumed was a prayer.

The woman looked up as Pò came through the door. She stopped praying and shuffled over to him. Nora gasped when the woman bowed. She was even more surprised when he bowed in return. Nora stared at Pò but he shoved her forward again, toward the back of the store.

As they reached the doors that led into the storage room, Nora looked back at the old woman. Master Héng stood before her and she bowed deeply. As she straightened, Héng laid his hands on either side of her head and twisted with one hard jerk. The old woman slumped to the floor like a sack of rocks. Nora gasped.

Master Héng may have broken the woman's neck but she wasn't dead. Nora could see her mouth open and close as she tried to command her paralyzed lungs to take in air. It would be several long agonizing minutes before she would die.

Pò never deviated from his path and remained unaware of what had happened. Nora struggled against him. She couldn't help the old woman but she wanted to beat her fists against Master Héng's chest. Pò dragged her through the doors and into the storage room.

More corpses lay scattered here as well and Nora almost vomited. As she clutched her stomach, Pò pushed her ahead until they stood outside the walk-in freezer. His men stayed by the entry way and she stared back at them, waiting for Master Héng to come through. When he did, she lunged for him, aware she couldn't hurt him but her conscience would allow for no less effort.

It didn't matter anyway because Pò grabbed her from behind and held her in place while Master Héng sauntered over. He patronized her with a pompous glare then smiled like they were friends, sharing a secret known only to them. It made her feel dirty.

When he was close enough Nora spat in his face. Master Héng's calm smug exterior never fell away but he backhanded her across the face. White spots swam in an inky darkness as she slumped in Pò's grip. He released her and she settled on her knees. She could taste blood in her mouth.

Nora looked up at Master Héng and smiled. She tried to spit at him again but only managed to dribble on herself. She wiped the bloody spittle from her chin and reached out to wipe it on Héng's pants.

"That'll have to do," she muttered as she grinned up at him.

His eyes flashed red as he raised his hand again. She welcomed the darkness.

****

Xīn lay still as he listened to his surroundings. He'd regained consciousness just as he overheard Pò ask Master Héng what to do. Xīn wanted to confront them both but he'd have to play dead for now so he could have a chance at saving Nora later.

He heard two línghún moving toward him through the grass. Two cars had left moments before taking Héng, Pò, and Nora back to the city. Xīn only had to deal with the two left behind. He listened to their conversation as he lay on the porch.

"Why do we have to clean up the mess?"

"Because you are a hopeless idiot and it's my turn to watch you."

"What the hell is that supposed to mean?"

"Just shut up. Let's hurry and finish with him so we can get back in time."

Xīn could hear their steps as they walked up on the porch. One stood at his head, the other at his feet. They continued to bicker.

"In time for what?" the first asked.

Xīn heard the second one blow out a sigh.

"The ritual, you idiot."

"Oh, right. What do you think will happen?"

"Nothing that will affect either of us, I'm sure."

"What do you mean?"

Xīn felt hands grab his shoulders and legs and within a few seconds he was flipped on his back. Before the second henchman could answer his companion's question, Xīn scissor-kicked and knocked him down. Rolling up onto his shoulders, Xīn kicked his feet up and back and slammed them into the jaw of the other one.

Whipping his legs forward, Xīn landed on his feet and brought his head and torso upright. He crouched in front of the first línghún just as he stood. Xīn kicked out his right leg and knocked him back down. By now the other one had recovered and Xīn heard him pull out a short sword from a sheath.

He lunged and Xīn grabbed the hand holding the sword, flipping the attacker onto his back. He plucked the sword away and decapitated him. The other one, it seemed, was not ready to go down just yet.

After grabbing two short swords from hidden sheaths, Pò's man whipped and twirled them through the air, screaming a war cry. He leaped into the air, swords pointed outward. Xīn rolled beneath him and stood behind him as he landed. Xīn swung the sword and beheaded the wú lài in one motion.

Xīn stood over the bodies. He was puzzled. Surely Master Héng knew he wasn't dead so why did he lead Pò to believe otherwise? Was Master Héng playing Pò for a fool, secretly counting on Xīn to destroy Pò's operation while he was occupied? Or was the Master planning to betray Pò as well? He'd never have any answers until he found Master Héng.

He pulled his cell phone from his back pocket and flipped it open. He dialed Taelin's number.

"Taelin, it's Xīn. I need your help. Tell Mǐn to head over to my home. Nora was taken captive by Master Héng and Líng Pò."

"What?"

"You heard me. They're working together. They're going to perform the yàn zi ritual. We need to save Nora before tomorrow night."

"I understand."

"We need to gather the best soldiers we have," Xīn continued. "We'll be up against the Master."

"All right. What else do you need?"

"Come pick me up."

Four hours later, Xīn, Taelin, Mǐn, and dozens of línghún stood around a long wooden table in Xīn's loft. Various weapons, modern and ancient, lay amidst the nylon and canvas duffle bags, holsters, ammunition, leather sheaths and straps. Bullets can't kill a línghún but if he needed to slow one down, guns would come in handy for that, as would tasers.

As Xīn honed an ancient dagger, he spoke to the assembled group.

"I'm sure you'd all like to know what's going on. And personally, so would I. But the least I can tell you is that Master Héng and Líng Pò are working together to perform the yàn zi ritual."

Many of the group mumbled and talked to each other, the surprise on their faces obvious. Every línghún knew the legend of the ritual but what appeared to be the biggest betrayal since Líng Pò went rogue is what disturbed all of them the most, Xīn included.

"Tomorrow night is the most auspicious time for the ritual but I'd rather us get in there to save Nora sooner. This isn't a movie. We can't swoop in at the last minute and expect all to turn out how we planned.

"Unfortunately, I don't know where they'll perform the ritual. Somewhere in the Enclave, definitely, but it's a large refuge. We'll need to break up into teams to search the entire place. Understood?"

All nodded at him as they continued to pack their individual bags with weapons and supplies. They had become so quiet, concentrating on the tasks at hand and the battle to come, but with all that had happened these past few days, Xīn wondered if the hurt and fear he felt had transferred to the group as well.

CHAPTER SIXTEEN

Nora struggled against the pressing darkness. Each cut and bruise throbbed to life as she surfaced toward consciousness. First her lower lip, then her cheek below her right eye, then the back of her head. As each injury called for her attention, she remembered the beating her captors had given her. Her neck ached from when the Master yanked her head back.

"Ah, you're awake. How lovely. I'd hate for you to miss anything."

The sound of Master Héng's voice focused her attention and Nora opened her eyes. He stood over her, his hands steepled under his chin. The image of Mr. Burns from *The Simpsons* popped into her head and she snorted. When his mouth turned down and his eyes flashed red, she snapped her mouth closed and looked away.

Nora took in the dark paneled walls, the cumbersome desk opposite her chair, and the ornate carvings of the room. She realized she was in the inner sanctum where she had met Master Héng the first time. Was it just yesterday?

Pò stood off to the side conferring with one of his men. He looked at Nora, though, never stopping his conversation. He appeared disturbed; his brow furrowed as if he had just received some bad news. She sure hoped it didn't involve her although at this point it was pretty obvious she was screwed. Whether it would be at Master Héng's hands or Pò's was still up for debate at this point.

A muffled crash echoed through one of the doors behind the desk. Nora saw that Pò still gazed at her but she broke his stare and turned to look toward the sound. Someone she assumed to be one of Pò's men burst through the door dragging a bloodied and battered man. Aside from his injuries Nora noted his clothing: dark burgundy robe and what looked like white pajamas underneath. His shaved head reminded Nora of a Buddhist monk.

Perhaps he was one of the dào rén, or holy men, mortals that protected the línghún secrets and traditions, the only ones allowed access to the sacred scrolls that Xīn mentioned. She knew there was more than one so what happened to the others? Nora's heart sank as she feared the worst.

The other man walked to Pò and stood by his side. Pò whispered something to him. Nora struggled to read his expression but he remained stoic. He and the other of Pò's men disappeared behind one of the doors to her right. She looked back at the holy man and was surprised to see him staring back at her. Awe and fear passed across his features as he knelt.

Despite the obvious pain that wracked his body he shuffled over to her on his knees. He reached a trembling hand toward her as if to touch her leg but at the last moment he pulled away, shame pinching his mouth. He clasped his hands together and held them under his chin as his lips moved in a silent prayer. Nora looked over at Pò who switched his gaze between the holy man and her then back again. She turned toward Master Héng and she cringed against the chair.

Master Héng's eyes flashed blood red, a color Nora had come to recognize as anger. She feared the holy man's life would quickly come to an end if she, or anybody else, didn't do something. She didn't have to wait long.

Pò moved forward and stood by the dào rén. He seemed to take little notice of Pò as he continued to stare at Nora and began muttering in Chinese. He pressed his hands to the floor and bowed before her, touching his forehead to his hands. Nora saw Master Héng tense, ready to pounce on the prostrate man and shred his body. But Pò stepped over him and put himself between Héng and the holy man. He held up his hands.

"Before you continue, let me remind you that you we need at least one holy man to help you with the ritual."

Master Héng pulled up short but it was clear he needed to use all his restraint to keep from tearing both Pò and the holy man to pieces. He sneered down at the man but spoke to Pò.

"You are correct but silence his ramblings or I will kill you both, consequences be damned."

He moved to a door behind the desk and then turned back to Pò.

"Is there anyone left?"

Pò nodded. "We kept half a dozen or so dào rén alive as a backup plan. Why?"

"I need to release," Master Héng replied. "Watch them."

As Master Héng slipped behind the door, Nora relaxed a little. Pò raised a hand to quiet the holy man at her feet. She feared he would be beaten into silence and she stopped Pò before he could do anything.

"Wait! Wait, please don't hurt him."

Pò stared at her, incredulous. "Why do you care?"

"The question is why don't you?"

He opened his mouth to respond but the holy man sat up and grabbed Pò's arm and said something Nora didn't understand. Technically she hadn't understood anything he said because she didn't speak Chinese. Whatever it was, though, this time Pò stopped before he completed the swing of his fist.

It sounded like the man was repeating the same phrase over and over as Nora started to pick out syllables and sounds. She looked at Pò who seemed rooted to the floor.

"What is he saying?"

He ignored her and conversed with the holy man instead. He nodded several times then called to one of his men who stood nearby. Pò spoke so low that Nora couldn't hear him, even though she sat only a few feet away. The man motioned to several of Pò's cronies and they took off through the door at the back of the room.

Pò returned to the holy man on the floor and Nora feared he still planned to hurt him. To her surprise, Pò lifted the man to his feet and helped him to a chair off to the left. When he came back to stand before Nora, despite his previous kindness to the holy man, she thought he was going to kill her. Again he surprised her when he reached behind the chair and cut the ropes that bound her wrists.

As she rubbed her raw skin, Pò knelt at her feet and cut the ropes there as well. He stayed on his knees for several long seconds and stared up at her. Nora looked down at him and a moment of understanding passed between them. As the moment grew, she could almost feel a sense of calm and peacefulness fill her heart and it looked the same for Pò. His expression softened and if it was possible his mouth curled into a smile. She felt an overwhelming urge to reach out to him but before she could he blinked and stared down at the floor. He mumbled something and she had to ask him to repeat it.

"I'm sorry," he said.

Before she could respond, Pò stood then conferred with his second in command, Gàn. They looked at Nora from time to time and she wondered what plan they were forming. Gàn bowed low to Pò then walked over to Nora. He held out his hand, indicating that she should precede him to the exit. She looked at Pò, confused.

"Please, Nora. Go with Gàn. He will facilitate your escape."

"My what?"

"There's no time to explain. Go with Gàn and he will protect you until Xīn and I can come for you."

Nora's breath hitched. "Fā Xīn? But how?"

Gàn grabbed her arm and gently pulled her toward the door. After opening it and guiding her through, he turned back and gave one last nod to Pò. Nora could just see the top of Pò's head bob up and down before Gàn closed the door.

****

Master Héng had sequestered himself in one of the cells deep in the heart of the Enclave. No one would disturb him or the three dào rén he locked in with him. There were three more still alive so if anything unfortunate happened to these, backup was available. As much as he wished he could tear all of them to pieces, Pò and his men included, he had to keep himself under control for as long as possible. Once he had all the elements in place, he could dispose of as many as he desired.

He stared at the man hanging from a large iron hook suspended from the ceiling. Master Héng had bound his wrists in thick rope and slipped the knotted loop over the hook. His feet dangled an inch off the floor so all the weight and pressure pulled at his shoulder joints.

It had been quite painful for the holy man, while he lived.

Master Héng studied every slash, every tear he'd inflicted on the man. Blood had pooled under his victim between the slabs of skin and flesh Héng had torn from him. What hung before him could have been a side of beef as much as a man. He felt his mouth curl up in satisfaction then turned his attention to the remaining dào rén.

Both men were tied at the ankles and wrists and knelt at the far end of the room. The one on the right cringed when Master Héng approached but the other stared him down, defiant to the last.

"You will never succeed," the man spoke. Master Héng grinned.

"Of course. Whatever you say."

"You may succeed in performing the ritual but you will still fail."

"And why is that?"

The holy man straightened his back and lifted his chin. He smiled keeping some secret knowledge to himself. Héng grabbed the kneeling man by his throat and lifted him until they were eye to eye.

"What aren't you telling me, holy man?" Master Héng sneered at the word 'holy'.

But the man clamped his mouth closed even as his eyes bulged and his lips turned blue from lack of oxygen. He refused to struggle against Master Héng's grip or even try to suck in air through his constricted windpipe. He did keep eye contact, though, and that infuriated Héng even more. He never understood why the línghún allowed these mortals amidst them. They couldn't be easily influenced and Héng saw that as a stumbling block to his plan.

Before he even realized it was done, Héng snapped the man's neck and dropped his limp body to the floor. He closed his eyes and tried to calm the rising anger in his chest. Sometimes his emotions did get away from him and in these moments, he almost wished he'd never been made immortal.

He opened his eyes again and turned his attention to the remaining holy man but before he considered what horror he could inflict, there was a knock at the door.

"What?" Héng shouted.

"Master, there's trouble," came the muffled reply.

Forgetting his anger for a moment, worry now replacing it, he moved to the door. After yanking it open, he stared into the face of one of Pò's men, Yǎn. Héng had secured him as a mole in Pò's operation with a promise of a reward from the power of the ritual.

"I told you I was not to be disturbed. What is so urgent?"

"I beg your forgiveness, Master, but she has escaped."

Master Héng felt his fangs descend as fury exploded through him. He managed to stay calm long enough to get the details from Yǎn. Once he learned that Pò was now working against him, and possibly with Xīn, he thanked Yǎn for his loyalty then tore his head from his body.

After dropping Yǎn's head to the floor, Héng made his way toward the tunnels that led to the exit. His only hope was to get them before they left the Enclave. He took one last look over his shoulder, realizing he left one holy man alive back in the cell but he didn't have time for more fun now. He'd take care of him, and all the others, later.

CHAPTER SEVENTEEN

Xīn barely registered Mǐn and Taelin as they entered the store behind him. The smell of blood choked his senses. It covered the floor, walls, the shelves of packaged noodles, spices, and dried meats. Most of the displays, if they hadn't been destroyed, glistened with the sticky residue of drying blood. Even the ceiling sported a few ink blot designs, leaving Xīn to wonder how they got there though in his heart, he didn't really want to know.

"What," Taelin began to ask before he doubled over, wretching. Despite the fact that línghún never ingested food or blood, unless they intended to turn someone, some scenes of extreme violence could move even the most stoic vampire to vomiting in disgust or anguish at the loss of life. Mǐn walked past him after laying a hand on his back in an uncharacteristic show of sympathy. She suddenly stopped moving and stared down at the floor. She jerked her head back and looked at Xīn.

"What is it?" he asked.

Mǐn didn't respond but looked back down at the floor. Xīn moved next to her. The old woman's corpse lay in a crumpled heap, her neck twisted at a severe angle. Her eyes were open wide, as if her last moments were spent looking into the maw of some hell beast. Xīn knelt beside her and brushed his hands over her eyes, closing them.

He stayed beside the old woman, his hand resting on her shoulder, as he whispered a prayer for the dead. When he stood,

Xīn wiped a tear from his cheek before he turned back to this team.

"It seems Master Héng has lost respect for all life, save his own. He deserves no mercy."

As they all nodded in agreement, a loud thud sounded from the storage area at the back of the store. Each pì rén went into battle mode and Xīn took the lead as they went to investigate.

Before they had covered half of the distance, two línghún burst through the double doors. When they saw Xīn they held their weapons above their heads. Xīn raised his hand to stay his team, hoping the fighting wouldn't begin until he found out what was going on.

He recognized the two as belonging to Pò's group but they had not been sent here to fight or stop Xīn. He approached them after lowering his weapon.

"What are you doing here? Why aren't you with Pò?"

They bowed to Xīn and the one on the right spoke.

"Pò sent us to find you before you entered the Enclave. I am Wū Yā. This is Xióng Jī."

Xīn nodded to Xióng and turned back to Wū Yā, who continued his explanation.

"Gàn has taken Nora and is trying to remove her from the premises while Héng is distracted. We had hoped Gàn had already made it out."

Xīn could guess what that distraction might be.

"Nora has not been through here, at least not recently." Xīn could smell her lingering scent even over all of the blood.

"Where's Pò?"

"I believe he is waiting for you at the center. We will escort you there."

Mǐn stepped forward, her hands gripping her blades. "Why should we believe you?"

"We shouldn't," Xīn answered for Wū Yā, "but I'd rather get moving and not stand here arguing aesthetics. Besides, we're more than equipped to handle an ambush."

The team nodded their affirmation and Wū Yā and Xióng Jī led the way back to the storage room.

****

Gàn led Nora down the main tunnel away from the center. She remembered the route from her first visit and offered to go on alone so Gàn could go back and help Pò but he refused, muttering something about shredded entrails and decapitation. As they reached the long flight of stairs back up to the entrance, Master Héng appeared out of the hallway to their right.

Nora could have sworn that when she looked down there a half of a minute ago, the tunnel was empty. She gasped in shock and within a fraction of a second, Gàn placed himself between her and Héng. He pushed her back, out of Héng's immediate reach, and slipped a silver blade out of the sheath at his back. He turned his head, never taking his eyes off Héng, and shouted a command to her.

"Run!"

She hesitated, wanting to save herself but not wanting to abandon Gàn to Master Héng, even if she was physically incapable of helping. Before Gàn could instruct her again, Master Héng flew forward, arms extended, eyes flaming red. Gàn leaped up, thrusting with his blade. It hit Héng in the stomach but he may as well have thrown a snowball at him for all the good the weapon did.

Héng grabbed Gàn's hand and crushed it against the hilt of the blade still buried in his stomach. Gàn cried out and they twisted in the air, Gàn landing on his back and Héng pressing down on him. With his free hand, Master Héng reached back to prepare for a deadly swipe with his clawed nails. Surely he'd eviscerate Gàn.

Nora bit her lip as she looked around for something, anything that she could use as a weapon. A loose stone, about the size of a softball, sat among smaller rubble at the base of the stairs. She ran to it, picked it up, and hurled it at Master Héng, hoping her aim was true.

It was. The stone cracked Master Héng in the forehead, just above his left eye. He twisted to look at her, allowing Gàn to slip out from beneath him. Master Héng touched a hand to his head and studied the blood that colored his fingertips. Gàn looked at him and then turned to Nora. A slight smile twitched the corner of his mouth. Nora jumped in triumph.

"Ha!"

When Gàn faced Master Héng again, Héng was already on his feet and stood inches away. Nora screamed when his fist broke through Gàn's back, bloody and holding Gàn's heart.

"No!"

Master Héng wrenched his hand back through Gàn's chest and held the heart to his lips. As Héng bit deeply into the lump of tissue, Gàn slowly held his knife out to Nora. With a trembling hand she took it as he slipped to his knees. He looked up at her.

"Tell Pò…I'm sorry I…failed you."

Gàn fell forward over his knees. It looked like he was bowing to her like the holy man did earlier. Tears streamed down her face as she looked from Gàn's body to the bloody knife in her hands.

Master Héng caught her attention when he moved to stand over Gàn's body. He grabbed Gàn's arms and pulled while pressing his foot against Gàn's back. Nora didn't wait to see what Héng planned to do and she fled down the tunnel to her right. She knew she couldn't outrun Héng up the stairs, even with a head start. As she heard the crunch of bones and the tearing of flesh, she hoped she'd be able to hide from him long enough for Xīn to find her – alive.

****

Wū Yā and Xióng Jī reached the bottom of the steps and stopped. Xīn ran into Xióng, not expecting him to be stationary as they entered the Enclave.

"What's the matter?" Xīn questioned but neither línghún answered. Wū Yā moved to the left and Xióng to the right then each knelt at either end of Gàn's body. Xīn stepped forward and saw Gàn's corpse. As he stared at it, Mǐn, Taelin, and the others moved out from the stairwell into the hallway, surrounding Pò's men. Though he had considered Pò and all his men as enemies, Xīn would never have wished such a gruesome death on anyone.

Gàn's arms and legs had been torn from his body, the ragged stumps still glistening in the torch light. His torso looked crushed by a great force and his clothes were shredded, the long tears mirroring the gashed flesh beneath. His head was the worst. Not only had the ears, lips, and nose been removed, they looked like they had been chewed off. The eye sockets lay empty and Gàn's tongue was missing. And the neck also appeared to have been chewed, as if the attacker ate his way through it in order to remove the head from the body.

For the second time that night, Taelin gagged and doubled over in disgust. Mǐn moved to stand beside him while the others moved away to give them room. Xīn stood by the body and spoke to Wū Yā.

"This was Gàn, yes? Pò's second?"

He nodded then looked from body part to body part as if trying to figure out how to put Gàn back together. Master Héng's scent permeated the enclosed space and Xīn's stomach twisted with agony. Gàn's flesh suddenly shriveled and dried, transforming into separate piles of dust. Xīn knelt beside Wū Yā and put a hand on his shoulder.

"I am truly sorry about your friend but we need to find Pò."

Wū Yā nodded and looked at Xióng. They shared some silent understanding and stood in unison. Wū Yā looked at Xīn.

"Follow me."

The two línghún led Xīn and his group towards the heart of the Enclave. They encountered dozens of bodies along the way: holy men, rogue línghún, and soldiers alike. Wū Yā and Xióng seemed surprised by some of the corpses.

"What is it?" Xīn asked.

"Many of these corpses weren't here when we came to meet you. I don't understand," Xióng said.

Wū Yā nodded. "I know we fought through some soldiers but no holy men. And none of ours were killed here when we attacked."

Xīn ground his teeth. The fact that Pò and his men attacked in the first place angered him. But he supposed they thought they were going to share in some grand design for their kind, a higher purpose. They didn't know they were being played the fools.

"Let's just get to the inner sanctum," Xīn said. "We need to talk to Pò and figure out how to find Nora."

They pushed on and finally entered the center room to find Pò, another one of his men, and a dào rén in deep conversation. Pò looked up as they entered. A brief flash of relief and happiness crossed his features when he looked at Xīn but his smile quickly faded.

"Nora never made it out, did she?" Pò asked.

Xīn shook his head. "But she could be hiding in the Enclave somewhere."

"And Gàn?"

Xīn stared at his feet unsure of what to say. When he looked up, Pò was wiping tears from his eyes. Xīn walked to his side and laid a hand on Pò's shoulder. Pò stared at him, surprised.

"I am sorry, Pò."

Pò studied Xīn for a moment before he spoke.

"You really are sorry, aren't you?"

Xīn nodded and Pò sighed. "I've been such an idiot. Master Héng made me believe this ritual would be good for all línghún," Pò laughed. "Or maybe that's what I wanted to believe. All those men," he stopped.

"Pò, you can feel guilty later. Right now we have to figure out our next step."

Pò nodded. "You're right. First we need to see if Nora is hiding somewhere down here."

Xīn moved to the door but Pò stepped over to the holy man.

"Pò, what are you doing?"

"Chún Míng can help us. He can tune into Nora's energy to help us find her."

Pò motioned to the holy man sitting in a chair in the middle of the room. He'd been beaten but was able and eager to help. When Xīn moved closer, the man stared up at him then stood. He bowed.

"You are the Protector," the holy man said.

"Excuse me?"

"You are the Protector. You are here to keep the sacred vessel safe."

"Vessel. You mean Nora?"

The holy man nodded. "As a sacred vessel is born, the gods will choose one among the línghún to be its sanctuary. Have not your dreams told you this?"

"I don't remember my dreams. But that explains why Nora looked so familiar when I first saw her."

"You must keep the vessel safe at all costs or all will perish."

"All línghún?"

"Seems if Master Héng succeeds in the ritual," Pò continued, "not only will he destroy all the línghún but he could possibly destroy everyone else, too."

"How is that possible?" Xīn asked.

"Part of the ritual is to make one invincible. That is what most línghún have been told. But there's another aspect," Pò replied.

The holy man nodded. "Only the destined vessel may possess the power of all the past souls. By taking that away from the vessel, the scales of balance will be disturbed. Once Master Héng performs the ritual, all the *future* souls will die as well."

"We can be sure that once Héng's successful, he will destroy any and all línghún that oppose him. After that, despite what may feel like a never ending supply of humans to be available for his consumption, it is only a finite number," Pò spoke.

Xīn frowned, still not quite grasping the whole truth. Pò signed in exasperation and Chún Míng explained.

"Don't you see? Héng consumes all the souls of the past in the ritual. The gods will not bestow any future souls upon this world in order to maintain the balance. As each soul of the present dies, there will be no more to take its place. No other living creature will be born ever again."

Xīn could feel his eyes widen. "All of humanity, all life, will cease to exist. A hundred years from now, this planet will be dead."

"You must protect her," the holy man said. He clutched Xīn's shirt and the fear in his eyes shone with a bright intensity. "You must."

Xīn held the man's hands. "I will. Can you help me find her?"

The holy man nodded and moved back to the chair. He sat down and dug a string of red wooden beads from somewhere inside his robes. A braided red tassel hung from one end. He pressed the beads between his hands, closed his eyes, and began to chant. It was an ancient dialect that Xīn didn't recognize.

Within a few minutes, the dào rén stopped chanting but his eyes remained closed.

"The vessel is still here but in great danger. Move quickly to the northwest corridor, one level below us. Héng is almost upon her."

Xīn and Pò nodded to each other. Each one assigned a man to stay behind then rallied their groups and headed out from the center to find Nora before Master Héng did.

CHAPTER EIGHTEEN

Nora ran from one corridor to the next. She hoped her erratic movements might throw Master Héng off her scent long enough for her to find a hiding place. Though scared and exhausted, Nora had to keep moving but at the same time try not to panic and do something stupid, like end up back where she started.

She turned down a hallway on her right and stumbled over a corpse. At least she managed not to scream, especially after seeing the head lying off to the side. She tiptoed around the body and stared through the open door next to it. One holy man hung from a hook in the ceiling and another lay in a crumpled heap on the floor.

When she gasped at seeing the carnage a third holy man stood. He had been kneeling next to the body on the floor and she hadn't noticed him. He walked toward her then bowed.

"Oh, great. Another one. Um, please don't do that."

Nora grabbed his shoulders and eased him back to a standing position. He seemed surprised but did as she directed. Looking back at his dead colleagues and then out the door to see the headless corpse, he began to speak in Chinese, a tumult of words spilling out of his mouth.

She tried to interrupt him, to let him know she didn't understand, but he continued. He pointed at the dead holy men, then out the door. Nora shook her head and he did something surprising. He straightened his posture, possibly to appear taller, and used his fingers to mimic fangs in his mouth. Moving to the man hung from the ceiling, he pantomimed actions that would have caused his injuries. He then walked to the man on the floor and reached down to grab his neck. He made a snapping noise with his tongue.

Still chattering in Chinese, the holy man moved to the hallway and imitated someone pulling the head off a body. He came back to Nora and put his fingers back in fang position. Nora clapped her hands.

"Master Héng! You're imitating Master Héng. He did all this," she spoke as she pointed to each corpse.

The holy man nodded and smiled but it faded when he looked out the door. He started talking again, motioning for Nora to hide somewhere in the room. Before she could move, he held up his hand and studied the room.

He walked over to a puddle of blood on the floor and dipped his hand into it. Walking back to Nora, he reached forward as if to paint it on her skin. She recoiled and shook her head.

"Nuh uh. No way. Why the hell would you want to put blood all over me?"

The holy man thought about it. He spread it on his own arm and then pointed to his nose. Nora was still confused. The holy man imitated Héng again but pretended to sniff the air, the bodies, his bloodied arm. When he sniffed his clean arm, he pretended to be a línghún and gnashed his teeth together.

"By spreading the dead man's blood on me it will cover up my scent, making it easier to hide from Master Héng," Nora said.

The holy man looked at her expectantly. She swallowed the nausea churning at the back of her throat and held up her arm. He smiled and began slathering her bare skin with blood. Nora pinched her eyes closed and turned her head away. If she watched the process, the nausea would do more than churn – it would project.

He continued to smear blood not just on her exposed skin but her jeans and shirt as well. *Guess he just wants to be thorough.* When she didn't feel him touching her anymore, she opened her eyes. The holy man stood before her, holding up his bloody hands, making motions of spreading the blood on her face. She nodded and closed her eyes again.

When he finished, he spread blood over himself as well. Once they both looked like extras in the latest horror remake, he pointed to the darkest corner of the room. Nora nodded and they moved to it, hoping the darkness and the blood would help them elude Master Héng. Nora feared no one would be able to help her, except maybe Xīn, but would he find her in time?

A loud snarl echoed in the hallway. It could have been right outside the door or a mile away, Nora couldn't tell. The holy man tensed beside her. Someone screamed in pain, followed by a loud rip, then silence. A faint slurping sound carried into their dark corner and nausea threatened to make a comeback.

Without thinking she grabbed the holy man's hand. Once she did she thought it might be inappropriate or he'd start bowing again. To her surprise, though, he gripped her hand in return and she smiled in the dark.

Suddenly the light from the doorway disappeared and she looked up. A large hulking figure darkened the entrance and Nora's breath caught in her throat. Master Héng. He moved into the room, turning his head left and right. Nora could hear him sniffing the air and she gripped the holy man's hand tighter, thankful for his quick albeit disgusting thinking.

Master Héng walked from one end of the room to the other, ending his search at their hiding place. Nora leaned away from him and toward the holy man who pulled her close. He was probably worried that she would betray their position so he pressed his hand over her mouth. She didn't mind. In fact she clamped her hand over his to make doubly sure she didn't make a sound. And the thought of his gore covered hand against her lips only passed through her mind for a fraction of a second. Master Héng was a much bigger concern right now. She could always throw up later.

Master Héng seemed convinced that the room was empty and stalked out. Nora still held the holy man's hand in place for a solid minute before moving. They each shifted and stood as quietly as possible then inched their way toward the door. Stopping just short of the entrance, they stared at each other and listened for any sounds of movement. The holy man held up his hand, motioning for her to stay put while he checked the hallway. She nodded.

His soundless steps passed through the doorway. First he checked to the right then left. Nothing happened and he turned back to look at her. Nora released the breath she'd been holding and took a step forward.

In the second it took her to breathe, the holy man's head vanished though his body remained upright. Perhaps the light was playing tricks on her eyes or maybe the stress of the whole situation made her hallucinate. But when the blood gushed forth from the stump of his neck and his body collapsed in a heap, Nora knew it was no trick.

Master Héng stepped over the body while holding the man's head in his hand like a pro ball player palming a basketball and she started screaming. She didn't stop until Héng grabbed her by the neck and slammed her against the wall.

The last thought before blackness took over was, "Xīn, where are you?"

****

Pò and Xīn stood over the decapitated holy man. His blood hadn't yet coagulated so they'd missed the fight by minutes. Xīn growled in frustration.

"Master Héng could be anywhere in this maze of tunnels and hallways. We could search for days and never find him. We can't afford to lose any more time."

"He'll have to take Nora off-site," Pò replied. "But where?"

"What about that cabin, north of here?"

Pò shook his head. "No, he'd have thought of that. It'd be the first place we'd look."

They wracked their brains for several minutes, suggesting different places that might work. Ultimately, they were all useless.

"What about your building, Pò?" Mǐn suggested.

They all turned to look at her and Pò shook his head.

"No. Master Héng said he'd never perform the ritual there."

"Exactly why we should look, correct?" she countered.

Pò opened his mouth to argue but snapped it closed. He looked at Xīn and shrugged.

"It's probably the best bet right now."

Xīn agreed. "Let's get everyone topside and plan our attack."

After gathering their ranks, they moved back up the stairs and into the storage area of the store. Pò instructed his men to go outside ahead of him and ready the cars. He turned to Xīn.

"I should probably tell you, we've got a fā kuáng."

Xīn stared at him. "You can't be serious."

"It actually comes in handy with any intruders or insubordinates."

"Pò! How could you be so cruel?"

Mǐn spoke up. "What's a fā kuáng?"

"A fā kuáng is a vampire that has overdosed, for lack of a better word, on emotion," Xīn explained. "But instead of death, they find insanity. They are trapped in a permanent state of madness. Though they are capable of some reasoning abilities, all they know, all they want, is blood. Human, animal, or línghún, it doesn't matter to a fā kuáng."

Mǐn nodded. Now that she had been away from Nora for a while, the few emotions she'd been showing had completely faded. As a matter of fact, all Xīn's soldiers seemed back to normal. Xīn wasn't sure if he liked that.

Before they could move through the double doors back into

the store, the door opened as one of Pò's men burst through. He blocked the group's way and Pò questioned him.

"Hóng, what are you doing?"

"Pò, I," he started but had to swallow before he could continue. "It's Madam Lài. She's…" He couldn't finish his thought and looked down at the floor.

Xīn studied Pò's face. Fear pinched Pò's eyes into slits. Pò pushed past his man and into the store. When Xīn followed, he saw Pò standing over the body of the elderly woman that worked behind the counter. He remembered how, despite the fear in her eyes, she always showed great respect to the línghún as they passed through the store.

When Pò fell to his knees beside her body, Xīn saw there was more than respect between them. Something more akin to love. Whether it was familial or romantic, Xīn couldn't say. He wondered if he'd ever find out.

Xīn stood beside Pò and laid a hand on his shoulder.

"Pò, we don't have time to mourn her right now."

Pò nodded but didn't stand. He traced his finger along her cheek first then whispered good bye. When he stood, he barked an order at two of his men.

"You two. Stay here and guard the body. No one is to touch her until I get back, understand?"

The two men nodded and moved next to the old woman's corpse. Pò turned to Xīn.

"Master Héng dies tonight. No matter what else happens, promise me you'll help me kill him."

"I promise."

Pò squeezed Xīn's shoulder. "Then let's go."

He took one last look at the old woman before he turned and headed out the front door. Xīn watched his men follow Pò and not one glanced down at the body, as if they didn't understand or care. That saddened him and said a quick prayer for Madam Lài before he caught up to the group.

****

Nora woke with a pounding headache. She rolled onto her side and tried to clutch her head. Her hands stopped short and through the fog of pain she saw the shackles. Great thick chains, bolted into the wall behind her, ran along the floor and ended at heavy, rusted metal circles surrounding her wrists and ankles.

"Shit, I hope I don't get lock-jaw," was the first thought that popped into her muddled mind.

She shook her head to help clear it but that only made the headache worse. She did manage to sit up and when she did she was able to take in her surroundings. The small cramped room held several other pairs of chains and shackles bolted to the walls. One set hung from the ceiling and though they were empty now, an image of a woman hanging from them popped into Nora's head. She didn't know how or why but she knew the woman was real and not a product of her imagination.

"Yes, she was real, my dear," Master Héng's voice slithered over her through the darkened room. "Yet another in a long string of Pò's victims."

Master Héng appeared in the doorway. He moved like oil,

slithering through the shadowy room until he stood next to the hanging shackles. He ran his hands along the rusty metal and the links clinked and clacked a rhythm that sent shivers through Nora's muscles. She scooched backwards, away from Héng, but bumped against the wall sooner than she liked.

In a flash, Héng was crouched in front of her and had his hands clamped on either side of her face.

"You're beginning to feel them, aren't you? The souls. The souls of all that ever were and that are, don't you?"

Even in the dark Nora could see the fanatical gleam in his eyes. She tried to pull away but he held her fast.

"*As the auspicious time draws near, the vessel will become more receptive to the energies around it and will fill with the souls of the world.*"

It sounded like he was reciting an information pamphlet or instruction manual. Nora tsked at him.

"Wow, you've really gone off your rickshaw haven't you, Héng?"

She heard a low growl sneak past his bared teeth before he backhanded her. Despite the pain, she managed to laugh.

"Guess I hit a nerve. Part of you must agree with me, eh?"

Before he could hit her again, a wave of images flooded her brain. It didn't hurt but it felt like someone was trying to cram a thousand marshmallows into her head through her ears. She managed a short 'ah' before she slumped against the wall. Her body went limp, against her wishes, possibly to help her acclimate the images into her mind without a struggle.

Nora recognized two faces, Héng and Xīn, in a sea of

strangers at an unfamiliar location. Pictures began to form a story in her mind.

CHAPTER NINETEEN

"You've done well, my son," Master Héng spoke to Fā Xīn. "Though you've only been línghún for a sliver of time, already you set yourself above the others."

Xīn bowed. "Thank you, Master."

"So well have you done that I desire you to lead the duì on its mission in the north."

"I will do as you command."

Master Héng laid a hand on Xīn's shoulder. "This is not a command. You may refuse the assignment, of course, but I would," he paused for effect, "feel better if you went."

Xīn nodded. "What are the details?"

"A group of wú lài have taken over a small town in the north called Linhuang. We don't know exactly where they've nested so it will be difficult to end their scourge. The humans there are no match for the rogues. They're just a pitiful weak band of mortals that need our help."

"Do we know how many there are?"

"Unfortunately no, but most wú lài band together with no fewer than ten individuals."

"If we plan on double that number, at least," Xīn continued, "it might be helpful if…"

Héng shut out Xīn's annoying prattling. He couldn't possibly care less about the details of this mission. He just wanted Xīn out of the way for a while. It's not that he wanted Xīn to fail or didn't care about him. He loved Xīn like a son, or how he supposed a father would love a son. Héng's father had been more interested in war than parenting.

When Héng realized Xīn had stopped talking, he turned toward the young vampire.

"Yes, yes. That all sounds good. Thank you, Xīn."

Xīn nodded and turned to leave to make the necessary preparations but Héng stopped him.

"Xīn, if you approve, I would like to visit your family."

Xīn appeared confused. "If I approve? Master, you know that you are welcome in my family's home any time you desire."

Héng smiled. "I know, but it never hurts to be polite, yes?"

"I suppose you are correct. Shall I let them know you plan to visit?"

"Yes, please. I would like to see them tomorrow if it's no trouble."

"I'm sure they will be very happy to see you. It has been a while."

"I know," Héng replied. "That's why I want to visit. I want to explain why I've been sending you away on so many missions, tell them how well you're doing."

Xīn bowed and left Master Héng's quarters. He watched his young protégé through the window as he moved through the compound toward the main gates. It was always nice to have such loyal, if somewhat oblivious, subjects. Once Xīn was off on another mission, Héng would have plenty of time for his latest obsession.

The following evening, Master Héng, accompanied by Xīn, traveled to the humble village of Xīn's family. Before he could knock, Xīn's father, Rú, opened the door to the simple wooden home. He bowed once and welcomed them both inside.

"Rú, thank you for allowing me to visit you," Héng said. Xīn's father blushed in embarrassment and he simply waved his hand at him. He pointed to the floor, motioning for Héng to sit. Xīn's mother, Lán, came in moments later with a tray of simple yet hearty foods. As soon as she set it down, she realized her mistake and her face drained of color. She started to stammer out an apology but Master Héng raised his hand.

"My dear woman, please don't worry. Though Xīn and I no longer require food to sustain us, you and your family do. Please feel free to consume what you desire."

That helped ease her embarrassment. Héng looked around.

"But where is the rest of your family?"

"Chāo and Dá are finishing up in the fields. They should be home soon. As you know, Huǎng recently married and lives with his wife's family in the next village. He will be sorry he missed you, I'm sure. And Ài, oh here she is now."

The beautiful young woman that walked through the door and embraced Xīn took Héng's breath away. There was nothing left of the awkward shy little girl from ten years ago when Xīn was transformed into one of the línghún. She moved with a graceful fluidity despite her years of a farming life in this little hovel of a village.

Though streaked with dried mud, her skin glowed with a

golden hue. Her black hair shone even in the dim light of the modest home. And when she looked at Master Héng, her eyes sparkled with awe and joy. She bowed deeply.

"Master Héng, it is so wonderful to see you again. Please forgive my appearance. I've just come from the fields. Allow me to clean up and I will be back soon. Ma, I will use the water from the barrel out back. Please don't let Master Héng leave until I return."

"Truly, my child, you do not need to change a thing just for me," Héng protested.

"Oh but I do," she explained. "I cannot give you a present looking like this. I will return soon."

Before he could ask what she meant, Ài bounced off to the back of the house. Héng heard the back door open and close as she headed outside to clean up. In his mind he could already see the water as it flowed over her body, a rough cloth scrubbing away the dirt from her face, her breasts, her legs. Rú's irritating voice interrupted his fantasy.

"So what brings you to our humble home, Master Héng? Everything is all right, yes? Qíng Shēng, I mean, Fā Xīn, is doing well, isn't he?"

"Of course he is. That is exactly why I am here. It is my responsibility to keep you abreast of Xīn's progress. Even though I'm no longer capable of true emotion, I thought you might be unhappy that I keep sending him away."

Rú and Lán seemed dumbfounded. Their cow-like countenances displayed their uneducated roughness. If they ask me what I mean, Héng thought, I'll rip their throats out and suck their bones clean.

"What do you mean, Master?" Rú asked.

With all the self control he could muster, Héng tried not to kill him. "I just mean that I don't want you to think that I send Xīn away because he isn't doing well. Quite the opposite. For such a young línghún, he has adapted faster and showed more promise than any other I have known."

"Master, I thank you but I know I'm not the only one. Pò is also," Xīn tried to play down his worth but Héng stopped him.

"Do not interrupt me, Xīn. I speak the truth in this matter. Yes, Pò is a great warrior but even after twenty years, he has not quite learned the art of loyalty as you have."

Héng turned to Xīn's parents who now looked pleased. "I say these things for two reasons. One, I truly want you to know how precious Xīn is to me and if I had been able to have a son myself, I would have wanted him to be like him."

Rú and Lán turned to look at each other, the obvious pride they felt showing on their faces. Before Héng crushed their heads into crimson stains, he continued.

"And two…"

Héng's thought flew out of his head as he looked up and saw Ài enter the room, freshly cleaned and dressed. Her simple white hemp tunic covered her from her neck to her ankles. She stood barefoot and Héng silently thanked the heavens that Ài's parents never bound their daughter's feet like those fools in the Emperor's court.

Ài knelt next to her mother. "Forgive me for interrupting you, Master Héng. Please continue."

He looked down at the box in her hands then back up to her radiant face. She smiled, a soft pink blush colored her cheeks. It was all he could do not to grab her and run out the door.

"And two, I must send him away again. There is a band of wú lài in the north and Fā Xīn would be the best candidate to quell their rebellion."

"Of course we understand," Rú spoke. "He is your son now. You are free to use him as you please."

Héng looked over at Xīn who simply stared at the floor. He laid a hand on the boy's shoulder then looked to his parents.

"I may be like a father to him, and he a son to me, but he will always be your blood. Your family. Though I do not ask your permission for anything involving Fā Xīn, you deserve to be made aware of the events of his life now."

As he hoped, the insinuation of insult by their comment hit home. Rú and Lán both threw themselves forward, pressing their heads to the floor and begged for forgiveness. Though he would have enjoyed their groveling for much longer, the look of shame on Ài's face forced him to forgive her parents sooner rather than later.

"Please, please. Do not trouble yourselves with any more guilt. We are all friends here. That is why I wanted to visit you. Just keep this in your minds. Xīn is being well cared for and has done his family proud by being such an honest and loyal línghún."

That seemed to relieve everyone so Héng turned to Ài.

"Now, what is this present you spoke of? Is that it, in your lap?"

Ài nodded and blushed again. Héng smiled, honestly more interested in her lap than the gift that lay upon it.

"I made this for you, Master. There's a carver in our village who has been teaching me his craft for a few years now. Though this is too simplistic and novice for a great man such as you, I wish for you to have it."

Héng took the wooden box from her hands. His fingers brushed hers for the briefest of moments but as they did, her emotions flooded him like fire: nervousness, awe, humility, a snip of pride, and a hint of desire. He twitched as that last feeling washed over him and fed his own lust.

He stared down at the box as he tried to control himself. Though Ài wasn't a willing sacrifice for any kind of ritual, her eagerness for something deeper was intoxicating. Héng licked his lips and lifted the lid. Inside laid a pale green and amber colored bowl. He lifted it out and was surprised by the delicate dragon carvings that adorned the outside. He turned the bowl around and counted nine different images carved into the jade.

When he looked back at Ài, she didn't lower her gaze. She held his eyes with her own for several seconds. He could feel so much passion emanating from her he thought he might go mad if he didn't have her. Soon. Fā Xīn broke the spell.

"Ài, that's beautiful. How long did it take you to make it?"

"I worked on it all winter. Do you like it, Master Héng?"

Héng opened his mouth to respond but couldn't find the

words. Even as a child living in the palace he had never received anything like it. As he struggled to answer, Ài laughed.

"I would say the Master does like it, wouldn't you, Xīn?"

Xīn's family all shared a good laugh then fell into a comfortable rhythm of talking, laughing, and sharing stories just as they did when Xīn was still human. Héng nodded and smiled when appropriate but most of his thoughts were about Ài. The way she looked at him all evening, a casual flip of her hair. He could have sworn that she let the hem of her tunic ride up enough to flash her bare ankle and calf, just for Héng's benefit.

By the end of the night, Héng was in such an emotional and physical frenzy that he excused himself ahead of Xīn under the pretense for them all to spend more time together before Xīn set off on his travels. As he left the house, he took in a deep breath and catalogued all the smells around him to help distract his thoughts: wood, dirt, trampled grass, excrement from a nearby farm animal.

All the smells of the earth blanketed him as he walked and he felt himself calming. Suddenly he caught a whiff of jasmine and the hemp fabric used to make clothing. He spun around and came face to face with Ài. He had been working so hard to distract himself that he never heard her approach. The moonlight lit up her face, glowed along the line of her tunic, and shone in her eyes that looked as black as the still water of a lake.

"Ài, what," he started but she held up her hand then pointed back to her home only a few feet away. She motioned forward and once they walked down the road a bit, she spoke.

"Forgive me. I told my parents I needed to relieve myself so I only have a few minutes. And I don't want them to overhear."

"Overhear what, my dear?"

"Since Fā Xīn will be going away for a while, does that mean you won't be coming by to visit us?"

"I suppose it doesn't have to mean that. Would you like me to visit?"

She smiled up at him and nodded. "Aside from my carving lessons, life around here can be rather dull. Believe me, I love and honor my parents and the life I have because of them. It would be much better, though, to have other things to do once in awhile."

Ài emphasized the word 'other' and looked up at him from under her lashes, trying hard to be coy. Héng hid a smile under his hand and frowned, pretending to mull over the idea.

"Well, if it is all right with Rú and Lán, then I shall have to visit from time to time."

Ài jumped up and down, her smile impossibly large. "Thank you so much, Master."

Then she did something Héng never expected. She stood up on her tiptoes and kissed him on the cheek. As he stood, hand on his face and dumbfounded, she cleared her throat and stepped back. Even by the light of the moon he could see her blush. Finally she bowed and made her way back home.

Héng stood in the middle of the road and watched her slip behind the house. Even after she had disappeared from his sight, he continued to stare at the space she had occupied and could feel his fangs protrude from his gums. He ran his tongue over them, cutting it open and tasting his own blood as it painted the inside of his mouth. He would have such fun with her.

The following week Xīn left with a contingent of línghún to help quell the wú lài uprising in the north. No sooner had he left did Héng move in for Ài. Under the pretense of checking in on them since Xīn would be gone for a while, Héng visited Rú and Lán one evening. He pretended to care about the small talk they made and gave them bland assurances that Xīn would be successful in his mission and return safely.

He was only biding his time until he could be alone with Ài. She stared at him all evening, between the banal conversations, the meal, and helping clear the dishes for her mother. Her eyes sparkled with a mischievous glint and when her parents tried to stifle their yawns, she told them to go to bed and offered to sit with Master Héng as long as he wished to visit.

"Don't worry, Ma. I will make sure Master Héng is taken care of."

Rú and Lán wished them both good night and went into their bedroom. Ài motioned toward the door.

"Master Héng, would you like to take a walk? It's such a beautiful evening."

Perfect. "Yes, Ài. That would be nice. And please, we're not in polite society now. Call me Wěi."

A soft pink blush colored her cheeks but she nodded in agreement. They stood and he motioned for her to precede him out the door. After bowing, she moved forward and he stared at her back. Her shoulders were pulled up and back and her hips swayed slightly under her tunic. She pushed through the doorway and he followed, licking his lips in anticipation.

He guided her south, away from the rest of town. Her relaxed shoulders and light walk showed the complete ease she felt with him. No fear or tension showed on her face, just her natural beauty shone in the moonlight. When they had reached a small river, Héng stopped on its bank and looked up at the moon.

"What a glorious night. I haven't felt this alive since the night I was turned!"

Héng looked down at Ài and for the first time that evening, Ài appeared nervous. She smiled as if to hide it.

"Wěi, you seem rather animated for a línghún. Normally you are so stoic and serious."

He smiled down at her. "Oh, I'm sure it's the remnants of the peasant I ate on the way over. Feisty little man with such passion for life. How he struggled and fought me. Ah, it just made him that much more delicious."

Ài's smile fell from her face. She took a step backward but Héng reached out and grabbed her arms.

"Oh, now my dear, why are you backing away? You're not afraid of me, are you?"

"But you're not supposed to attack people who aren't willing to give themselves to you."

"So you aren't willing? Come, come. You've been giving looks of lust and want for a while. Don't pretend to be shy now."

Ài tried to pull free from his grasp but to no avail. She shook her head back and forth in protest.

"No! I never did any such thing."

"Oh, then my mistake. When you told your mother you'd take care of me, what exactly did you mean?"

She opened her mouth to reply but nothing came out. Her eyes took on the look of resignation as she realized she'd done everything of which he'd accused her. Caught in his grasp Ài could do nothing to escape. The need to absorb her soul was stronger than it ever had been now that he had her in his hands.

He pushed his forehead against hers. He could feel her brow crinkle against him and he smiled at how it tickled. Soon Ài began to tremble as the soul energy was drawn through her body. She opened her mouth and a flash of light burst forth. Héng opened his mouth to receive it then shuddered with pleasure once he consumed her soul. Normally he would have given it to the gods, as was required in the transformation ritual, but what had they ever done for him? No, Ài's energy would be for him alone.

Now that her soul was extracted it was time to feed on her visceral life force. Héng dragged her into the river, the cold water nothing to him but Ài would soon start to shiver.

"Sometimes I prefer my drink to be chilled. You don't mind, do you?"

He pushed her down, submerging her entire body by pressing on her head. She kicked and thrashed but could do nothing else to rectify her predicament. After a minute he pulled her out and she gasped and choked for air.

"Don't worry. I only need to do this a few more times to get your blood the correct temperature."

He dunked her into the water over and over for several minutes. Only when she exhausted her struggles did he stop. Pulling her close and holding her against his chest, he whispered in her ear.

"This will only hurt for a moment. Or possibly longer. It depends on how well I can control myself."

He felt his fangs protrude then opened his mouth wide. Plunging his teeth into the soft tissue of her neck, into the main blood vessel there, he squeezed his arms to keep her from slipping away. Her blood flowed into his mouth and down his throat. The ecstasy that rushed into every tissue of his body from her pure fluid was like a million fireflies dancing through the night sky. He arched his back as a bolt of energy flowed from her into him.

Within moments Ài began to slump against him, her body drained of too much vital energy to fight any more. Still clamped onto her neck, Héng eased her down to the ground on the bank of the river. The soft bubbling sound of the water, the ants moving in the ground beneath them, the swishing wings of the night birds as they flew overhead boomed in his ears. Even the moonlight was more vibrant after he took his fill of her.

Héng stopped drinking just short of her heart's collapse. He knelt over her, sniffing the skin of her neck and face then moved until they were nose to nose. The usual golden glow of her skin was wan and pale, her hair lay flat and lifeless. Though her eyes had dulled, there was still a spark of life left in them.

"The only question my dear is this: will you die now or live forever?"

She wasn't expecting to be given a choice. That small spark grew as she considered the option.

"Consider carefully but don't take too long. You haven't much time."

Ài pressed her lips together in determination and nodded her agreement. Héng could feel his lips curling into a vicious smile.

"Wonderful."

He raised his arm and bit into his wrist. Dark crimson blood flowed out and he placed it against her mouth.

"Drink. Quickly, before the wound heals."

She obeyed his command, weak at first, but soon her teeth clamped onto his wrist and he could feel the pull against his skin as she suckled at his torn flesh. The fireflies were gone and replaced with pure fire. His wrist burned as his own blood flowed out and into Ài. Though he wanted to pull away he knew it wasn't time yet. She needed a few more seconds to drink enough to make her turn.

When the time came, he pried her off without too much difficulty and she laid back on the grass. Her body arched and contorted as her tissues absorbed Héng's blood and transformed. The glow came back to her skin, albeit with a little less gold sheen to it. Her eyes flew open and transformed from black to gold to green then red. They finally settled on a soft brown shade that complemented her new beauty.

Once Ài stopped twisting and thrashing, she sat up and stared at the world around her. Héng sat back and watched her as she watched the night, tracking flies and tilting her head from side to side as each new sound pricked her ears. He remembered how it was when he was turned and could imagine what was going on in her mind at this moment. He smiled.

Though she was now an emotionless línghún, Héng was riding high from her energy. It would be a few hours before he could come down so he needed to find a place for her to rest and continue adjusting. He would take her back to his home but keep her hidden from anyone who might remember her as Xīn's sister. Once Xīn returned, he'd figure out what to do about her then.

"My dear, we must get you back home so you can rest. You've been through quite an ordeal tonight."

"Yes, I suppose I have. I will head back now. I hope my parents will be all right with this."

"Oh, no. Not your home. Mine. I'm afraid that because we were a bit... impulsive... you must stay in my home until we can resolve any complications that might arise."

She thought about it. "But surely I should at least inform my parents."

"Don't worry. I will speak to them. It's only right that I explain the situation. Now, let's get you home and then I will return and talk with Rú and Lán."

Ài nodded her agreement and they walked to his home. He didn't want to scare her by moving too fast, what mortals thought was flying. It was her first night as a línghún. She'd learn of all her abilities soon enough. Or at least what he chose to teach her. After securing her inside his bed chamber, he returned to Rú and Lán's home with a handful of his lesser followers.

Of course he had no intention of speaking to either of them. He needed for them to just go away. If Ài's parents simply disappeared, though, it might look suspicious. If the entire village were to perish, then it would be seen as a tragic accident, and one only the gods could have ordained.

A fire. If he set several of them, the village would burn much more quickly. The wind had picked up in the last hour and that would help. He ordered his men to spread out through the village and burn it to the ground.

"Kill anyone who tries to escape. Your reward will be great if you succeed. Do not fail me."

They moved in different directions while Héng slipped into Rú's and Lán's home. He found them both asleep in the back room, unaware of their fates. Héng stepped beside Rú and stared down at the man. Ài's life was doomed if she stayed tied to these peasants. He raised his foot and held it over Rú's head then slammed it down. The force caused Rú's head to explode and brain, bone, and blood sprayed in all directions. Much of it onto Lán's face and she jerked awake.

"What?" was all she could say before she saw Rú's ruined skull next to her. She wiped at her face. When her fingers came away with blood and goo she began to scream. Héng swooped down and grabbed her throat in one hand, cutting off her air and, thankfully, her screeching. He leaned in close and whispered.

"Take comfort in knowing that Ài belongs to me now. She is línghún and will do great things in the centuries to come, which is more than I can say for you two dirty, lowly peasants. You never deserved her."

Héng jerked his hand and snapped Lán's neck in one quick movement. He didn't even want to taste their blood. It was probably tainted with dirt and manure. Before he could stand, though, someone jumped on his back, screaming in rage. Héng twisted his head to see Chāo's face, red and sweaty. He'd almost forgotten about him and his brother, Dá.

Throwing Chāo off his back, Héng could smell Dá coming before he saw him. Dung, dirt, and sweat clogged his nostrils just before Dá burst into the room. With a quick swing, Héng shoved his arm into Dá's chest and tore out the boy's heart. When he dropped to the floor, Chāo was back up on his feet and running at Héng. He was dispatched as easily as his brother.

Leaving them as they lay, Héng stepped out of the small hut and waved down one of his men. He held out his hand.

"Give me your torch. I'll handle this home."

Setting the simple house ablaze lifted his heart, even more so than Ài's blood had. He moved out to the street and watched the wooden structure burn with great satisfaction. Soon the entire village was on fire and his men had gathered around him, awaiting praise or further instruction. He pointed at two of them.

"I need you to head over to the next village. It needs cleansing as much as this one. When you've finished, report back to me."

The two men bowed and ran off into the night. Héng decided they didn't need to know that Ài's brother, Huǎng, was the only one in need of cleansing. As long as Ài's family was dead that's all that mattered to Héng. He turned to his remaining men.

"You have all done well. Thank you. Now I no longer have need of your services."

The four línghún looked at each other. While they stood there, trying to puzzle out Héng's meaning, he moved so quickly among them, slicing and tearing, that they never knew they were dead until their heads fell to the ground. Now that all the loose ends were tied up, he could head home and enjoy his new acquisition.

CHAPTER TWENTY

Nora shook her head to clear the images from her brain. She looked around and found herself in chains, with Héng standing over her, in some room of Pò's building downtown. Héng looked down at her, a small smile of triumph on his face. Nora grimaced.

"You know, this auspicious time sucks. Feels like I've been hit by a freight train. I guess that's what comes with the memory of finding out exactly how much of a monster you really are."

"I don't know what you mean, my dear," Héng replied.

"Ugh. Please don't call me that. That's what you called Ài and look what happened to her."

The smug satisfaction that had become Héng's usual countenance fell away. His eyes flashed red in the dark room.

"What did you say?"

"That was her name, wasn't it? Ài? Xīn's sister? I assume he has no idea what you did to her. Although I suppose she was lucky, in the sense you didn't rape her. At least not sexually. Weren't feeling it, were you?"

Héng lifted Nora by her throat, pulling her up until the chains around her wrists and ankles popped free of their secure anchors then threw her across the room. She crashed against the far wall and pain shot up her spine and exploded out her eyes. Stunned, she expected Héng to attack her again but when nothing happened, she dared to look up.

She could see him pacing the floor and it sounded like he was talking to himself. Nora sat up and when her head didn't swivel off her shoulders, she took stock of her body. Nothing seemed to be broken but she'd be seven kinds of purple in the morning. If she lived that long. Her chains had broken free from the wall but they were so heavy she knew she'd never be able to escape while dragging them behind her.

Nora couldn't make out what Héng was saying but the tone sounded like anger and regret. She snorted and he stopped mumbling.

"What?"

"Um, nothing."

He flew to her side and crouched down, pushing his face close to hers.

"You have something to say, vessel?"

"Well, I just had a funny thought, that's all."

"Funny? Pray, share with me this funny thought."

Nora cleared her throat before answering. "I don't think you'll find it as funny as I do."

Héng backhanded her across the face. "Why don't you tell me anyway and let me be the judge."

She rubbed her jaw. "If you don't stop hitting me, I won't be able to talk at all."

"From your lips to the gods' ears."

"Ha ha. All I was thinking was that when I brought up Ài's name, you may have started to feel regret."

Héng didn't respond and continued to stare at her. Nora raised her hand to protect her face in preparation for another strike.

"I said that you wouldn't find it funny."

When nothing happened, she lowered her hand and looked at him. He was looking in her direction but not seeing her. He must be lost in some long-ago memory of Ài. Nora really did see regret in his face this time and she was tempted to reach out to comfort him. It was a reflex, really, but she never imagined that Héng could be so human. Once she remembered that he planned to kill her, all sympathy flew out the window.

"Well, well. How the mighty have fallen."

Nora knew it was a risk to piss him off even further but maybe she could distract him into missing the deadline for the ritual. Unfortunately, he was already on to her plan.

"Tsk tsk, Nora. You work to provoke me. Don't worry. The auspicious time draws near but we can still entertain ourselves until then."

"Oh my God, enough with the auspicious time. You sound like a bad kung-fu movie."

Héng growled and picked her up by her shoulders. Nora barely had time to scream before he slammed her against the ground and pressed himself on top of her. He pressed his lips to her ear.

"To have raped Ài before I turned her would have soiled her essence. So to answer your question, no, I wasn't feeling it. But believe me. I had plenty of fun with her afterward."

He ground his hips against Nora's and she grimaced. Héng drew his tongue along her jaw and up to her ear. He whispered and Nora's body broke out in goose bumps of fear.

"Are *you* feeling me, vessel?"

Nora indeed felt him and she almost threw up. He laughed against her cheek.

"Don't worry. To rape you before the ritual would also soil your essence. And mine. But that doesn't mean there aren't other things I can do."

He nipped the bundle of muscles at her jaw. Nora could feel a small trickle of warm fluid work its way down her neck and behind her ear. Héng lapped at it like a dog with a steak bone.

"I thought you didn't want me damaged before the ritual?"

"Oh, my dear, I didn't want anyone else to harm you. What fun is there in playing with a toy that's already broken?"

Nora clenched her teeth as Héng gouged his fingernail against the flesh just under her ribcage. Though the pain was like having molten lava poured over her, she refused to scream. She didn't want to give Héng that satisfaction. He chuckled as he brought his bloodied finger to his lips.

"So, we've decided to be the strong silent type all of a sudden, hmm? We shall see about that."

He wrenched up the chains and dragged her over to the set of hooks in the ceiling. It only took him moments to attach them and have her hanging by her wrists, helpless. The yoga clothes she put on earlier made her feel naked as she hung from the ceiling. She was aware of how the stretch pants hugged her curves and that the flimsy t-shirt she had pulled on may as well have been saran wrap. The jacket she wore helped give her a sense of protection but Héng had his fingernail hooked through the end of the zipper and he ripped it off in seconds.

Nora's skin tingled as Héng dragged his sharp nails across the skin of her stomach. He flattened his palm against her and moved is slowly up toward her chest. Fearing this may end up a sexual assault after all, she squeezed her eyes shut and turned her head away. She heard him grumble with laughter.

"Still worried I plan to soil you, my dear? Think again."

Héng flipped his hand so the back of it was pressed against the skin between her breasts. He punctured the cloth of the t-shirt with his nails and pulled, shredding the flimsy garment to ribbons. He left the tattered remains hanging in place. The fabric was barely enough to cover her naked chest and Nora wanted to cry. She bit her lip hard enough to draw blood but she was able to keep silent.

Unfortunately, the small amount of blood on her lip seemed to work Master Héng further into a frenzy. He gripped her waist and pulled her body against him. He sniffed the drop of crimson on her lip and Nora wanted to vomit when his tongue flicked out and licked it off. He closed his mouth to savor her blood, his eyes flickering from black to gold then red. If she wasn't ready to pee her pants, this would be fascinating to watch.

As he leaned his head back in ecstasy, his fangs slowly extended until they almost reached past his lower lip. When he looked at her again, his eyes ringed with fiery reds and oranges, Nora cringed. She tried to pull away but he still had her by the waist and trying to wriggle free only strengthened his grip. He pulled up on her hips, raising them to his mouth, and slipped a finger underneath the elastic waistband of her pants.

He pulled the top of her pants down just enough to expose the left hip. She could do nothing but stare in horror as he leaned back, mouth open and teeth gleaming. With a growl of hunger Héng clamped his mouth against the point of her hipbone and plunged his fangs in. Nora's courage fled and she screamed.

****

Xīn ushered his group, as well as Pò and his men, into the loft. Because the ritual couldn't be performed until midnight, they had some time to reorganize their plan of attack. Despite the fact they outnumbered Master Héng, it was never prudent to underestimate him, as they learned tonight.

Pò had one of his men draw up the schematics of his building so they could study it. He pointed to several locations, describing each one.

"On the first floor is the main lobby. It's very open and spacious, perfect place to get slaughtered. So we might want to enter here instead." He pointed to a small entrance at the rear of the building. "It opens onto a three-pronged hallway, one straight through the building and the other two head east and west."

"Where do those two corridors lead?" Xīn asked.

"The east one turns south about a hundred meters down and follows behind what used to be the administrative offices. It eventually turns west and empties into the lobby. The west does the same thing but the rooms there are for storage and electrical supplies."

Xīn thought about it. "We can split the group into thirds and each one take a corridor. Then meet back in the lobby once we've secured the first floor. What about the second?"

Pò indicated the main staircase. "These are the main stairs that access the upper floors. Not too wide but still has potential to get us picked off, one by one. We'll need a few spotters while the rest of the team makes its way up.

"If we make it through that, all the upper floors are the same. The stairwell opens up in the middle each hallway. Ten rooms on each side. A second stairwell is accessible at the north end of each floor."

Mǐn shook her head. "Do we have enough men to set up guards at each end of these hallways? It looks rather easy for someone to get the jump on us if we're spread too thin."

"I think so," Xīn answered. "We may even have enough to leave at least one behind on each floor in case someone tries to sneak in behind us after we've cleared an area."

"The roof is the most likely place for Héng to perform the ritual," Pò said as he pointed to the roof on the map. "Only one access point in or out if no one plans to jump off or climb up the side of the building, that is."

Xīn glared at him. "Yes, if no one plans to do that. What about the fã kuáng?"

Pò frowned. "What about it?"

"Where is it?" Xīn asked between clenched teeth.

"Oh, it's in the basement. Here." Pò pointed to it. "The only door is off the main lobby, just at the end of the hallway that enters from the back of the building. Why?"

"Héng knows you have it?"

"Yeah, he does."

"We have to assume that he'll use it against us." Xīn stared at Pò. "Exactly how old is this thing?"

"From what I was told it's almost as old as us. Even though it's younger, and insane, it's extraordinarily powerful. The door to the basement is scribed with ancient powerful spells to keep it in place, as are the shackles."

Xīn shook his head in disgust. "Do you have any weapons that can kill it, Pò?"

"Yes," Pò nodded. "The only thing that will destroy it is to pierce its heart. I've always kept a heavy steel sword on hand just in case it ever got loose. It should do the trick. It's in my quarters."

"Let's hope we can get to the fā kuáng before it gets to us. So, assuming we aren't all slaughtered before we even begin the fight, our goal is to get to the roof."

"Do we know what time the ritual will occur?" Taelin asked.

The holy man they brought from the Enclave spoke. "From all the writings and tablets I've seen and studied, at precisely 11:52pm, all the planets will align and the energy of the cosmos will be at its peak. Only then can Héng perform the ritual. Any earlier or later, even a fraction of a second, and he will fail."

"What exactly does this ritual entail?" Xīn asked.

The dào rén closed his eyes as he recited his teachings. "When the moon is dark and the fixed stars of the heavens touch hands, all the souls of all the worlds unite in one purpose, to fill the well of life once again and empower the vessel to rule over it. With a sacrifice of sacred blood, and permission from the intended one, however, a línghún may take the power for his own.

"But if there be no vessel, and one with a heart corrupted is in its place, then all life will extinguish, forever."

"So basically if Héng kills Nora then takes her place, the whole world goes to hell?" Mǐn asked.

"No. It will cease to exist. No heaven. No hell. Nothing at all," the dào rén answered.

Xīn interjected. "But it won't happen right away. From what I understand, life will continue and seem normal until no new souls are born. Which means no children. Everyone who has already been born will live on but once they die, there will be no one to continue the cycle of life, correct?"

"That is correct. So it is of vital importance that the vessel remain unharmed."

Xīn nodded. "The only way Héng can take her power is by killing her, yes?"

The dào rén nodded. Pò pulled out a long silver blade and held it up to the overhead lights. The razor edge gleamed.

"Then we'll just have to kill him first."

"What time is it?" Xīn asked.

Pò looked down at his watch. "Almost nine a.m. Why?"

"Let's finish up our plan and get the weapons together. Then we have to get some rest. We can't go against Héng, and anyone else he might have working for him, unless we're at a hundred percent. We've got to get Nora before he can perform the ritual.

"You all know what we're up against. Now multiply that times ten and factor in a hundred things we don't know about. Héng may be my maker, and I've known him for centuries, but he has so many tricks up his sleeve that even I can't know them all."

They finished the rest of their prep work in silence. Mǐn, Taelin, and two of Pò's trusted men volunteered to stay awake and keep watch, just in case. The rest hunkered down in separate corners and spaces to get some sleep. As Xīn closed his eyes and drifted off, he tried to get a sense, a feel, for Nora. Though they had a powerful connection, he couldn't get a grasp on anything that was definitively her. And that scared him – more than Héng, more than defeat. More than anything else, Xīn wasn't sure if he could, or wanted, to go on if he lost her.

He opened his eyes as he sensed someone watching him. Pò stared at him from across the room. Xīn nodded at him and Pò rose, walked over then sat down. He leaned his head back against the wall while he spoke.

"Xīn, I…"

"You don't have to say anything, Pò."

"Yes I do. I'm so sorry, Xīn. If I hadn't been so selfish, so blind, none of this would have happened."

"Oh, I doubt that," Xīn said. "I have a feeling that Héng would have found a way to kidnap Nora, perform the ritual, and doom us all. He's been planning this for centuries, Pò. It's not your doing."

Pò stared at him and Xīn managed a little chuckle. "Okay, it's not *all* your doing. Feel better?"

"That's funny coming from you."

"What is?" Xīn asked.

"Asking me how I feel. Last week you would have cut off my head, and probably your own, before allowing that kind of sympathy. Now look. We're working together to save the world."

"Yeah, I suppose that is rather amusing. I've been trained for so long to keep emotions at bay, always obey the rules, be Héng's," he paused. He couldn't find a word to sum up his predicament.

"Bitch?" Pò offered.

Xīn laughed. "Nora would have said the same thing, I bet. I don't know, Pò. Maybe I've had it all wrong. There is something to be said about being impulsive, throwing the rule book out the window."

"You don't mean that, Xīn. There's nothing wrong with order. Nothing wrong with following the rules. Look at me for crying out loud. I've constantly fought against order and I've done some terrible things. And I can't change that. Maybe if I had a little more order in my life, I could face each day without so much guilt."

"Guilt? For all the people you killed, you mean?"

Pò opened his mouth then closed it. He looked like he wanted to confess something.

"What is it, Pò?"

He shook his head. "Nothing that needs to be discussed right now."

Xīn clapped a hand on Pò's shoulder. "Maybe we both need

to learn compromise, eh?"

Pò smiled. "Maybe you're right. Look, enough chit chat. We need to get some rest if we're going to save the world in a few hours. We can talk after we've lived through this."

Xīn nodded and watched Pò walk back across the room and find a comfortable spot to sleep. He smiled again, hoping that he and Pò would live to have that talk later. Xīn closed his eyes and slept.

CHAPTER TWENTY-ONE

Nora stood in an open field as dull green grass swayed in the dusk breeze. The sky to the west held the slightest tint of orange at the horizon while overhead the stars began to peek through the violet and dark blue night. She closed her eyes as the scent of jasmine washed over her on the wind. For a moment she felt utterly at peace.

The hairs on the back of her neck stood up when the wind died. She opened her eyes and came face to face with Ài, Xīn's sister. Her golden skin picked up the last bits of light in the sky and absorbed them, making her glow. Nora thought she looked despondent.

"What's wrong, Ài?"

"We don't have much time, Nora."

"Why? What's going on?"

"Héng is coming. He's coming for us both."

Before Nora could ask her to clarify, she saw Héng appear off to the right, holding a large burlap sack. Whatever was in it was struggling something fierce but it didn't seem to bother Héng. He swung it over his head and smashed it against the ground and the wriggling stopped. Dragging the sack over to Ài, he paid no attention to Nora.

"I have a gift for you, my dear."

Ài sighed. "What now?"

"You are going to learn what it's like to turn someone."

"What?"

"You heard me."

"You can't be serious," Ài protested. "I've only been línghún for a few years. I'm not ready for this."

"Nonsense. You are more talented and capable than even your brother. Why do you think I've never offered to help him do this?"

Ài flinched at the mention of Xīn. She bit her lip as she considered it. Finally a smile broke across her face.

"Truly? Well, I suppose it can't hurt to try."

Ài bent over the sack and poked at it. The person inside began twitching again and pleading in Chinese. Even though Nora didn't speak the language, she understood everything he said.

"Please, please don't kill me! I'll do anything just please don't kill me!"

"Don't worry, my little friend. I won't."

As she opened the bag, Héng stood behind her with a strange look on his face. Part pride but part something else that Nora couldn't quite put her finger on. He stepped back a few paces as Ài released the man from the sack. The man looked up at Ài and surprise choked back his pleading. He looked at her as if a child had just released him.

Héng moved so quickly to stand behind the man that he never noticed Héng was even there. At least not until Héng grabbed him by the hair and pulled him into a standing position. He tried to twist his head around to see his captor but couldn't quite do it. Héng pushed the man toward Ài, still holding on to his hair.

"Now, Ài. First you must drain his blood. Not so much as to kill him. That would defeat the purpose. You'll hear his heart slow, almost come to rest. That's when you must stop. Understand?"

Ài nodded and moved closer. She caressed the man's cheek and spoke in a soft, childlike voice.

"What is your name?"

"Bu Xīng."

"Bu Xīng. Please don't be afraid. I won't hurt you. I'm going to set you free."

She put one hand against the side of the man's face and the other on his shoulder, pushing it down and stretching out the surface of his neck. Nora heard the snick of Ài's fangs as they descended then watched as she plunged them into the man's flesh. He screamed but even that couldn't cover up the slurping sounds as Ài drained him.

Soon the man quieted and began to slump. Héng helped lower him to the ground while Ài continued to feast. When the man's eyes closed, Ài released him and stood up. Héng smiled at her.

"You see? And I didn't even have to tell you to stop. Well done, my dear."

"Now what do I do?"

Héng reached for her arm and brought it up to his mouth. He bit into it, slicing the tissues deep enough to get them to bleed. Ài gasped.

"Feed him from your wound. He must drink the blood of a

línghún in order to be turned. Quickly, before your arm heals."

Ài knelt down next to the man and propped his head up with her uninjured arm. She held the open wound against his mouth.

"Drink. And live."

At first the man didn't respond but soon his eyes snapped open and Nora could hear him drinking. Within seconds his eyes opened wider and he clutched Ài's arm. It looked like he was trying to cram the entire appendage into his mouth. Ài's breathing became fast and heavy and her eyes drooped closed. Héng moved in and pulled the man off. He picked Ài up and laid her down a few feet away.

When he turned back, the man had rolled over onto his side and was screaming. He arched his back and curled forward several times then flailed his arms and legs. He grabbed at the grass surrounding him and pulled it out by the roots, flinging dirt in all directions. When his screams turned to laughter, Ài sat up and clutched at Master Héng.

"Is that supposed to happen?"

Héng shook his head and continued to stare at the man. The look crossed his face again and Nora finally figured out it was fascination. It was like he knew this could happen and had hoped it would. Nora looked at Ài and the fear and disgust was obvious on her face.

The man continued laughing but instead of pulling at the grass, he pulled at his clothes, his hair then started scratching at his face. Each gash he opened quickly healed before the next one could be made. When he tried to gouge out his own eyes, Héng swooped in and held his wrists. The man writhed against Héng and started screaming again. Héng shouted above the cacophony.

"Ài, I will take care of him. Stay hidden in the grass until your strength returns then go home. I will see you there."

In seconds, Héng picked up the man, still screaming, and disappeared from sight. Ài lay back in the grass and Nora walked over to her. She knelt down and laid a hand on Ài's arm.

"Are you all right?"

Ài covered her face with her hands and wept, oblivious to Nora, who was at a loss. How exactly was she supposed to comfort a vampire that made a man go insane with her blood? As she opened her mouth to say anything that might help, Nora felt a wave of dizziness wash over her. She clamped a hand over her eyes and tried to steady herself.

When she reached down to the ground, she felt carpet beneath her fingers. Opening her eyes, Nora was shocked to find she wasn't in the field anymore. Héng stood on the other side of the room talking to someone she couldn't see. She stood up, the dizziness gone now, and moved closer. Another shock hit her as she recognized Pò.

"It's locked in the back store room. Take it someplace secure, someplace Ài won't see it, but don't kill it."

"But Master," Pò said. "Isn't it dangerous?"

"If properly contained, no. And imagine what we might be able to learn from it."

Pò shrugged then bowed. "Yes, Master."

"Oh, and Pò? I don't need to remind you to keep all of this

from Xīn, yes?"

"Of course, Master."

"As far as he's concerned, his entire family died in the fire."

Pò nodded and Héng smiled.

"Thank you, Pò. I know I can always count on you."

Pò left and Master Héng watched him through the main window as he laughed. Nora squeezed her eyes shut as another sensation of dizziness crashed down on her. She collapsed to the floor and the world went black.

When she opened her eyes again, Nora was lying on the hard linoleum floor of her modern day prison. She reached up to rub her face and felt the tug of the shackles on her wrists. With a growl she yanked on the attached chain which made her feel a little better.

Her entire body ached. She couldn't remember everything Héng did to her, mostly because she'd passed in and out of consciousness several times. But the scratching, the metal tools he used to scrape up her skin, and the biting were all vivid in her mind. She felt groggy as well so Héng must have drained enough of her blood to keep her weak. There's no way she could fight against him anyway even if she did have any strength.

The most vivid image she had in her mind, though, was of Ài. Nora relived another memory while she was unconscious. Her heart broke for Ài and for Xīn. Neither one really knew how Héng played them for his own purposes. She wondered how Xīn would react once he found out.

Nora knew Ài was dead, though she only had vague visions

of it: Ài throwing herself on a large steel sword, her head rolling off to the side, and Héng throwing her corpse onto a large fire. The memories from Héng's life seemed brighter, more vivid but Ài's were cast in grey and blue tones, almost muted. As if their energy was no longer linked to a living creature and could not sustain themselves without the original life force.

"Ah, good. You're awake, my dear."

Nora looked up to see Héng towering over her in his usual stance of superiority.

"It won't be long now. The time for the ritual is almost upon us."

"You know Xīn will stop you, right?" Nora growled at him with a confidence she didn't feel.

"Oh, my dear. Is this the point where I'm supposed to quake in my shoes at the possibility that Xīn and his piss poor followers will ruin my plans? I think not."

Nora was worried that Xīn and the others wouldn't get here in time. She wasn't so worried about her own life at this point. She was terrified for the rest of the world. If Héng succeeded with the ritual what kind of hell would he bring down on everyone?

"It will be glorious," he continued. "I'm afraid you won't be around to see it. Behind every great man is a woman who had to be sacrificed."

Nora stared up at him and he grinned.

"Or something to that effect. No one will understand or even appreciate what I am about to do but they will. In time they will bow to me and revere me above all else."

Nora had stopped listening to Héng's rant. He'd been babbling on and on about the glorious ritual, how his power would increase, and how her sacrifice would make it all possible. Was she supposed to be grateful or something? So she tuned him out after twenty minutes of his ramble.

She thought of Xīn. Was he coming for her? Was he even still alive? Something in her chest told her he was all right and he was on his way. She wasn't going to sit here, like a fairy tale damsel in distress, though, until Héng dragged her away for this ritual. The problem was she had no idea what she could do to help herself.

As she concentrated on finding a solution to her predicament, Nora failed to notice that Héng had stopped speaking. It wasn't until he picked her up by her shoulders and pressed his face close to hers, his eyes burning red.

"Have you been listening to a word I've said?" he demanded. His anger and ego were barely contained behind his whispered question. Maybe if she pissed him off enough she'd find a way to escape.

"Listening to what? You were talking?"

Héng ground his teeth even as his fangs slipped down. Nora smiled.

"Careful, you might chip a tooth. And long term clenching like that can lead to TMJ, headaches, broken or cracked teeth."

He howled in anger and threw her against the far wall. Her breath whooshed out as pain exploded in her shoulders and back. Gasping, Nora thought she'd die from lack of oxygen right here. No such luck, she thought as her breath returned and the pain took center stage.

As she struggled to stand, leaning against the wall for support, the chains slipped from her shackles. With the repeated temper tantrums from her gracious host, one of the links in the chain securing her broke. The chain slipped free from the metal loops in the shackles. Nora stared at her hands as she lifted them above her head, unfettered now without the chain to secure them.

She looked up at Héng, whose back was to her. He was muttering something but she didn't want to waste time figuring out what it was. She moved slowly, careful not to clank the shackles against anything. Each step caused every muscle to scream in protest and it was difficult not to give voice to their pain.

Just as Nora reached the door, Héng chuckled.

"Did you honestly believe I couldn't hear your every step, every shallow breath, every hair on your body as you moved?"

In a moment, Héng stood before her, blocking the exit. In another he thrust his hands into her hair and pulled her close. Nora could feel the tears welling up in her eyes as defeat settled into her bones. Héng grinned as her tears spilled onto her cheeks. He licked them away with great relish. As he savored them, like one would a rare vintage of wine, his eyes flared gold.

"Ahh. Tastes like hopelessness. My favorite."

As quickly as he'd found his delight, it faded. Héng tilted his head at a sound only he could hear. When his eyes flashed to black, his smile returned.

"It appears your knight has come for you, my dear."

Nora swiveled her head from side to side, trying to see Xīn. Héng snorted.

"He's not here yet but he is coming. Not that he'll get to you in time, of course. He'll have his hands full."

"What do you mean?" Nora asked, not liking the fear in her voice.

"You didn't think I'd make it easy for him, did you? That he could just walk right in, take you by the hand, and walk out again?"

Héng called out and two línghún that Nora never knew had been nearby stood before Héng awaiting orders.

"Get the others. Xīn, Pò, and their people are coming."

The two nodded and turned to leave. Héng stopped them.

"In case you end up being more incompetent than you look, release the fā kuáng."

"Master?"

Héng backhanded the one that spoke and sent him sprawling to the floor. The other shook as Héng leaned into him and screamed.

"Release it!"

He nodded and went to help his comrade but Héng growled.

"Leave him."

He scrambled away and down the hall. Héng moved to the línghún on the floor and pressed a foot against his head. With a crack, Héng destroyed his skull with little effort. Blood and brains popped out and sprayed along the hallway floor. Héng turned to Nora.

"Come, my dear. We must get you ready."

She spat in his face, the only thing she could do. At the very least, perhaps Héng would beat her unconscious so she'd never feel the death blow he would be delivering later. He only smiled as he wiped the spittle from his cheek.

"Desperation. How wonderful."

He grabbed her wrist and pulled her down the hall. Despite her struggles, Héng had no trouble dragging her away. Each punch or kick she delivered either missed him or bounced off harmlessly but it was undignified for him to deal with her in this manner. She could see his jaw muscles working each time she flailed at him. He caught the attention of four of his men as they made their way down the hall.

"Take her to the roof. Secure her next to the altar and whatever you do, don't let her escape. Keep her conscious. I want her awake and aware of everything until the final moment, understand?"

"What are you planning?" Nora asked. When Héng didn't answer, only motioned for his men to take her, she twisted and turned to look back at him, and screamed as she was hauled away.

"What are you going to do?"

The last thing she heard before being pulled into the stairwell was the low rumble of Héng's laughter.

****

Xīn and Pò stood two blocks down the street from the abandoned apartment building as they studied the rear entrance. They had already decided to combine both their troops to create three main arteries – one for each hallway leading into the center of the building. Pò demanded to take the main hallway that went straight through to the lobby since he felt responsible for them being in this situation in the first place. Xīn argued that as protector of the vessel it was his job to take the lead.

"Why don't you both take the main hallway?" Taelin chimed in. "The rest of us are capable of handling the other two. It will also keep us from standing here arguing all night and allowing Héng to succeed with his plans."

Xīn turned to Pò who raised an eyebrow at him. He looked at Mǐn who simply nodded her agreement. Xīn clapped a hand on Taelin's shoulder.

"So be it. You and Mǐn take the north hallway."

"And you take the other," Pò said as he pointed at two of his men.

Xīn continued. "Everyone be on the lookout for guards posted at every exit, every window, every possible turn. Héng won't make this easy for us and we need to be stealthy for as long as possible, understand?"

Everyone agreed then Pò reminded them about the fā kuáng.

"That just might interfere with our stealthy plans."

"True," Xīn said. "But we'll do what we have to for as long as we can."

Xīn and Pò led them toward the back entrance of the building. Several silent hand motions from both alerted the team to the línghún standing guard. Mǐn moved to the front of the group, her crossbow at the ready.

She looked down the silver tipped arrows, their wooden

shafts soaked with corpse blood for extra potency, as she took aim. Her speed and accuracy allowed her to take down all the guards within seconds without raising any alarms from inside. Once dispatched, the group moved forward again.

Slipping inside, the team split into three groups and took their assigned corridors. Xīn walked shoulder to shoulder with Pò as they crept forward. It didn't take long to reach the lobby since they didn't encounter any further resistance than the men outside. The hairs on the back of Xīn's neck prickled as the lobby opened up before them.

From the hallways on their left and right the other two teams appeared almost simultaneously. Now Pò turned to Xīn, his face wrinkled with worry.

"That was a bit too easy, wasn't it? Where the hell is everyone?"

Xīn turned to Taelin and motioned him closer. "Did you see anyone?"

Taelin shook his head as did Pò's men. Before Xīn could voice his concern, a great horrifying scream echoed through the lobby. Without seeing its source it was hard to know what could make such a sound, a sound filled with rage, insanity, and sorrow. But it could only be one thing – the fā kuáng.

The group moved to the center of the room with military precision, backs to each other, and scanned every corner and shadow. A loud thump sounded overhead. All of them turned their faces toward the ceiling as they tracked each bump and crash. It was moving closer at an alarming speed even for a línghún.

When it first came into sight, it leaped onto the top landing of the stairs before them. Xīn realized why it was able to move so fast. It wasn't running from step to step. It was jumping from landing to landing, skipping the stairs at each level. It flew at the wall, sticking to it like a spider then crawled several feet before it leaped onto the ceiling.

Mǐn aimed her crossbow with a steady hand but her voice shook with a hint of shock.

"I assume that's the fā kuáng."

"Yes, it is," Pò responded. "Seems Héng has given it freedom in order to distract us."

"It's working," Mǐn replied.

Xīn shook his head. "That thing will never be free until it's dead." He turned to Pò. "You never should have- "

"Whoa! I didn't make it, Xīn," Pò interrupted him. "I only inherited it."

Xīn stared at Pò and he shrugged. "Okay, so I stole it but I didn't create it."

"Then where?"

Pò pointed at the fā kuáng as it crawled across the ceiling above them. "I don't think now is the best time to get into this, Xīn."

Xīn stared up at the creature as it hissed at the group. "All right, the subject is dropped. For now."

Mǐn pointed her crossbow at the fā kuáng but spoke to Xīn. "Sir?"

"Kill it," he ordered.

He detected a slight nod from Mǐn out of the corner of his eye then heard the quiet whoosh as the arrow flew free toward its target. The fā kuáng easily dodged it. Xīn turned to look at Mǐn, her eyes wide in disbelief. She'd never missed before.

Pursing her lips she tried again. And again. And three more times. She shot until all her preloaded arrows were gone. The fā kuáng sprang from the ceiling to the wall, down to the floor and back to the ceiling. It skipped and jumped faster than anything Xīn had ever encountered before. He didn't know much about a fā kuáng, but he assumed their increased speed was a part of their sickness.

Xīn was afraid to find out what else this thing could do.

As if reading Xīn's mind, the fā kuáng released its hold from the ceiling and launched itself at the group. It landed on the línghún next to Mǐn, who was trying to reload her weapon. The group dispersed, backing away several feet, except for Mǐn who continued filling the crossbow with arrows.

The fā kuáng reared back its head as four three-inch fangs elongated in its mouth. Most of its bottom teeth were either needle sharp points or broken jagged stumps. It clamped onto the línghún's neck with fierce power. Even as it drained its victim, the fā kuáng's hands flew and tore at the body beneath it.

It pulled fistfuls of clothing so fast that the línghún was half naked in seconds. Soon it ripped and tore skin, flesh, and bone. Its screams of rage and bloodlust drowned out the meek whimpers of its victim.

Despite being spattered with gore from her fellow línghún,

Mǐn finally loaded her crossbow to maximum capacity and raised it. She aimed at the fā kuáng. After pressing the trigger, the arrow flew and hit the fā kuáng in the right hand, piercing it through. The creature howled and stared at the arrow. Its face became a mask of bewilderment as if it didn't understand why it was in pain.

It turned its hand back and forth as it studied the arrow. Using its left hand, the creature reached down into the body beneath it, pulling a loop of intestines free then put them in its mouth. It chewed on the entrails like a student would chew on the end of a pencil while puzzling out a difficult homework problem.

While it concentrated on this enigma, Mǐn shot another arrow at it. It hit the creature in the left shoulder and it immediately dropped the flesh it was holding as it screamed. It craned its neck around to see what was causing the new pain and its eyes fell on Mǐn.

It saw the crossbow she held then stared at the arrow in its hand. Looking back at Mǐn, the fā kuáng snarled. It stood then stepped away from the corpse at its feet. The creature hissed at her as more wicked fangs extended in its mouth.

Xīn motioned for half of the group to move upstairs while the creature was distracted. As he moved the other half behind the fā kuáng, Mǐn held up her hand.

"No. We don't have the time or luxury to split up. You've got to find Nora and Héng and end this. I'll take care of him."

"Mǐn, I can't leave you alone."

She stepped away as the creature hissed again. "Just go!"

Xīn motioned to three other línghún. "Back her up. We're

heading upstairs. Find us when you're done."

They nodded then inched their way around the creature to stand next to Mǐn. She took her eyes off the fā kuáng long enough to look at Xīn. She nodded at him and he bowed to her.

Once she turned back to the task in front of her, Xīn moved to the stairs and led the rest of the team away from the lobby. He heard the fā kuáng howl with rage and he almost turned back. As capable as Mǐn was, she couldn't defeat the creature. And somewhere deep down, she knew it, too. Xīn could only hope he lived through this to offer a proper tribute to her sacrifice.

****

Mǐn felt more than saw the three soldiers move to her side. She also registered Xīn's hesitation on the stairs. 'Just keep going, please,' she thought. Though she knew she wouldn't defeat the fā kuáng, they couldn't afford to lose Xīn. He was the only one who could save Nora. She just hoped she could buy him enough time before the creature tore her to pieces.

The fā kuáng hissed at her and she shot another arrow at it. Now that it was concentrating on her it dodged the projectile easily. She knew it was useless to continue utilizing the crossbow so she dropped it. It clanged to the dirty tile floor with a crash that echoed through the entire lobby. The creature smiled at her as if it understood.

Mǐn nodded at each soldier, a small swift movement to indicate she wanted them to flank the fā kuáng. They quickly responded. The creature smiled again, never taking its eyes off Mǐn, its jagged teeth glistening with saliva.

It moved so fast that Mǐn could barely track it. Before she could even twitch, the fā kuáng spun and jumped, its arms pin wheeling out and around. Within seconds, it stood across from her again and the other línghún were dead. She didn't dare take her eyes off the creature but from the smell of blood and the distinct clattering of a rolling head, she knew.

"You will die here," it spoke to Mǐn. Its voice was sweet, almost melodic, with just a hint of insanity. Mǐn could feel her mouth open in surprise and the creature laughed.

"Just because I'm mad doesn't mean I'm stupid."

It jumped and landed behind her, wrapping one arm around her waist and the other across her chest. She gasped and turned but the fā kuáng held tight. Before it tore her apart, Mǐn spoke.

"You know what Héng is up to then?"

"I do, I do" it said.

"If you help me, if we work together," Mǐn began but it clamped a hand on her head, pulling it to the side and exposing her neck.

"We can stop him from ending all existence forever?"

Mǐn swallowed and rasped out an affirmative. It licked her exposed skin from the base of her neck to her ear. Its breath was fetid with rot.

"Why would you wish something so cruel? What have I ever done to you?"

It giggled at its own joke and Mǐn struggled against it.

"But he's responsible for you."

"No. She did this to me. She did. She…but I can't find her.

Can't make her pay. Perhaps if Héng succeeds, I'll finally be able to rest."

Before Mǐn could question it, the fā kuáng clamped its hand over her mouth and pulled her head further to the side. She felt her neck crack in protest and she whimpered in pain. She heard the creature's teeth extend.

"Don't worry. I'll be sure to send Xīn your regards."

CHAPTER TWENTY-TWO

Nora pulled against the ropes that tied her to one of the metal ladders leading from the roof of the building to the ground. A holy man sat nearby, bound and gagged. He rocked back and forth, eyes closed, as if in prayer. Two of Héng's men stood on either side of her and another two assisted Héng, fussing over a low table covered with colorful cloths, multiple bowls and candles, and some wicked cutlery. She'd peppered Héng with question after question, watching him as his anger grew and his temper shortened. After he nearly knocked her unconscious, she realized she couldn't agitate him enough to screw up the ritual. So she'd been struggling silently for the past ten minutes.

"What were you guys, in the Chinese Navy before becoming vampires?" Nora cursed as she tried to loosen the knots of her bindings.

"The one on your right helped set up the naval forces in the 12th century," Héng replied. "And the other, on your left, fought in the Battle of Lake Póyáng, under the command of the man who became the first emperor of the Ming dynasty."

Nora rolled her eyes. "A simple 'yes' would have been enough."

Héng chuckled like a predator who knows the end is near even if the prey does not. He reached down to the altar behind him and picked up a large gold chalice, adorned with red stones, and a matching dagger. Though he stared at Nora somehow she knew those implements weren't for her. She whipped her head to look over at the dào rén, who continued to pray and rock then back at Héng.

"No. You can't. He's a holy man!"

"That is exactly why I can. If he weren't, he would be of no use to me."

Héng nodded at the two línghún guarding her and they swiftly moved to either side of the seated man, hauling him to his feet. The holy man didn't open his eyes until he felt the sharp edge of the blade pressed against his throat. He looked up at Héng then slid his eyes over to Nora. She struggled against her bonds but could do nothing else.

The man smiled at her. Nora held her breath in astonishment when he turned back to Héng and tipped his head back to expose more of his throat. Héng's jaw muscles bunched. With his lips pressed together in anger, Héng slid the golden knife across the exposed flesh of the dào rén's neck. A flash of bright red blood burst forth and Héng held up the chalice to catch as much of it as he could. When it would hold no more, he nodded at the two línghún again and they tossed the man aside.

Nora could feel fresh tears stream down her face as she stared at the dào rén, his wide eyes staring back at her. He still smiled, as if unafraid, as if he knew a secret about life after death and was eager to experience it. His fingers reached for her but her bonds wouldn't allow her to extend her hands to him. Soon his eyelids drooped and his breathing became shallow. A crimson and ever widening pool formed around his body until his heart stopped beating and there was no more blood to spill.

Nora thrashed her legs out at the nearest línghún and succeeded in tripping him. He sprawled to the roof, cracking his head on the brick ledge and she swung her legs at the other one. But he was ready for it and jumped out of the way. She continued to kick, hoping she would connect with one of them again, until Héng swooped down before her, jamming his knees into her thighs and grabbing her hair. He raised his hand, his eyes radiating a fierce red light.

Before Héng could strike her, two línghún burst through the access door on the other side of the roof. They ran up to Héng, bowed, and the one on the left spoke.

"They've arrived, Master. After encountering the fā kuáng, the group broke in two. Only four stayed behind to fight it. The rest moved up into the building."

"Then why aren't you inside?"

The línghún stammered like a student struggling to guess the right answer on a pop quiz. "I, uh, I have my men," he started but Héng screamed and grabbed him by the throat.

"*Your* men? You have *my* men at your disposal, insect. They follow your commands because I command you."

The soldier gasped and sucked, trying to reply. "Yes, Master. Forgive me. I have your men scattered throughout the building with orders to kill anyone on sight who opposes them."

Héng nodded then crushed the línghún's neck. He flung the vampire away as if he were nothing more than a scrap of paper. Héng turned to the other one and hissed.

"Get back inside and stop Xīn and his men from reaching the roof. If you don't, you might consider killing yourself as a viable alternative to rejoining me."

The línghún grimaced in fear. He nodded and rushed back to the roof door then disappeared into the building. Nora swallowed as she looked over at the corpse lying off to the side. She whistled at Héng's back while he watched the other man run back inside.

"Wow. You should be a motivational speaker. Tony Robbins has nothing on you."

Héng slowly turned around to stare down at her. The smile that crawled across his face made everything he'd done to her up until now seem like a child pulling the wings off a dragon fly. Simple amusement. When he lowered himself to one knee next to her, not only did the hairs on the back of her neck and every other inch of her body stand up, they froze in place. Nora felt her bravado vanish like smoke on the wind.

"My dear, be thankful. If I didn't need your sacrifice for this ritual, I would keep you as my pet for as long as I desired. And believe me, I don't bore easily. Just imagine what we could do together if we had years to play."

Nora's heart felt like a lump of glass in her chest. If she didn't feel all the blood drain from her face she would have sworn she was dead already. She couldn't even flinch when Héng drew his finger across her brow, down her cheek, and caressed her neck. If Xīn couldn't save her, Nora hoped her death would be quick.

****

"We have to assume that Héng has his men scattered

throughout the building to stop us at every turn," Pò said to Xīn as they led their collective group up the main stairwell.

Xīn agreed. "Don't forget the fā kuáng."

"You have so little faith in your people?" Pò asked.

Xīn turned his head to look at Pò. "We both know that Mǐn is already dead."

As he finished saying the thought aloud, a shrill scream floated up to them. They stopped moving but Xīn couldn't bear to look back. It pained him to hear her death cry. He finally turned to look back at his men and caught Taelin's gaze. The other línghún was trying and failing to hold back tears.

Xīn had sensed a growing emotional bond between him and Mǐn but until this moment, he thought it was simple camaraderie between soldiers. Over the past several days, he saw that the more his people interacted with Nora, or even Pò and his men, the more they experienced emotions. Despite all his training, despite everything he'd believed, Xīn hoped they could all continue to explore this new dimension of existence.

If anything existed at all ever again.

"I," Xīn started to apologize as if that would make Mǐn's death all right. But now wasn't the time. "Let's keep moving. We don't have all night, and who know what Héng set up for us? The ritual will have to take place within the hour. We can't afford any mistakes."

Everyone in the group nodded and they continued up. Once they reached the third floor, Pò pointed to the right.

"We have to go down this hall. There's no direct access to

the roof from the main stairwell. Once we get to the stairs at the end, we can take them all the way up."

Xīn nodded then turned to the group. "Once we enter the hallway, we need to move quickly. Every other man go left and secure the east end. The rest move forward with us."

Xīn didn't wait to get confirmation. He and Pò pushed through the double doors to the third floor. After looking left and right and seeing nothing, they moved ahead. Xīn looked back to make sure the línghún behind him went to the left to secure the other end of the hallway. When they did, he concentrated on the west wing ahead of him. Pò stopped him after a few feet. He motioned to a couple soldiers behind him and two moved ahead. Xīn frowned at Pò.

"You can't go first, Xīn," Pò explained. "We need to keep you safe until we can get to the roof."

"But," Xīn protested but Pò held up a hand.

"You're the protector, remember? I don't know exactly what that means but nothing can happen to you before we get to Nora."

A loud crash sounded behind them and they both turned to look. A half dozen of Héng's men rushed out from two separate rooms at the other end of the hall. It didn't take long for Taelin and a few of the others to cut them all down. Taelin looked surprised at the ease of the fight but before he could say as much, two more doors opened and more of Héng's men burst forth.

This second group kept up their end of the fight better than the first and Xīn couldn't stay to see who would win. Pò ordered a couple of his men to guard Xīn as they moved forward. Just as he did a door on their right burst open and four línghún flew out. Pò took point and had killed two of them before one of his men killed the others.

Pò pointed at several men. "Move ahead and help me clear these rooms. We're wasting too much time waiting to see who will pop out where. It's like a giant hallway of jack-in-the-boxes. Let's go."

They cleared the remaining ten rooms in minutes. No more surprises, ahead or behind. Only Héng's men lay dead as Xīn reached the stairwell. Pò ordered half the group to move through first. The rest secured the rear in case of a sneak attack.

Xīn growled. "I feel completely useless in the middle here, Pò."

"It's a necessary evil, my friend. Just keep thinking of Nora. We'll take care of the rest."

Xīn pictured Nora's face – the freckles on her nose, long dark lashes that framed her blue eyes, the way her cheeks dimpled when she smiled. His heart felt like it beat for the first time in eight hundred years on the day he first saw her. And now his chest felt like it would burst if he never saw her alive again. He supposed this was what love must feel like.

He'd be damned if he let Héng take that away from him.

****

The fā kuáng walked among the corpses that littered the hallway. The other línghún had moved through here only minutes ahead. Even among all the dead, all the blood and carnage, the creature picked up a familiar scent. A scent not identical but similar to the one who did this to him. The brother of the one responsible.

Xīn.

Ài's brother, Xīn. The bitch Ài. Ài. She did this to me. She killed me. She did. She did.

Now that it was on Xīn's trail, the creature found it difficult to concentrate. It raised its chin and sniffed the air, zeroing in on the wall to its left up ahead. Here. It brushed its hand across the pockmarked drywall then lifted it to its nose. Inhaling deeply, it took in the scent as well as the dust of the empty years here. The creature sneezed then rubbed its hand under its nose to clear it.

Xīn. Xīn. Xīn. Xīn.

It shook its head and moved down the hall again. The scent disappeared behind the metal door at the end. The fā kuáng pressed its face against the cool steel and inhaled.

Nothing. No scent. Gone. Where? Where?

It bent down as it sniffed the entire door. Finally, through the narrow gap at the bottom of the door, a tiny fragment of the scent entered its nose.

There. Follow. Find the scent. Find Xīn.

It pulled the door open and what felt like a solid wall knocked against it as the full force of the familiar scent hit it. It could feel the drool as it slipped past its lips and chin as a ravenous hunger raged in its belly. It turned back and searched for the closest body. Seeing one only a few feet away, it approached then punched through the corpse's chest.

The creature pulled the chest cavity open, flinging skin, tissue and ribs over its shoulder until it got to the heart. It ripped it free from the body and laughed at its conquest. Before it could bite into it, though, the fā kuáng dropped its slippery prize onto the carpet.

A quiet moan of disappointment escaped its lips but it quickly picked up the organ again. After pulling off bits of dirt and fibers it wiped the heart against its filthy shirt to clean it off. Satisfied, the creature stuffed the heart into its mouth and tore off a large chunk, chewing it noisily as viscous fluid dripped down its chin to mingle with the saliva already there.

Within seconds, though, the tissue turned to ash in its mouth and the creature spit the slurry out. It shuffled back to the now disintegrated corpse from where it took the heart. The creature knelt down and dug through the pile of dust searching for more food. When it found none, it whimpered with disappointment.

It moved back to the stairwell then stood in the open doorway before moving forward, tilting its head to catch any sounds from the group ahead. They were a few floors above so it moved to the first step.

Quiet now. Quiet. Don't let them hear. Don't let Xīn know.

Its thoughts jumbled and rattled in its head but it knew enough to keep the element of surprise as long as possible. It took one last forlorn look at the desiccated body before following Xīn's scent.

CHAPTER TWENTY-THREE

Héng's hand was like ice against Nora's skin. She tried to pull away. She even kicked out at him as he approached but he was quicker and stronger and within seconds, he subdued her protests. With a quick flick of his fingers, the knots in her bindings loosened and Héng yanked her to her feet. Still she tried to put on a brave face.

"Hey, watch it. I just got my hair the way I like it."

Héng laughed and reached up to grab a handful of her hair. He pulled her head back and pressed his cheek against hers.

"My dear, the dead don't need to worry about such things."

He dragged her across the rooftop toward the altar his men built. It was a makeshift structure of wood and stone, from bits and pieces they'd found strewn throughout the building. It was adorned with objects and items of such beauty Nora had never seen before.

A large square of bright red silk covered the top and dragons of every shape, size, and color dotted its surface. Stone, wood, rock, metal – dozens of different materials Nora recognized, and some she didn't. Golden bowls of various sizes, colored glass vases and containers, burning oil lamps and candles, smoking cones of incense, gold and silver coins, and small cakes. Were they all offerings?

Nora didn't understand the meaning behind all the items but it was obvious that Héng took great care to make the altar perfect.

Just as she marveled at his dedication she took note of the long steel blade lying on a matching platter as they reflected the stars above. She tried to dig in her heels, to stop their approach in any way, but Héng overpowered her.

He instructed one of his men to retie her hands behind her back. After doing so, the man pushed her to her knees. He slipped another rope around her neck, holding on to the two ends behind her head, then anchored her in place by standing on her calves. Nora winced in pain.

Héng stood before her. She refused to look up at him and give him the satisfaction of seeing the utter terror she felt reflected on her face. When he snapped his fingers, the man behind her secured the rope under her chin and pulled back, forcing her to look up at Héng. His form blended with the blackness of the night sky so all she could see were his eyes, two blood red dots floating above her.

"You have no idea how long I've waited for this moment. For you. Now it is here, and I will be magnificent."

He knelt down in front of her and the man loosened the rope. Héng grabbed her face in his hands, his eyes bright, his voice reverent.

"My beautiful vessel. To be confined to such an imperfect pitiful form. Give me your power and I will see it eradicate this insignificant race to dust."

Nora blinked. "Are…are you asking for my permission?"

Héng didn't respond but she saw his jaw muscles tighten. She couldn't help but snort.

"Are you seriously asking permission?"

"But of course," he replied. He was trying to sound nonchalant but the frustration in his voice was unmistakable. "Any great ritual must be based on a mutual understanding and consent."

"Oh, well, naturally. Then I must decline."

"I can make you," Héng threatened but Nora was tired of being a victim.

"Yes, I'm sure you can. Untie me and we'll talk about it. I promise to listen to your side of the story before I make any final decisions, okay?"

Nora could hear the growl building in his throat. He grabbed her by the shoulders and pulled her to her feet, knocking the man behind her down to the ground. Héng hissed at her face.

"You dare refuse me? I can shred you like tissue paper. I can crush you like the insect you are. I can make your entire existence a living hell and still you play coy?"

"I know what you're capable of, Héng. I've seen it. I've felt it. But I know you won't hurt me. Wanna know why?"

He shook with visible rage but said nothing. Nora took that as an assent to continue.

"For starters, bo-ring! Sure, if you don't get your way, you can torture me to your heart's content. But how long will that keep your interest? You'll tire soon enough, kill me, then move on to your next diversion. And you don't get your ritualistic groove on.

"But more importantly, you'd end up being the biggest cosmic joke this side of the Great Wall. Imagine, the great Master

Héng, waiting all these years, tracking down stories and legends. Finding the vessel, securing her, and bringing her to the brink of the ritual only to be shot down. Couldn't close the deal. Denied. A failure! All on a technicality!"

Nora knew she was risking her life by belittling his ego. She'd understood from the moment he took her that he was all about the glory this feat would bring to his name. But if she was going to die, she'd rather die alone and keep the rest of the world safe. Either way, she'd win and Héng would lose.

"You're nothing but a pathetic, weak-minded creature. You only find pleasure in the pain and suffering of others, particularly young girls like Ài. What's the matter, Héng? Couldn't function as a man so you had to become a vampire?"

His rage had reached the boiling point now and his grip on her shoulders was excruciating, as if her bones would turn to dust inside her flesh. She didn't dare stop now.

"That's it, isn't it, Héng? How typically average. Same old story, eh? Even now, over a millennia since you were last human, and it all comes back to your wang. If that wasn't so pitiable it would be funny."

The primal, almost animal, scream that came from him chilled her blood. He lifted her off the ground and she prepared herself for whatever death blow he would deliver. It was then that she saw Pò and Xīn, and their soldiers, standing near the roof entrance. The closest of Héng's men were watching Nora and hadn't noticed their security had been breached.

Several of the group had separated at Pò's direction and

snuck up behind their closest enemies. Only a half a dozen or so of Héng's men remained and Nora didn't want them to know about Xīn's arrival.

"Go ahead, Héng. Do it. Kill me. Do what you always do when someone gets in the way of what you want. Like Xīn's whole family. Like Ài when she drove that man insane with her blood. When she refused to be your plaything anymore."

Nora worried that Xīn may not know about his family or his sister but Ài was a soft spot with Héng. Under all his bravado and ego, something like guilt stirred within him whenever Ài was brought up. So she pushed on.

"Ài was different, wasn't she, Héng? She wasn't like all the other humans you'd encountered over the years. She was special. That's why you pursued her. Why you slaughtered her family then burned their villages to the ground. It's why you made her a vampire, isn't it?"

Héng released Nora's shoulders without warning and she slammed to the ground. He paced a few steps away from her, then back. Then paced away again. Nora had really rattled him this time but not enough. When he turned away from her again he saw Xīn and Pò. His back straightened and he pointed at them, yelling orders to his men.

"Get them!"

As Héng's men turned and dashed to fight the intruders, Héng moved swiftly to Nora's side. He grabbed her arm and yanked her back to her feet. Dragging her over to the altar, he cursed her every step of the way.

"I will get your permission. One way or another, I will."

A shriek echoed through the night and Nora turned to see the most pitiful frightening creature she'd ever seen. Though it was bloody, dirty, and clearly insane, Nora recognized the man from her vision, the man that Ài had created with her blood. She racked her brain, trying to think through the fear so she could remember his name. What was it?

The creature leaped into the air. It tore and ripped at every línghún it encountered, whether they belonged to Héng or Pò. Body parts flew through the air and blood splattered every surface. Héng's men quit fighting and scattered, trying to find any possible hiding place. Pò and Xīn yelled at each other in Chinese then Xīn headed towards Nora while the others squared off to fight.

Héng turned to face Xīn. The pain on Xīn's face was hard for Nora to bear, since it was likely she who put it there. She only hoped he could use it to defeat Héng.

Xīn pulled a long silver sword from a sheath strapped to his back. It gleamed in the lights from the altar. He held it out, its point at eye level with Héng.

"I trusted you. I gave you my life and my dedication. But that wasn't enough for you. You had to have Ài's, too?"

Héng held up his hands. "It's hard for you to understand, my son."

"I. Am not. Your son," Xīn spat.

Héng lowered his hands. His mouth split open in a wide grin as his fangs descended.

"No, I suppose not. You never were good enough. Neither

was your sister."

"Ahhh!" Xīn screamed as he leaped into the air. He held the sword above his head and brought it down in a flashing arc towards Héng's neck. His former master moved easily out of the way and Xīn rolled when he hit the ground. In seconds he was up again and running at Héng.

This run, slash, dodge, miss, turn, run again ballet continued for several minutes. Nora inched her way toward the low wall at the edge of the roof, as far from the fight as she could get. She bumped into the corpse of the holy man, eyes still staring off into eternity, and shivered.

Nora looked past Xīn and saw Pò facing off with the creature. Just as Pò tripped and fell onto his back, Xīn did the same. With Héng standing over Xīn and the creature standing over Pò, it looked as if the bad guys were going to win.

Before either could deliver a fatal blow, Nora remembered the man's name. It popped into her head with sudden clarity along with the kernel of an idea that might save them all.

"Bu Xīng!"

Héng snapped his head to look at her. She registered his shock from the corner of her eye as she stared over at the creature. He stood over Pò, arms raised in readiness to fall on his enemy and tear him to pieces but at the sound of his name he froze. He turned his head slowly in her direction. She said his name again.

"Bu Xīng."

Bu Xīng's hands fell to his sides and he stumbled toward her, tripping over Pò's legs, and other body parts, as he went. He barely registered Héng's presence when he moved past him, pushing him aside to get to Nora. Bu Xīng knelt beside her.

"I don't know you. I don't know you. Do I?"

Nora shook her head. "No, but I know you. I saw what happened to you."

Bu Xīng's eyes widened with disbelief. "You weren't there. You didn't do this to me. It was her."

He pointed back at Xīn. Nora shook her head and reached out to take his hand. She moved it so he pointed at Héng.

"He did this to you. He knew what could happen but told Ài to turn you anyway. It's not her fault. It's Héng's."

"Héng? Héng."

Bu Xīng turned to look back at Héng. Nora got up on her knees next to him and pointed.

"Yes, he did this to you."

Bu Xīng snarled and stood up. "You…you took me from my farm. You put me in that sack. My family, my children. Gone. Gone. Gone. Because of you."

Héng snorted. "Enough of this."

He turned on Xīn, pulling the silver sword from his hand. He swung it back at Bu Xīng and pierced the man through his heart. Héng held the hilt at arm's length and pushed the blade further into the man's chest. Nora screamed and reached for him but Xīn had grabbed her from behind and pulled her away. She struggled but Xīn's strength outmatched hers and she finally allowed him to drag her out of Héng's and Bu Xīng's confrontation.

Bu Xīng looked at her for a brief moment, a small smile

curling his lips. He turned back to Héng and growled. Stepping forward, forcing the sword to move further through his body, he grabbed Héng's hand and pulled. Once the hilt of the sword hit his chest, and could move no further, Bu Xīng reached out both arms and grabbed Héng by the neck.

The expression of surprise locked in place once Bu Xīng crushed Héng's throat and ripped his head free from his body. As Bu Xīng clutched the head, Héng's body remained upright. Nora waited for it to run around in blind circles, like a chicken after being decapitated. After a few moments the corpse's knees buckled and the whole body crumpled to the ground and lay still.

After everything that had happened, for some reason Nora expected Héng's demise to be a bit more dramatic. Not that a bare-handed decapitation wasn't worthy but Nora found herself disappointed, wanting Héng to suffer more and be dead less. She freed herself from Xīn's embrace and moved to stand over Héng's body. She kicked the corpse but that only hurt her foot.

"Ow! Dammit, even dead this bastard still manages to get the upper hand."

"Nora," Xīn spoke softly to her.

She turned away from the body and saw Bu Xīng clutching Héng's head to his chest. Nora moved toward him and reached out to touch his hand. When she did, he dropped the head. He watched it roll away and when it came to a stop he slumped forward.

Nora rushed to catch him, ignoring the blood and gore that smeared over her. She eased him down to his knees since the sword sticking out of his chest and back prevented her from laying him down. She placed her hand on the hilt and looked into Bu Xīng's eyes. He nodded and she yanked the sword out as quickly as possible. He uttered a soft grunt then fell onto his back.

Xīn knelt on the other side of Bu Xīng as Nora leaned over him and held his hand. He looked up at her, tears pooling in his eyes, and nodded. When he turned to look at Xīn, Bu Xīng inhaled through his nose. He struggled to speak.

"The scent. Ài's scent."

Xīn did his best to hide his surprise or anger or whatever he was feeling right now. Nora couldn't be sure but to his credit, he simply nodded.

"Yes, Ài was my sister."

"She didn't mean to. Didn't know," Bu Xīng gasped.

"I know, Bu Xīng. Héng was responsible and you honor my sister's memory by exacting justice upon him. Thank you."

Bu Xīng's smiled. He closed his eyes and took a deep breath, the madness that plagued him finally relaxing as he neared death.

"Can I sleep now?"

Nora squeezed his hand as tears rolled down her face.

"Yes, Bu Xīng. Sleep. When you wake up, you'll be with your family again."

He smiled and squeezed her hand in return. Nora released his hand and it fell to his chest. She couldn't tell if he was dead until his skin started to crinkle and peel. In seconds, the papery texture that used to be his skin flaked off and swirled about in the wind. His flesh dried and sunk against his bones, turning to ash. Within minutes, all that remained of him were his ragged and bloody clothes and a pile of dust.

Nora gulped back the lump in her throat. "Is that what happens to you guys when you die, I mean, really die?"

Xīn nodded but said nothing. He was looking over Nora's shoulder. She turned to see Héng's clothes lying in a rumpled pile. Like Bu Xīng's, there was nothing in them but ashes. Nora looked back at Xīn. The firm set of his lips showed his satisfaction with Héng's death, but the tears in his eyes proved he mourned for his maker as well.

"There now, that wasn't so hard, was it?" Pò asked as he stood over them. Nora never heard him approach and she jumped at the sound of his voice. She stared up at him as he shrugged.

"You have got to learn *not* to sneak up on mortals like that, Pò."

"Sorry, Nora," he mumbled under his breath.

"Yeah, yeah. Just help me up, would you?"

She held her hand out to him. Pò grabbed it and pulled her to her feet. She stumbled then arched an eyebrow at him and he held up his hands. When he smiled then moved away to see to his men, Nora turned to Xīn. She held her hand out to him.

"Need a hand?"

Xīn smiled. He didn't need her help to stand but she wanted to touch him so he could feel that she was all right and that it was over. Nora feared that since the ritual was no longer possible, the feelings she'd been having for Xīn, and he for her, would dissipate. That maybe all the auspicious whatever-it-was was responsible for hyper activating their emotions. When Xīn pulled her into him arms and crushed her with an embrace, she thought maybe it wasn't.

"Can't…breathe…" she gasped.

He held on for another second before releasing her. She sucked in a lungful of air but managed to smile up at him. When she could breathe normally again, she looked around the rooftop. Piles of clothing, filled with ashes, lay strewn about. The altar had been knocked over at some point, spilling oils and offerings everywhere. She looked back at Xīn.

"It's really over now, isn't it?"

Xīn nodded. "No one can perform the ritual now. It's only once every thousand years that everything aligns as it should, making the ritual possible. So you're safe. From that at least."

"What do you mean?"

"Well, the ritual can't be performed but you are still a vessel, Nora. Who knows what else can be done in order to steal that power or destroy it?"

Nora hadn't considered that possibility. "So what am I supposed to do, hide in my house for the rest of my life?"

Xīn smiled. "I'm sure that won't be necessary. I'll talk to the dào rén. Consult the archives. Find out as much as I can. For your immediate future, though, I think sleep is in order."

Nora smiled and nodded. "Yeah, I feel like I could sleep for a month."

"Well, I don't want you to sleep for that long."

She looked up at him and he winked. Laughing, she wrapped

her arms around his waist and leaned against him as they headed for the roof exit.

EPILOGUE

Nora swung her legs back and forth as she sat on the low wall next to the river. She nibbled on a peanut butter and jelly sandwich and watched a large freighter drift by.

"So it looks like you're over that bug."

Nora turned to look at her friend, Janet. "Huh?"

"You've been sick, right? That's why you've missed a week of work?"

Nora swallowed the lump of food at the back of her throat. "Oh, yeah. Right. I'm feeling much better now. Got my appetite back and everything."

"Uh huh," Janet sounded doubtful.

"Well, what else would I have been doing?" Nora demanded.

Just then, someone tapped her on the shoulder. She screamed and swiveled her head around. Xīn bowed.

"I'm so sorry. I didn't mean to frighten you. Are you all right?"

Nora pressed a hand to her chest, trying to keep her heart from busting through her ribcage. "No. I mean, yeah. I'm fine. Sorry, I didn't hear you walk over."

He smiled. "I'll be sure to work on that."

Janet cleared her throat and Nora turned to look at her. She'd almost forgotten about her friend.

"Ah, Xīn this is my friend, Janet. Janet, this is my, I mean, this is Xīn."

"Nice to meet you, Xīn," Janet smiled as she extended her

hand. He grasped it and bowed at the same time.

"An honor to meet one of Nora's friends."

When he let go of her hand, Janet looked at Nora. She arched an eyebrow at her.

"What would you have been doing indeed?"

"What?"

Janet looked at Xīn. "You probably want to talk to her alone for a minute, am I right?"

He smiled and nodded and Janet picked up her lunch. She pointed to a picnic table a few yards away.

"I'll be over here when you're done, my dear. So nice to have met you, Xīn."

He bowed again as Janet left then sat next to Nora. He slipped his hand into hers and he frowned when he felt her shaking.

"What's wrong?"

Nora shook her head. "It's just that no one will ever be able to call me 'my dear' again without me hearing Héng's voice."

Xīn wrapped his arm around her shoulders and pulled her close. She closed her eyes and tried to will away the memories of the past week. When she began to relax, she spoke.

"So have you talked to the dào rén?"

"There are a lot of conflicting stories. So many legends that contradict one another. It will take a while to rifle through it all. A group of the holy men are looking into it. We wish there could be more but there are so many other problems out there we need to handle as well."

"I know," Nora said. "What can I do to help?"

"For one thing, you need to learn how to defend yourself."

Nora pulled away. "You mean screaming for my mother and slapping at my attacker isn't good enough? What is this world coming to?"

Xīn laughed. "Surprising, I know. I could help you, if you'd like."

She smiled. "You'll teach me how to fight?"

"Of course. I've got a few hundred years of experience. I'm sure you'll find it invaluable."

"And a humbling experience to boot. All right, you're on. When do we start?"

"Friday night?"

"It's a date."

Xīn frowned. "A what?"

"Never mind. I should get back to work."

"Nora?"

"Yes?"

"Could you do me a favor?"

"Of course, Xīn. Anything."

He chewed on his bottom lip, another emotional tic Nora noticed he had picked up since he met her.

"Can you tell me more about Ài?"

"Are you sure you really want to know about what happened between her and Héng?"

Xīn paused then nodded. Nora grasped his hand and squeezed it.

"All right. I assume you'd rather wait until Friday to talk about it."

"Yes. I don't think this is an appropriate venue to discuss my sister's," he paused as he searched for the right word. "Transformation. But can you tell me one thing?"

"What's that?"

"Ài's dead, isn't she? I mean, truly dead."

Nora sighed. "I'm afraid so. It was the last memory I had of her before the ritual."

Xīn clenched his hands into fists, his knuckles gleaming white with the strain. Nora placed her hands over his hoping she could put him at ease.

"Don't worry, Xīn. Not everything I saw about her was awful. I did experience quite a few pleasant memories."

That seemed to help and he smiled. "Good."

They both slid off of the wall and turned to see Pò sitting next to Janet at the picnic table. She laughed and playfully slapped at Pò's arm. Nora looked at Xīn.

"Um, what is he doing here?"

Pò looked up and waved at them. He whispered something to Janet and she laughed again. He stood and walked over to Xīn and Nora, leaving Janet at the table.

"Well, well, well. Fancy meeting you folks here."

"I could same the same for you, Pò," Xīn said.

"Now don't get your boxers in a twist. I just came to let you know that I took care of everything at my building."

Xīn frowned. "You took care of it?"

"Yeah, you know. Cleaned it up, got rid of all that altar stuff. It looks like it always did."

"Like a giant crap hole?" Nora asked.

Pò frowned at her. Nora studied her feet before looking back up at him. Pò spoke to Xīn.

"I just wanted to let you know that I, well, I'm sorry. For everything."

He extended his hand. Xīn hesitated for a moment then shook it.

"Thank you, Pò. Are you going to stay out of trouble from now on?"

Pò laughed then looked back at Janet. He waggled his fingers at her then turned back to Xīn.

"No promises. Are you going to get *into* trouble from time to time?"

Xīn looked at Nora and smiled. She blushed before Xīn looked back at Pò.

"No promises."

Pò smiled and looked at Nora. He bowed deeply at the waist. Nora nodded.

"Thanks for saving my ass, Pò."

"You're quite welcome, Nora."

"Hey, I know that woman over there." She pointed at Janet. "Please don't do anything-"

Pò raised his hands. "I got it. I got it. I won't hurt her, all right?"

Nora nodded. "Thanks."

As Pò walked back to the picnic table, he spoke over his shoulder. “Not unless she wants me to.”

Before Nora could yell at his back, Xīn pulled her close. “Don’t worry. He’s just trying to bait you, Nora. Don’t fall for it.”

Nora bit her bottom lip. “You think so?”

They watched as Janet and Pò got up from the table. Janet called over to Nora.

“I’ll see you back at work, okay, Nora?”

Nora nodded and waved. She looked at Xīn.

“Maybe we could teach her a few defense moves, too. Just in case.”

Xīn smiled. “Good idea.”

THE END

ABOUT THE AUTHOR

Peggy Christie is an author of horror and dark fiction. Her work has appeared in dozens of websites, magazines, and anthologies, including *13 Little Hells*, *Necrotic Tissue*, and *Fearotica: An Anthology of Erotic Horror*. In 2016, Dragons Roost Press re-released her short story collection, *Hell Hath No Fury*. Peggy is also the Secretary of the Great Lakes Association of Horror Writers as well as a contributing writer for websites like Cinema Head Cheese and Slack Jaw Punks. Visit her website, themonkeyisin.com, for more information on publications and appearances.

Peggy loves Korean dramas, survival horror video games, and chocolate (not necessarily in that order). She lives in Michigan with her husband and their dog, Dozer.

CPSIA information can be obtained
at www.ICGtesting.com
Printed in the USA
FSHW01n0306110718
50081FS

9 781945 940163